JUN 2013

AR MAY 2015
SU JUN 2015
MI MAR 2017

OPEN PIT

A NOVEL

MARGUERITE PIGEON

NeWest Press

Library and Archives Canada Cataloguing in Publication

Pigeon, Marguerite

Open pit / Marguerite Pigeon.

Also issued in electronic format. ISBN 978-1-927063-32-3

I. Title.

PS8631.I4769O64 2013   C813'.6   C2012-906588-9

Editor for the Board: Douglas Barbour
Cover and interior design: Natalie Olsen, Kisscut Design
Cover image: coal mining facility © Jan Hyrman / Shutterstock.com
Author photo: Edward Pond

NeWest Press acknowledges the financial support of the Alberta Multimedia Development Fund and the Edmonton Arts Council for our publishing program. We further acknowledge the financial support of the Government of Canada through the Canada Book Fund (CBF) for our publishing activities. We acknowledge the support of the Canada Council for the Arts which last year invested $24.3 million in writing and publishing throughout Canada.

#201, 8540–109 Street
Edmonton, Alberta T6G 1E6
780.432.9427

NeWest Press www.newestpress.com

No bison were harmed in the making of this book.
printed and bound in Canada 1 2 3 4 5   14 13

For Mirna Perla, Carlos Amador, Berta Caceres
and the groups they serve in El Salvador and Honduras

AUTHOR'S NOTE: Los Pampanos and the Mil Sueños mine, while based on real places, are fictional.

2005

SUNDAY
APRIL 3

11:50 AM. *Hwy 18, Morazán province, El Salvador*

The bus passes yet another struggling 4×4. On the truck's open flatbed a half dozen passengers bump knees and press hats and scarves to their heads against the wind. One man briefly lifts his frayed Stetson and smiles, no front teeth. Danielle forces herself to smile back. Ahead of her, Antoine waves and grabs a shot with his phone as the man falls from view. The hard green school bus seat squeaks as he turns to show her.

"They used to call them '*peek-ups*,'" Danielle says, remembering, but she doesn't like what's happening here. The bus driver, Ramón, is going way too fast, overtaking *peek-ups*, sedans, motorcycles — everything chugging upwards on the narrow highway. The others seem oblivious, enjoying the foreignness, but Danielle can't concentrate on her schedule for intrusive fantasies of crawling from the wreckage of the bus to check for their pulses. She's had it with Ramón's music too, going BOOM da-da-dah. *Sí, ma-mi, sí!* BOOM da-da-da-da-dah.

"Reggaeton," Tina said earlier, the end of the word sucked out the open upper half of her window with a few stray hairs from her tidy ponytail. "It's like Latin American hip hop. Pretty raunchy." Tina rightly assumed Danielle hadn't identified the style. Tina has all kinds of pop culture references at her fingertips. She drops them like crumbs, letting you know where she's been and you have not. She also looks like a yoga instructor, which is fine, because she is one. But her stretch-fit top is a distraction. After she sat down at breakfast no one in the group heard a word of Danielle's review of drinking water safety.

Danielle looks back at her page. Six days' worth of meetings, tours, talks and sleeping in hammocks. Six days between her and getting what she needs. She checks her watch. At least Ramón is making up time. They left San Salvador late thanks to Martin, the chubby-faced stock analyst two rows up. Danielle has no idea why he's on this delegation, never mind what could've taken him so long to get ready. Let it not have been prayers. Neela did mention that he's a serious Christian.

Now Ramón gestures to Danielle to come forward. She hesitates. The road, straight and smooth all the way from the capital city, is winding and bumpy as they head north into the foothills. She would prefer not to fall on her ass on her first day. But Ramón cranks his arm more insistently and Danielle cautiously gets up, putting a hand on Antoine's seat back.

"We close?" he asks.

"Very."

"Then what he want?" says Pierre, seated directly across from Antoine. The francophones joined the delegation together while travelling in Nicaragua. Grew up neighbours in Quebec City. Best friends for life. So said Neela. Danielle has a hard time seeing it. Antoine is sweet, Pierre imperious. He could pass for a cult leader in training this morning, all intensity, curly hair and bony bod. A tan abdomen and the nub of an outie show where his t-shirt has drawn up above his drawstring pants.

"I'm going up to find out," says Danielle, a bit terse.

Arriving alongside Ramón she is disconcerted to see that he is sweating profusely, looking wound up. "We'll stop soon," he says, nodding at the shoulder of the highway. The familiar sound of his quick singsong Spanish pulls Danielle back through time.

"I don't know. . . . We're already late."

Ramón's hands curl more tightly around the steering wheel, his knuckles blanching. "This is special. A stand for cane juice."

"I'm sure we can get something similar at the market in Los Pampanos. Our host is —"

"You can't get this," Ramón interrupts, freeing a hand and flapping it at her, shooing.

Danielle wants to object, but she won't be *that* foreigner. The one who assumes everyone in the developing world has an agenda, steering you to their cousin's restaurant. Not in front of these kids. She hears the voice of her friend Neela, who organized the delegation. "Whatever happens afterwards, enjoy the first week. Relax. Be open. Learn something about yourself." This was her final pep talk as she dropped Danielle at Departures yesterday morning with a folderful of papers, flight information for the others, directions to their hostel and the neatly typed schedule. Everything Danielle needed to take over. Except Neela's confidence.

"Alright," says Danielle to Ramón. "As long as it's quick."

Without waiting for her to sit down, he speeds up even more, cruising past a truck stacked high with water bottles, then a tragic, stuttering moped coughing blue exhaust. The music goes on, BOOM dah-dah. *O Mami!* BOOM BOOM BOOM.

Teetering back towards the others, Danielle hollers over it. "Ramón says we can get fresh cane sugar juice up ahead, a local delicacy. Stretch our legs a bit."

Everyone but Pierre nods.

"My doctor of Chinese medicine says it's awesome for digestion," says Tina, searching the highway for such a wondrous place.

A few minutes later Ramón pulls into a semicircular dirt driveway and parks behind a rickety wooden structure encrusted along its bottom half with dried mud.

"Is *that* it?" Tina asks.

Martin has his wallet out. "How much do they charge?"

"Eets closed," Pierre says to him, his accent thickening with irritation. He rolls his eyes towards Danielle like she should have known.

She's about to tell him to back off, there's been some mistake, but she's distracted by Ramón. He pulls the keys from the ignition, but instead of turning to offer an explanation, he levers the creaky folding door open and gets out. The group is silent as he disappears without looking back. Danielle thinks of an actor leaving a stage. Something about it makes her rise in her seat. She tries to hide her concern, to look like she can manage. Nothing's wrong here.

But stepping outside, she isn't so sure. Ramón is gone.

A thin honk. Pedro is early, as usual, and Marta Ramos hurries to gather her things. She shuts the office door, testing the lock with a few hard tugs. Ever since the mine's goons forced their way in last year she wishes the Committee could afford an alarm. No one was charged, of course. But Marta has no doubt. If she weren't so *loca* about backing up data, the water sampling numbers would have vanished with her laptop.

She stands on the threshold until Pedro has thoroughly checked the area, then steps into the car. Pedro closes her door. "They haven't called," she says, perplexed, as he takes the wheel and backs them out. "Neela was very clear that they would call. I better see if I can reach the one in charge — Neela's friend from Toronto. Is it possible I met her once?" Pedro is not a talker, and Marta long ago stopped waiting for answers from him. "Red hair," she adds, fumbling for her cell, noticing that she's missed two callers. "*Díos mío!*" she says, reviewing her messages. "Members. . . trying to get out of tomorrow's meeting." She snaps the phone shut. "Do they think El Pico will be magically spared while they're out dancing?"

Pedro shakes his head in shared dismay at the weak links in the fight against the Mil Sueños gold mine. He keeps a steady speed as they cruise along the main highway that cuts through Los Pampanos, past *Clic-Clic*, the Internet café and ice cream joint, then the steep driveway leading to the crumbling community radio station, after which comes the cinderblock former office of decommissioned guerrillas, now meeting place for AA, NA, Alateen. Opposite that is the giant new evangelical church where, if the windows were open, Marta can guarantee she would hear determinedly cheery singing. Finally, the market comes into view. It's silly, really. The whole distance would take fifteen minutes on foot. But Pedro doesn't like her to walk, and anyway, Marta prefers air conditioning. They park and head to the main doors, where Marta speed dials one of her delinquent committee members. "We can't give up now," she tells him, though she's said this too many times, to too many supporters.

"*Licenciada Ramos!*" shouts a man near the market doors, smiling broadly. "*Adios! Adios!*"

Marta waves, acknowledging the salutation even as she continues her call. One last stab at convincing the member to show up to the meeting. "It will be short — just one hour."

Pedro taps his watch face and gives her a look.

"I know," she mouths. She hangs up to dial Neela's replacement — *Daniela* something — but someone else has just stepped out of the market: a former nurse and mother of four, now unemployed and sick, who lives downriver from the mine. Marta has been meaning to get a statement from her for months. She hustles over and hugs the woman, asking after her family. Then, as she does every time she comes to her home town, Marta completely loses track of time.

12:05 PM. *Roadside stop, Hwy 18*

"Ramón?"

Danielle waits for an answer. Long enough to become conscious of the specific feel of the air, remembering it with sudden clarity, its fragrance and weight, the way it once made her feel enclosed, like she was trapped in a zoo. "Ramón!"

She rounds the bus to face the homemade-looking juice stand. "Ramón!" she yells, feeling stupid.

"Go check the front," says Martin.

Danielle turns to see him pointing out a window of the bus towards the highway beyond the wooden structure. The other three delegates are looking out with the same concerned expression he wears. Danielle inspects the stand. Several boards are missing from the back wall. The inside is in deep shadow. "It looks abandoned," she calls back. Still, to be thorough, she starts walking towards the far side.

A loud crash to her right makes her glance in that direction. Two men appear from the trees beyond where the bus is parked. For half a second Danielle thinks: oh, they work here. But the men, one tall, one short, are carrying weapons. Each has his head covered in dark material. Their shoulders bend forward as they eat up the distance between the trees and the bus.

"Danielle!" someone shrieks from inside. Then Tina screams, "What going on? What's going on?"

The short man is within a foot of Danielle before she can form a thought. He sticks the tip of his gun to her chest. Danielle steps backwards, dumfounded, trips, ends up on her side. The man's black ski mask juts towards her as he reaches down to grip her upper arm. Behind two small holes in the material, his eyes are steady.

Danielle recoils. She scrambles, hands and feet forming a wall. The man is silent as he works to stay clear of her kicking boots.

"No no no no," she yells, aiming for him. But he simply releases her arm and grabs her by the hair. Danielle comes to standing in a split second, the pain leading her up like a winch. The man switches his hold, locking a forearm around her shoulders so that she faces away. Danielle looks over that big arm, down at her feet, which are still jerking. Her hiking boots appear idiotically new. The man walks her around the front of the bus, the engine tick-tick-ticking as it cools.

Up the steps, banging loudly. Everyone on the bus screaming, Danielle joining in. "Stop this, please! Stop!"

BOOM-da-BOOM BOOM. Dah-da-dah-dah. BOOM-da-BOOM. Ramón's reggaeton, pounding.

"Help!" Martin pleads. "Help!"

"*Non!*" cries Antoine.

The second, taller masked man is already aboard, yelling "*Callense! Callense!*" in a high-pitched tone. The one holding Danielle edges past him, repeating "*Abajo!*" His voice is a counter to the other's: deep, rumbling with an emotion Danielle can't name. "*Abajo!*" he says, over and over, his gun aimed at each of the delegates in turn. He doesn't seem angry. The voice is too even. More like certain. The way a doctor tells you how to treat your disease: if you want to live, just shut up and do it.

"*Abajo!*"

But Martin is upright, doesn't understand the Spanish. Still holding Danielle like a rag doll, the compact man rushes him. "*ABAJO, PUTO!*" he yells, shoving the butt of his gun into Martin's midsection. Martin folds in half with a sharp exhalation and collapses onto the floor, his shaking hands covering the back of his head. The taller man comes and pulls him up onto one of the seats.

Danielle screams. The man holding her backs up and forces her into a row nearer the front then joins his partner at the centre of the aisle. She hears the delegates breathing hard into their laps behind her, Tina making a squeaking sound, maybe hyperventilating.

A strong smell pervades the space. Piss. Danielle looks back. As she does, Pierre glances up the aisle towards her, sees her see him, sees her smell it, his face turning a deep red. Danielle looks away.

The music is shut off with a small click, and Danielle, bending, glimpses Ramón. He's back. He starts the bus and puts it in gear, pulls onto the highway, drives ten, maybe twenty minutes. Upwards. Up and around a lot of corners, then more slowly, as Danielle watches a handful of two-storey buildings cross through the windows above her. Los Pampanos. Then trees, a near stop, a sharp right — off the highway? Yes. Danielle hears gravel being dispersed, the road getting rougher, dust coming through the windows, everyone bouncing on their seats like freight. She has time to consider the irony of something this bad happening to her here, and now. She thinks of Neela, then of Aida.

The bus stops. *"Afuera!"* says the compact one, and the confusion starts up again as his tall partner starts seizing people's arms, forcing them to stand. They're marched off and lined up along the side, where the tall one searches their pockets, removing Danielle's papers, her phone, some loose change. When he gets to Ramón, he completely ignores him. Danielle swears she sees her driver smile.

Aida puts down her bag. The smell of her own childhood nearly overwhelms her. She turns on the hall light, takes off her coat and boots, makes enough room in the musty, overstuffed closet so nothing in there will touch them, loosens her scarf and goes into the kitchen. A blue sticky note curls on the stove: *REAR BURNERS OUT.* As if Aida is about to cook. She folds the note in half and puts it on the counter.

Nothing has changed. Even the same arrangement of fridge magnets Aida saw last time she was in the house, several months ago. Her grandfather's research books are still rotting on the built-in shelves under the stairs. She runs her hand along their weakening spines as she walks back down the hall, hoping she'll feel him. Nothing. It's been too long.

She wanders upstairs and sits on the bed in her old room. Hard as ever. She quickly gets up and checks her phone. André said he'd check in when he left the university. She goes into the bathroom, touches up her makeup, decides she could use a manicure, then pees. She lifts a book from the bin beside the toilet. *Excavating Your Authentic Self.* Is that what Danielle's doing? The book is pristine. Aida lets it drop back to where she expects it will remain, exactly that way, forever.

Back downstairs she searches the kitchen for the plant food her mother asked her to use. Opening the cupboard she locates the bag, which contains about a tablespoon of powder. Aida slams the door and sighs. The three-bar melody of her text notification chimes. She smiles, relieved. It's André.

STILL THERE?

Aida detects annoyance. TRAFFIC. BACK SOON, PROMISE.

KEEP YOUR PROMISE AND I'LL COOK FOR YOU. AT STORE NOW. SUPERB FIDDLEHEADS.

Aida prefers asparagus, but she loves when André makes a fuss for her. PERFECT, she replies. BUT ONE FAVOUR FIRST? Aida hates favours and feels strange texting for one, especially from André, who generally prefers to guess what she needs and offer it rather than to have her ask. But Danielle's plants should not pay the price for her mother's neglect. Aida asks him to buy some of the plant food, typing in the brand name.

There's a long pause before André returns the text. SHE EVER GOING TO SELL THAT PLACE?

Aida frowns. NOT SURE. Her mother will never sell. But Aida knows André isn't curious about the house. It's Danielle he's talking about. He doesn't try very hard to hide his dislike of her, which hurts a little, even if Aida understands. The less they discuss her mother, the better. Aida does enjoy a fiddlehead. FORGET THE PLANT FD. I'LL DO IT.

NO. IT'S FINE. I WILL, MON ANGE.

Aida smiles again. She's his angel. It's not André's fault he's huffy. He's French, from a rich-ish family in Paris. They loved Aida when they visited Toronto, let her know how much they're looking forward to getting to know her. If only Danielle had been so pleasant the first time she met André. Or ever been that way with Aida, for that matter.

But. Watering plants is a painless task requiring two visits to this relic, tops.

Aida goes to check out the fern in the dining room. On the way, she passes a pile of papers, stops to look. It's a stack of envelopes held together by a thick elastic band, another sticky on top. *Please read these in the spirit of forgiveness, which is what I hope for. We can discuss when I get back. Over a glass of wine? — Danielle*

Aida tugs off the elastic. Each envelope is addressed to Danielle's old friend Neela Hill, but at a street address Aida doesn't recognize. She takes the top envelope and pulls out a single sheet, unfolds it.

The paper is gritty and thin, nearly see-through, the handwriting rough, like Danielle was in a hurry. It's dated January 20, 1980.

Dear Neela,

This is first moment I've had to myself since we arrived. I'm writing you so you don't think I got lost, never to be seen again. I'll figure out later how the hell to send it. The trip here was weird and exhausting. We sort of went in circles. Turns out they have to switch up the routes they take, bringing journalists across. But no one explained that until later.

So here I am in guerrilla territory! This morning they handed me a Styrofoam plate of tortillas and beans and a tin mug with coffee so sweet my fillings nearly fell out. A woman our age (I think), very serious, shook my hand and said, "Compa." (Everyone calls everyone that.) "We are proud to have you witness our struggle." Not a bad start.

From what I can see Morazán is nothing like the places where I lived with my parents (Dad studies coastal soils, as in beaches).

Aida freezes at the mention of her grandparents. Is she prepared for more about them? About a young Danielle? Excavating her mother's "authentic self" isn't what she's had in mind. She glances back at the letter, but now the old wall phone rings in the kitchen. She gets up to answer, then changes her mind. No one knows she's here except André and Danielle, and they usually text — Danielle begrudgingly. Aida doesn't need any hassles about her mother's unpaid bills. She reopens the letter.

We're inland, so the mountains are dry and dramatic. You'd like the
pine trees — and the views.

So far, the faction seems. . . informal? Not sure what else to call it.
The guerrillas don't even have uniforms, so it's hard to tell who's who.
A lot of teenagers are sitting around with guns like they're waiting
for orders. My primary contact at Command is supposed to be here
tomorrow. He'll decide where they're sending me first.

I feel like I've made the right decision, Neela. I feel brave.

DB

Brave? Danielle? Aida tries to let the oxymoron sink in. The stack
of letters is suddenly unstable terrain, threatening an avalanche
of revelations. All she wanted to do was feed the plants and go
home to André.
    Her ringtone startles her. Unknown caller. "Hello?"
    "Aida?"
    "Yes?"
    "It's Neela. Hill. Have they called?"
    "Neela?"
    "Foreign Affairs. . ."
    "What? About these letters?"
    "Oh. Those letters. I forgot. No, Sweetie. It's your mother."

How long? How long can this fifty-year-old body walk? Danielle is not fit. She has a bunion, two so-so knees. All afternoon she's trudged, watching her shadow lengthen, eventually stretching all the way to Martin, ahead of her. Now the sun has gone behind a hill to her left, the evening air is cooling, and still no sign of a destination. Not a word from anyone — besides Pierre. He said, "*Sacré!*" when he tripped over a tree root and went down. The shorter masked man turned from where he's been all along, in the lead, and flicked him on the head with the back of his hand. Pierre was instantly on his feet, stiff with rage but walking.

As far as Danielle can tell, he hasn't made another misstep since. Pierre exudes determination, his wiry arms confidently pushing back branches. But determined to what, Danielle wonders? Has he considered that what happens next could be worse? Danielle's only clue to her future is Ramón, who looked extremely compliant when the short man shoved a paper into his hand and ordered him back to San Salvador. Ramón and that paper say these men aren't about to execute anyone. Not yet. They want something. Aren't the others bothered, not knowing what it is? Tina is fast on Pierre's heels, Antoine next. Only Martin looks as unsteady as Danielle feels. He's not good at anticipating oncoming twigs. Every so often he ducks awkwardly to avoid gouging out his eyes. But Danielle lags far behind even him, rejecting this madness with every step. The taller masked man is only further back there to avoid losing her altogether.

Now something strange. A faint rumbling. The ground shaking. Danielle puts her palms out to the sides, feels like she's hula-hooping as the earth shifts left, then right. Everyone stops, steadying themselves. Danielle thinks her luck cannot be this bad. There can't also be an earthquake today.

"Tell them it will pass," the short man calls out, completely calm. He moves a few steps to one side and makes eye contact with Danielle. "Tell them."

Danielle realizes he wants her to translate. She doesn't relish the responsibility, but no one else in the group has Spanish, and they look bewildered as motion continues under their boots. She repeats the man's words in English. Ten seconds later, the rumbling stops. Martin looks at her like, what the hell was that? Danielle can't begin to imagine.

The short one approaches, glaring around, apparently unhappy that the quake has interrupted his uphill marathon. "Give them water," he growls at his tall accomplice, who immediately removes the pack he's been carrying, unzipping its main compartment. He pulls out a cowboy hat and places it over his dark mask, which makes him look like a dummy in a hat store window. Then he lifts out a large canteen, handing it to Danielle without making eye contact. She sips eagerly, ignoring him as he hovers, waiting to grab it back.

"And you can piss over there," the shorter one adds, pointing behind a large tree.

Danielle says this in English and Tina beelines for the spot, Antoine right behind her. Danielle crosses her arms. She has no urge to piss on the ground like a dog, no desire at all except to get wherever they're going. The only place she can envision is the guerrilla camp she stayed in longest in 1980, which had a cook tent, bunkers, latrines.

By the time the short one tells them to get back in line, the last light of day is disappearing. Danielle changes her mind. The ground looks inviting. She's prepared to go K9, put her pack down and call it home, paw the bruise on her scalp where her hair was pulled. But the tall one reaches into his loot bag once more and pulls out a handful of battery-powered lights, each no bigger than a quarter. He attaches them near the bottom of every pack and gets the group moving, single file. The one on Martin's bag give off a dim, pulsing green flicker every other second. Danielle moves forward, following what rapidly becomes her sole sign of life.

Mitch Wall tells his new favourite joke, pausing before killing the punchline. "So the Quebecker yells back, '*Toilette* pepper! *Toilette* pepper!'"

For a moment it doesn't look like anyone besides the Danish call centre owner gets it. Then Carlos chuckles behind a slanted index finger and the rest, mostly locals, join in. Mitch laughs too. His wife subscribed him to some online outfit that sends one Canadian-themed joke a week to his inbox. This was the best so far.

A woman in a black vest and crisp white shirt comes around with a tray of mini quiches. Mitch takes two onto a napkin while Carlos heads to the bar, returning with Scotch glasses.

"*Salud*," says Mitch, taking one, then tells the Dane about the expansion at El Pico — more, probably, than the guy wants to hear. El Salvador is drowning in call centres and he's late to the party. Mitch is not normally a gloater, but he can't help going into detail about NorthOre's forecasted earnings.

Afterwards Carlos suggests they take a walk, and he and Mitch cross through French doors and wander towards the pool area where more guests are mingling, their clothes reflecting ripples of light from fixtures under the water's surface. A band whose female lead is stuffed into a tube dress plays a slow, romantic song in Spanish. The air is humid, flowery.

"You think those guys even knew where Canada is?" says Mitch to Carlos, shaking his head.

"Do most of your friends outside your industry know where El Salvador is? Anywhere in Latin America — besides Cancún? Or Veradero?"

Mitch grins. If his friends could see him now. Everyone knows he considers lefties to be one illogical opinion away from certifiable. But here he is, taking jibes from Carlos Reyes, a well-known former guerrilla strategist. "So listen, I'd really like to get you up to the site. Definitely before the launch."

"Of course. I'd have come sooner, but —"

"You're busy." Mitch nudges him. "Hey, Rome wasn't built in a day. Neither is a political career, right?"

"I will make time next week, Mitch."

"Machine's fueled and ready when you are." Mitch's BlackBerry vibrates. He pulls it from his jacket. "Hunh. Security. Hold on," he says, stepping away, a finger to his ear to listen over the band. "Everything alright, Manuel?"

"I am pulling into the hotel, *Señor* Wall. Please. Come to the entrance."

"Here? Why, what's going on?" Mitch looks back at Carlos, who's swirling his Scotch, deep in thought. The band has just put down their instruments for a break. Mitch sees the singer go out of her way to make eye contact with Carlos as she walks inside. He's a dapper man. Great suit.

"Please, *Jefe*. I will explain."

Twenty minutes later Carlos and Mitch sit across from one another in a tranquil, moody corner of the hotel's lobby, the drooping frond of a potted palm extending overhead. Manuel Sobero, Mitch's chief of security, is on his phone nearby, busy doubling his manpower at the mine.

"What can be taking them so long?" says Mitch, rechecking the screen of his handheld device for the email he's been expecting from the Canadian embassy.

"Probably they're verifying that it isn't a hoax," says Carlos. "Let me make my own calls, see what I can find out. We do not always have — receive — the best information through official channels."

Carlos is being extra-precise with his English. Mitch wants to tell him not to bother. He does better than ninety-nine percent of the Salvadorans Mitch deals with. And he's offering concrete help.

So far, the embassy has only doled out crumbs, saying some kid dropped a ransom note on their doorstep today from a man claiming that he's got five Canadian hostages and that he wants something from NorthOre. The embassy wouldn't say what. They were supposed to forward the note ten minutes ago.

Sobero approaches. "Someone will drive your car back to the apartment, *Jefe*. I've posted men there. You can ride with me." Sobero eyes Carlos, who's getting up to make his calls, then adds, "I cannot secure this location. We should go."

Mitch has the feeling Sobero doesn't like Carlos Reyes. The optics must be strange to a former military man like Manuel, Mitch chumming around with a man who was so firmly on the other side of El Salvador's civil war. It's strange for Mitch too. But he knows Carlos has undergone a complete transformation since the old days. He travels in powerful circles now. He's a leftie with a twist — and contacts.

"Thanks, Manuel. But I think I'll stick around while Carlos does his research." Mitch has worked too hard for anything to go wrong so close to the El Pico launch.

Carlos sits back down. "Mitch, let me tell you what I —" he stops, turning slightly.

Mitch understands. He nods towards Sobero, who obliges, withdrawing, giving them privacy. "Manuel is good at what he does, you know."

Carlos ignores the remark. "You need rest, Mitch. We can speak tomorrow."

"Rest? I can't go to bed. No offense, but your country's not exactly highly organized. Dealing with a kidnapping at home would be bad enough. On your turf, I'm screwed. How do I make this go away?"

Mitch's BlackBerry buzzes before Carlos can answer. "Fuck, finally," says Mitch, pulling up the embassy's email and forwarding it to Carlos and Sobero. All three are silent as they read the attached, scanned ransom note. Struggling through the Spanish, Mitch finishes last.

To the Ambassador,

Today I have detained five tourists from your country. They are unharmed. In exchange for their freedom, I demand the following:

1. NorthOre must cease operations at its Mil Sueños mine, including all blasting on the mountain called El Pico.

2. The Argentinean team led by Alejandro Reverte must be brought to the mine to exhume the remains of my family, who were murdered on El Pico before NorthOre took control of the land.

3. The remains must be given a Christian burial.

The first demand must be met no later than Monday, April 11. I will then send instructions for where to search for the remains and I will release one detainee. If the demands are not met, we will execute one of the foreigners and we will continue to take another life every day.

My family has been on El Pico in silence, without justice, for too long. I will not let their memory be destroyed along with the mountain.

A humble Salvadoran peasant

Mitch is at a loss. A shutdown. This close to the launch date. The very thought of it makes his stomach churn. He turns to Carlos, desperate for his take.

Carlos has a hand to his chin, running it back and forth, as he often does before speaking. In the six months Mitch has known him, he has never once seen Carlos rush. Eventually, leaning forward, Carlos puts both palms on the low coffee table between them and looks Mitch in the eye. "A hostage situation involving foreigners and your mine will be a big story here, in the press. You must appear relaxed and calm. Like this has nothing to do with you."

"But it doesn't!"

"Exactly." Carlos pauses again. "Why don't I come to the mine sooner — tomorrow, even? I'll keep making calls to my people close to the police. By then, I'll have more for you. We can discuss in person, prepare a strong response for the newspapers and TV."

Mitch smiles, regaining his balance slightly. "Probably this guy's bluffing, right?"

"He — or they — may be bluffing," says Carlos, sounding doubtful. "It's too soon to say."

Sobero is standing by patiently. Nothing has registered on his face since reading the note, and it's clear he's not about to share his thoughts with Carlos around. "For your safety, *Jefe*. We should leave."

Carlos nods, encouraging Mitch to listen.

Mitch gets up, thanking his stars that he knows both these Salvadoran insiders. That's his edge and he's got to use it. Because one thing is certain: El Pico will launch on schedule in two weeks' time. "Forget about the apartment," he says. "Send someone to pick up some clothes, Manuel. I'm going to my mine. Tonight."

February 19, 1980

Dear Neela,

A few things, if you ever get it in your head to cover a revolution in
Central America:

1. food sucks
2. fleas
3. tampon shortages
4. avoid being low woman on the totem pole

You don't want details on 1–3, trust me. But 4's even trickier.
The faction won't let me out of camp, even though I've heard Times
and Herald reporters are out there as we speak. A student paper
isn't high priority, I guess.

I'm trying to be patient — and to prove myself. I did a good interview
with a fifteen-year-old who joined up because her family couldn't afford
to feed her and the faction can (but see #1 to keep this in perspective).
She's training to be a fighter, says she wants to be a Comandante
one day.

I'm dying for more material like this, but camp only provides so much.
Most people our age are in the actual war. Here, it's older people (mostly
women) doing the cooking, laundry, etc., and young recruits who aren't
ready to be sent anywhere else. They're all from the countryside, very
shy and reserved. They stare at my red hair, which was funny for a while.
When I've tried to talk to them about the war, they just repeat clichés
like "You can't hold back the people." Nothing original for my stories.

Still figuring this place out, I guess.

DB

MONDAY
APRIL 4

DAYBREAK. *Foothills, Morazán province*

Step-step, step-step. Danielle stares at the outline of her boots as, improbably, they continue to carry her forward, the details of their laces and purple and brown seaming clarifying as the inky night recedes. She has not experienced this moment of the day in years. She once found it hopeful. Anything might be possible before the sun is up, before objects and people are cemented back into their static forms.

Suddenly, she ploughs into Martin's pack. He's come to a stop.

"Put your bags down there," says the short man, marching down the line and nodding at a grassy, nondescript area to their left. Danielle goes first, stepping into what can't even be called a clearing — no tents, no latrines. She unloads her pack with a thud to signal the others to let theirs down too. Her back is immediately cold as chilly air flows over copious sweat.

"Stand there," the man says, pointing away from the bags.

Robotically, Danielle obeys. These clipped instructions have got to end sooner or later, like the walking. As the rest of the group comes to huddle around her, the taller masked man steps away, disappearing through the trees. The shorter one remains. Antoine, on Danielle's right, is using his sleeve to wipe a runny nose. He has an honest face, and Danielle exchanges a glance with him that gives her a tiny burst of comfort. But Tina gasps, making Danielle look back. The tall one is returning, and he's not alone. Two people follow, cracking branches as they emerge from the trees. Both are masked, both women. Tina starts to cry. Danielle is too tired for an emotional response. She can only do the math. That's four altogether. Four bad guys against five weaklings.

The women come directly towards the group, gun straps pressed across their chests, their arms full of green plastic. "They're Rita and Delmi," says the short one as the first, Rita, steps up to Danielle and throws plastic at her feet like it's a bag of garbage, another chunk of it at Antoine. The other woman, Delmi, who's plump, spilling out of a tight t-shirt, more sheepishly deposits three bundles in front of the others, then backs away with a slight giggle.

"That's Cristóbal," the short man continues, nodding towards his tall accomplice, Mr. Hat Store Dummy. "And I'm Pepe." He pauses, giving the group time to take in these names. "Now you'll sleep," he adds.

The women accomplices eagerly pull up their guns, guarding closely as each member of the group unfolds a tarp. Danielle smoothes out the new-smelling plastic, creating a thin barrier between herself and the raw earth. Then she gets down and closes her eyelids tightly, blocking out the morning.

11 AM. Mil Sueños *mine, Municipality of Los Pampanos*

The photo caption in tomorrow's paper will read: "NorthOre owner Mitchell Wall, recently targeted by terrorist threats, preparing to tour *Mil Sueños* with probable Democratic Alliance Party candidate Carlos Mendoza Reyes." Mitch is banking on it. He and Carlos played around with the wording for some time. Now they tuck away their helmets, smile and shake on it. The camera snaps multiple frames.

"Okay," says the photographer, capping his lens, and Carlos walks over to run through the shots with him. Mitch stays put, trusting him to cherry-pick the very best, the one in which he looks his most cool, calm and collected.

Sobero, who has come outside to join them, signals modestly from the edge of the tarmac. Mitch waves him closer.

"*Jefe*. I've chosen two good men to begin making inquiries into where the foreigners might have gone. These individuals are very skilled. They will not fail."

"That's fantastic," says Mitch, though Carlos has brought news from his own contacts that suggests the hostages could be just about anywhere. It's been twenty-four hours and there are no witnesses besides their bus driver, who says he knows nothing. "Let's also see what the police can sniff out."

· "I have more freedom than the police."

Mitch looks Sobero over. The top button of his white work shirt reaches nearly his chin. His too-round eyes blink quickly. "I don't want anything dangerous, Manuel," says Mitch, feeling, as he has before, a bit sorry for Sobero and his reduced position. He was "somebody" in El Salvador before the war. After it ended, Sobero had to start from scratch.

"Nothing dangerous. Just what is necessary," says Sobero, running his hand, not much bigger than a child's, slowly down the lapel of his cheap jacket. He always speaks in general terms about his tactics, has ever since Mitch hired his fledgling firm, MaxSeguro, in '96 to clear out squatters from the site of the future mine. Sobero did a fast, thorough job, but never specified his methods.

Mitch looks towards Carlos, who's returning from escorting the photographer towards the guard assigned to see him out. Mitch meets Carlos halfway and slaps him on the back in gratitude. The photo shoot was Carlos's idea. The newspaper the photographer works for has the largest daily circulation in El Salvador. Carlos has known him for years and managed to talk him into driving up from the capital. Genius!

"Let's get some air," says Mitch, grinning, guiding his friend to the door of the helicopter and stepping up after him. Belting in, Mitch experiences a sharp anticipatory thrill. He loves aerial tours. Sure, they're costly. But this is Carlos's first visit to *Mil Sueños*. It would be rude not to take him around in style, exactly as the newspaper will report.

The pilot starts his engine and a deep buzz builds to a high-pitched squeal above them as the blades begin to turn. Mitch puts on his headset. He glances towards Sobero, who is still on the tarmac, his hands clasped behind his back, looking put out. Sobero can be loyal to a fault. Last night, on the drive to the mine, he peppered his conversation with unflattering anecdotes about Carlos Reyes: Carlos's history with women. His conniving politics. The unsavoury elements behind the new centrist political party, the Democratic Alliance, or DAP, that Carlos will represent if he runs in the next Salvadoran elections. Mitch took it all with a grain of salt. Sobero doesn't seem to get how important Carlos will be to the future of the mine if he wins a seat — for *any* party. Then, this morning, Sobero had the gall to suggest that Mitch should cancel Carlos's visit altogether for security reasons. Mitch told him to get a grip. Carlos Reyes is more than a contact. He's a friend.

Now Sobero's thin hair sweeps up into a pointed triangle as dust swirls around him. He remains on guard, looking rather puny, as they lift off. Mitch considers the final bit of gossip he pieced out about Carlos last night. "You know, *Jefe, Señor* Reyes has a unique history with helicopters? He enjoys shooting them out of the sky." When Mitch, stunned, asked Sobero to please expand, Sobero shook his head, blowing off the question, saying it was just an old war tale. Mitch didn't press. He sympathizes with Sobero's aversion to people, like Carlos, who've done so well since the Salvadoran war, even though they were once gun-wielding Marxists, while Sobero's own career was snuffed out because of some bogus allegations of war crimes. But as they leave the ground, Mitch wishes he'd asked for details. Carlos shot down an actual helicopter! That can't be easy. Especially considering the other tidbit Sobero passed along just before Carlos arrived: "He'll flaunt his *bravado*," Sobero predicted, exaggerating the word. "But *Señor* Reyes has a fear of flying. Poor man."

"Doing alright, there?" Mitch asks Carlos now, seeing sweat bead along the rim of his friend's helmet.

"Fine, thank you."

"We'll just do a quick go-round," Mitch assures him. He figures that if what Sobero says is true, getting airborne might actually help Carlos. No one can afford to indulge fear. If Carlos is going to get into politics, he'll definitely have to leave his comfort zone.

After lift-off they hover a moment above the boxcar-like portables housing NorthOre's offices. As the helicopter's nose straightens, Carlos wraps his fingers under the edge of his seat, his arms straight as boards. Mitch taps him on one taut shoulder and begins a running commentary, keeping the mood light. "This, my friend, is the power of believing."

After the portables, not far to the northeast, the helicopter next passes Mitch's processing plant, its jumble of uneven pipe lengths glinting silver in the sun. "We're retrofitting it to handle the output from the Pico expansion. Putting in the coin now so that this time next year, it'll have the most cost-efficient production of pavé bars south of Mexico. We'll get it all back in eighteen months at full production. Markets can't get enough."

Next come the leaching fields. Mitch has always thought they look like stairs to some giant's house. Reddish, several soccer fields long, made up of finely crushed ore, they are stacked storeys high, black tubing running down each enormous step. "With this kind of mine, you want to clear the overgrowth, blast loose the ore, crush it, spread it out, then distribute a mild cyanide solution over it." Even in Mitch's own ears, his explanation sounds too much like a geologist's summary. Getting a degree in the field was never his passion. More a matter of getting his father's dream out of the way before he could go after his own. He aims for a less technical tone. "Basically, we gotta grab the gold chemically. Suck it right from the ore. Then we drain it away and catch it at the bottom." Mitch points downhill. "But it's not what people think. It's harmless." As he says this, they fly directly over the pressurized tubes, pocked with a regular series of holes, from which the cyanide solution, diluted with a steady supply of groundwater, flies into the air, creating tremendous arcs, before landing on the crushed ore. Gravity has already drawn some of the solution, with the gold it has taken from the ore, down to vast collection ponds — pools lined with a special material designed to prevent leaking.

"If people could see how well-made these are. Maybe it would shut them up." Mitch knows that critics consider the ponds flawed, always harping about overflows during the annual rainy season, heavy metals seeping out. But anyone sitting where he is could see the system works. And where's their evidence? If the extremists had their way, everyone in this country would be sorting coffee beans for a living. If they want to talk about overflows, how about the local coffers overflowing with his tax dollars! "From there," he says, shaking away echoes of his opponents' constant whining, "the gold settles at the bottom, we gather it up, melt it into bars, ship it, and there you are. Quarterly results!"

Further along, an even rarer view: the open pit that has already made Mitch richer than he ever expected to get (not to mention his father's much humbler expectations, God rest his soul), and which has convinced his investors that he can successfully expand. From the air the pit looks like a moon crater, multiple rust-coloured layers deep. Around the edge run crude roadways where trucks on oversized wheels bump along, carrying out yet more ore to stack on the giant's steps.

"Quite the sight, eh?"

Carlos just stares out his window.

"Wait until you see what's next," says Mitch, though he wonders if Carlos is going to make it without tossing his cookies. The helicopter blades thwack as the pilot banks hard, bringing a mountain into view. "There she is. El Pico."

Mitch has never understood the name. To him, Pico looks more like a colossal tooth than a bird's beak. Its rocky tip, sharp and exposed, widens into green, more gently sloping sides, and finally into a slowly extending base where, because of the new road and stacks of cut trees and massive drilling equipment and tractors, it isn't easy to picture the settlement of Ixtán that Mitch knows was here before Manuel Sobero got rid of those squatters. Wait — is it them? Has one of the former squatters dreamed up these demands out of sour grapes? Mitch strains towards the window, examining his land, asking himself whether there really could be dead bodies here. Fifteen years ago, this was a war zone. But if you go back far enough, isn't every place? There's probably traces of conflict covering every square inch of the planet. Why should he be the one railroaded into putting the innards of his property on display?

"Incredible," says Carlos, admiring the mountain.

Mitch beams. Even now, Carlos looks handsome, more or less composed. The man is 1,200 feet above ground, flying against his better judgment, all to help out a friend. Comfort zone breached!

When the blades come to a stop, the pilot gets out and opens the door. He offers a hand to Carlos, who looks unsteady. Mitch invites his friend inside for coffee. "We'll save the champagne for the launch," he says, winking.

Carlos doesn't return the smile. "El Pico will be a great achievement, Mitch. But today, it is only an idea. It can only succeed if you handle this abduction."

Mitch smoothes his hair against the hot breeze. Any fear Carlos felt up above has apparently burned off. His voice is rock solid, and his warning strikes Mitch as overly dire. Usually they're too busy dreaming of the future — of the Pico expansion, of how they're going to help this shithole of a country grow — to get bogged down by obstacles. "Someone is trying to hurt me," he says, feeling wounded by the change in his friend's demeanour. Then he realizes. "It's not the squatters. It's that Committee!" Mitch doesn't like to use the full name of the group that's had it in for him since day one. The Committee for the Environment — like they know anything about it; he's the one with environmental science Ph.D.s on staff. "From Los Pampanos. The ones who are always bad-mouthing me," he says, recalling every trick, every ruse those nuts have tried against him so far — none successful. "They want to derail El Pico."

Carlos gives him a long, assessing look. "It is important to find out who took the hostages, obviously. But maybe not as important as it seems. The Canadians have to live, regardless of who is responsible. That is the priority. Your ambassador has already understood this. Her own reputation is at stake."

"The ambassador? What's she got to do with it?"

"One of my contacts tells me she's requested meetings at the top political levels. She's nervous about casualties if the police intercede."

"But she can't really — she's not a factor here."

"Oh?"

Just the way Carlos says it, Mitch begins to doubt.

"It would be worth deciding for yourself," Carlos adds as they begin walking towards the portables.

He often drops hints like this, morsels that Mitch will later conclude are in fact good ideas. Mitch recalls the first time he ever saw Carlos Reyes. He received an invitation out of the blue to a speech Carlos was giving and thought, why not? Carlos showed up looking elegant and told his audience that countries like El Salvador are being forced onto new ground, politically, that no one can afford to dwell in the past. He emphasized that El Salvador needs large-scale investment to survive. And then he used the example of Mitch's mine, saying the name, *Mil Sueños,* making it an example. Mitch was so pleased he proudly elbowed the man seated beside him. Carlos ended his speech by saying that too many Salvadoran ex-guerrillas are afraid of the future. But he isn't. He will be the first to take the leap, wear the brave face. Mitch approached him afterwards to shake his hand. They've been in touch ever since.

A guard opens the door. The air-conditioned hallway feels cold after the noonday heat. Mitch leads the way to his office.

"I'm seeing them tonight, by the way," says Carlos. "That Committee for the Environment."

Mitch stops, the air suddenly icy.

Carlos just laughs at Mitch's discomfort, coming alongside him and wrapping a warm palm around the base of Mitch's neck, a Latin move Mitch would normally find too intimate. Somehow, Carlos pulls it off.

"Don't worry," Carlos adds. "You need all the information you can get."

"First say your name."

"Tina Chiblow."

Danielle looks down at the handwritten note: "Now repeat: 'I am a member of the Partners for Justice in the Americas delegation to the municipality of Los Pampanos, El Salvador.'"

Tina says the words quietly, looking straight into the camera, the chords in her long neck clearly defined, her cheeks shining with tears or sweat. Probably both.

Danielle consults her paper again. "'I urge the government to do whatever is necessary to secure our release by Monday, April 11th, 2005. Otherwise, these people will take our lives one by one.'"

Tina pauses then lets the same words fall from her mouth like lead weights.

Danielle looks over at the kidnapper who calls himself Pepe. He pulls his attention away from the small viewing screen and nods her on. Danielle is struck all over again by the oddness of interacting with someone wearing a ski mask. "Now you have a minute to say something to your family," she says, looking away. She hates that steady pressure Pepe applies with his eyes.

Tina is on a low stump about five feet off, her hiking boots planted in a scatter of dry leaves, her kneecaps forced up near her chest. She looks momentarily horrified at the idea of addressing her family. Danielle wants to say that she understands; this is not exactly a cozy setting. Stuck out on an ant-eaten tree trunk in dirty clothes, underslept, hot, traumatized, strangers ogling you — four of them wearing balaclavas and carrying rifles. But Tina's eyes also seem angry, maybe at Danielle for overseeing the translation of the videotaping. And so Danielle also has the urge to defend herself. She can't exactly go off script here. Pepe's gun hangs with nauseating heft from the strap on his shoulder. So she nods at Tina as empathetically as she can and silently begs her to get on with it.

The young woman pulls nervously on the tip of her ponytail and looks back into the camera. "Um. Okay. Well. What can I say? Mom, I'm fine. I'm not hurt. I don't want you to worry."

This Tina is much more hesitant than the one Danielle spent a half day with in the capital city. The cool, knowing tone is gone. Tina continues ad-libbing what she seems to understand can't sound like the last message she'll ever send her family. "Uncle Ralph, we'll have to wait a while on that presentation I promised you. . . . John, looks like we're in the same boat now. At least you have a lawyer." She nearly smiles, touching her hair again, tilting her head.

So this is what full-time yoga does for you. Tina's shapely face (only slightly swollen with bug bites) and her body are simultan-eously soft and firm. Danielle wishes she could put up a barrier so that all the men — not just the kidnappers, but the other members of their group — couldn't gawk so blatantly. Danielle scans the faces of her fellow Canadians. Pierre is checking Tina out with a blend of judgment and boredom. Beside him Antoine has a wor-ried, questioning expression, like he's silently asking her to please tell him when he can go back to peaceful, self-contained Quebec City. A few feet away Martin shifts his rump and stares at Tina with open, hopeless attraction.

"I miss you lots, John. Call Mum. She hates it when you don't call."

Tina's done. Pepe must understand enough to know, because he straightens up and looks expectantly at Danielle, who repeats back Tina's statement in Spanish. How horrible! Reiterating these kids' personal messages has felt like spying. Martin, just before Tina, cried so hard Danielle could barely make out his words about how he still believed God would protect him. Antoine spoke to his parents with achingly straightforward affection. Pepe has listened closely through it all, his dark, almond-shaped eyes unwavering. Now something about them stirs a memory. Pepe reminds Danielle of someone she knew many years ago. But no. Not him. She tries to shake away the disturbing connection. More likely what she's remembering is just the choking atmosphere of violence.

Pepe sends Tina off. Danielle knows her turn is coming. She's going to have to say something to her daughter. She won't try for anything too lovey-dovey. That always backfires with Aida. But Pepe chooses Pierre instead. Wasting no time, Rita takes him by the arm. Rita, with her small head and tufts of bushy, dyed blonde hair that stick out from under her mask near chin level. She has a jerky way of moving and a meanness about her that seems to go beyond her role here. But she feels it again as Rita conveys intense pleasure in hauling Pierre up as roughly as possible. The cigarette he's been smoking falls to the ground. The kidnappers have been plying them with smokes — as pacifiers, presumably. Danielle gets it all too well. She sees herself crawl over to pick up Pierre's, brush it off, inhale. She quit a decade ago, but a slow, unhurried cig is still among the most desirable things she can think of. Fear keeps her glued to her spot beside the camera, of course, and Pierre doesn't try to reach for it either, even though it's practically begging to be rescued, right at his feet. Instead, he angles his head towards Antoine, trying to look like he's above it, then yanks his arm back from Rita so hard she loses her grip. Rita only snorts, content to clamp down doubly, but the interaction provokes a discernible spike in Danielle's anxiety.

Pierre comes to sit on the decayed log that faces the camera. Filling out the shot is a green tarp like the kind they all slept on. The kidnappers have strung it between low branches. Behind that, above the trees, Danielle can see the range of mountains that she remembers well, that mark the border between El Salvador and Honduras. A long, long way from Toronto.

When Pepe gives her the signal, she begins rereading the statement. "Start with your na —" but Pierre doesn't wait for her to finish.

"Elvis Presley," he says expressionlessly.

Danielle forces a smile, like he's joking. "Your *real* name."

"John Lennon."

Danielle's palms moisten. She glances around. The others all seem confused, except Antoine. The fingers of both hands are crawling up his face towards his temples as if he's scared, expecting something bad from his friend. The other kidnappers, Rita and Delmi, along with Pepe's gangly sidekick, Cristóbal, exchange quizzical looks.

"*No tengo patiencia para burlos,*" says Pepe without looking up from his screen.

"He's getting impatient, Pierre. Just say your name, please."

"Pierre Charbonneau, of *Québec.*"

"Now repeat . . ." Danielle reads out Pepe's script before pausing, waiting for Pierre to talk. He squints at her.

"*C'est d'la merde.*"

Danielle tries to understand. Could this be pride? Neela said Pierre is active in the Quebec nationalist movement. So he thinks he's a rogue? Sees himself as a grownup playing by his own rules, maybe. Her heart beats faster: she has been abducted alongside a man-child with delusions of difference.

"*Qué, cabrón?*" Pepe is standing straight now, addressing him.

Pierre looks right back at him. "*Me — erde,*" he repeats. "I'm not going to say his words." He turns to Danielle. "What's he going to do? Shoot us — every one? How's he going to get his million, or whatever he wants, if we're all dead? I'm here for El Salvador. For the people. To learn. Do they even know? Why we came 'ere?"

Pepe looks towards Danielle too, his eyes glowing with interest. He's waiting for the Spanish. But Danielle can't produce it.

Why is she here? Not for the same reasons as Pierre who, for all his bluster, probably really has come on this observational delegation because of his idealism and for its stated aim of seeing how rural Salvadorans live, listening to their stories about the trouble a foreign mine is causing them. Danielle's own agenda goes so far beyond this her tongue cannot form words for it. Which might be reasonable enough, except that Pepe is reaching for his gun — his second, smaller one. As he untucks it from the belt of his fatigues, Danielle flashes back to the moment on the bus, just after Pierre pissed his pants. His eyes weren't only red and scared. They were vicious. He was humiliated, belittled. He looks exactly like that now, as Pepe rushes him. He's still wearing the same pants.

"I am not a tourist," Pierre yells. "You have to listen."

Pepe picks the young man up by the collar with one fist. Pepe is shorter by nearly a foot, but he has heavy, muscular legs and those big, dense arms that Danielle knows firsthand are capable of applying crushing pressure. He pushes Pierre backwards, towards a tree, which the young man thumps against hard.

Antoine steps forward, as if to help, but Tina has the good sense to put a hand to his chest before any of the kidnappers can react.

"*Daniela!*" says Pepe, raising his voice to Pierre but addressing her.

Right. Translation. Danielle stutters out in Spanish everything Pierre has said about the delegation coming to El Salvador for the people, that they aren't tourists.

Taking in this information, Pepe still seems relatively calm, like he's confident that he can intimidate Pierre out of whatever notions of bravery have gripped his immature mind. He doesn't even raise his voice. "Tell this *desgraciado puto* that if he's ready to die for El Salvador, to say one more word."

Danielle translates through sudden tears.

"Tell him I think he's bluffing," says Pierre, seething.

"No, Pierre! Don't do this," Danielle says, but immediately regrets it. Her words sound chastising, parental. She imagines Aida hearing them, crossing her arms. "Just stop, please," she implores. "Stop talking."

"Why should I? He has to listen — to you especially. You're the one who wrote abou —" Pierre catches himself, changes tack. "You're supposed to be the leader!"

But it's too late. Pepe pins Pierre by the neck and turns to Danielle, his laser eyes finding hers. "What did he say?"

"He says. . ."

"Tell me!" Pepe yells, and Danielle can see that his calm is breaking, ready to splinter like a homemade bomb. His gun is pressed directly to Pierre's head.

Danielle knows that they are all going to suffer for Pierre's big mouth. For her past, too. She wishes she'd burned those letters. Then she wouldn't even be here. She and Aida could've gone on like before. "He says you should listen to us."

"He said 'wrote.' What about writing? Who wrote?" Then, though he seems already to understand, Pepe repeats at the top of his lungs "W HO?"

"I did," says Danielle.

"When?"

"I came to write about *la guerrilla*." She's scrambling again, needs to rescue herself. "It was just a student newspaper, and they took — I lost my notes. The articles never got published."

Danielle knows the others might be able to pick up stray words from her Spanish: *guerrilla*, or *estudiante*, or *publicados*. Will they guess the rest? She can feel them trying to weave together a meaning. Only Pierre really knows. He got the basics about her past, back in San Salvador, when he pressed her on why she was leading the delegation instead of Neela. Danielle was forced to confide how, back in the dinosaur age, in her last year of university, she'd applied for permission to live with one of the five guerrilla factions that were starting a war against El Salvador's oligarchy. She instinctively left out everything else. These omissions have now morphed into a dark mystery Danielle can feel the others trying to probe as much as Pepe. She can practically hear them asking themselves who this old woman in front of them really is. Rita, who has stepped in closer to the group, is listening intently with the energy of a vulture as she, too, probes the mystery, her gun pointed.

"Where were you?" says Pepe, still addressing Danielle.

"Here. In Morazán."

Pepe's eyes widen ever so slightly, their steadiness shaken. Then, suddenly, he swings back towards Pierre and puts so much pressure on his neck that the boy begins to choke. "Listen to me, *hijo de puta*. I am going to squeeze the life out of you in front of your friends. And then I'll leave a bullet in your skull so you understand. How much will it count for then, your devotion to El Salvador?"

Pierre, who clearly has only the vaguest idea of what is being said to him, tries to articulate words between gasps. No one makes them out. But just as abruptly, Pepe lets go, raises his chin, pulls back his shoulders and returns to his position behind the camera. "Tell him he has thirty seconds to talk or I'll shoot him," he says, bending down to adjust the LCD screen. He might as well be talking about the weather. The bomb has been abruptly defused.

Danielle numbly repeats these words. She watches Pierre pull his t-shirt collar away and rub his neck. He wobbles as he gets to his feet, looking smaller, rumpled, the cult leader dethroned. When he gets to the stump he puts down a hand, steadying himself before sitting.

Danielle can't stop crying. Stupid, stupid, she thinks, angry with herself for it — for everything. "'I urge the government to do whatever is necessary to secure our release by Monday, April 11th,

2005,'" she says. "'Otherwise, these people will take our lives one by one.'"

Repeating the statement, Pierre's voice is a clash of squeaks and croaks.

"Now something for his family," says Pepe, not moving his eyes from the camera.

When Danielle echoes this in English, Pierre just shakes his head. Danielle worries that another, worse explosion of anger will result — a mushroom cloud no one can survive. But Pepe mustn't care much either way about the personal stuff because he presses a button to end the recording.

"Now you," he says to her, as Cristóbal leaves the campsite, returning with a length of rope and a blue bandana. He pulls Pierre to one side and starts tying.

———

Pepe is putting the video camera back into its case.

Cristóbal approaches. "*Listo.*"

Pepe glances back at the hostages to assess whether Pierre's hands and mouth have been adequately bound. He gives the camera to his cousin. "Pack this away. And tell Rita to go easy on them."

Cristóbal tilts his hat, letting in some air. "*Sí*," he replies, but he keeps his eyes averted. He takes the case and turns it over absently.

"Your wife could be dangerous for us if she overreacts."

Cristóbal shakes his head. He knows Rita can put up a fuss. That's her way. Unlike Delmi, who has no spine, who will do whatever Rita or Pepe tells her.

"She will be," says Pepe, insisting.

Cristóbal still doesn't look back at him, and the men stand, just a foot from one another, in an edgy silence until, in a sudden move, Pepe lifts a fist towards Cristóbal, who flinches, his hand going up to protect himself. But the fist slows, coming to land with a light touch across Cristóbal's left bicep. "If she's hard on you, it's okay," Pepe says teasingly, and uses his knuckles to grind into the arm muscle.

Cristóbal smiles, relieved. Rita is their one source of conflict. Pepe has openly debated several times whether it's been a mistake to take advantage of her eagerness to be in on the plan, but Cristóbal always reminds him that it was better to include only people they know. His wife and her sister are both hard workers. And Cristóbal is as eager as Rita for the money Pepe is going to pay them. They'll use it to buy passage into the U.S. The best *coyotes* charge $8,000, and Cristóbal won't chance it on the cheaper kind, the ones who might leave you stranded halfway across a swollen river. He hopes Pepe will join them in *Los Estados*. But everything depends on Pepe placing a small amount of trust in Rita.

Pepe holds up the camera's memory card. "If Rita did her job, this will get to San Salvador."

"She did."

"We'll see." Pepe walks off. "I have to take the call. Don't wait. Pack up."

Cristóbal watches him leave and sees Pepe catch Delmi's eye. Cristóbal knows Rita has encouraged a relationship between the two. "He either fucks my sister or he'll end up fucking one of the foreigners. Which is easier for you?" she said, and Cristóbal conceded because he knew she was right. But he and Pepe have never discussed it. Delmi simply went to Pepe at some point, and Rita looks after the money. She's always thinking of money, but Cristóbal believes she's doing it for them, for their future.

As far as he knows, Pepe doesn't have any relations with women except paid ones. At least it's been that way since the war ended. That's when the cousins ran into one another at a construction site in San Miguel. "Missed a spot," said a man standing behind Cristóbal as he was washing his hands in a bucket. Turning around, Cristóbal couldn't believe his eyes. There was his childhood companion, José Molina Domingo, *Pepito*, smiling, teasing as he always had. They became inseparable. *"Puro Indio,"* Pepe always calls him. And it's true. Cristóbal looks Indian. But he doesn't know anything about the Lenca, the ancient people Pepe says they're descended from, and he always worries that Pepe is insulting him. Cristóbal only did a few years of school and doesn't read the way Pepe does — especially not the news, which Pepe has an insatiable appetite for. Pepe is much more capable than he is, but they manage to get along anyway. Better than manage. Cristóbal attributes this affinity to shared blood.

As Pepe disappears from the campsite and Cristóbal tucks the camera back into his large canvas bag, he remembers those early days after the war, when Pepe was still drinking. He'd get into fights. One time Cristóbal knew just from the face of the man challenging his cousin that he wanted to murder Pepe. The wounds from the war were still so fresh. People acted on impulse. Pepe took the first punch like he wasn't planning on doing much to stop the next, or the next. Like he wanted to see how many the man had in him. Cristóbal broke it up, but in the commotion Pepe hit him in the head several times. Later, Cristóbal couldn't tell whether it had been even partly accidental. A lot of ex-militants have calmed down in recent years. Not Pepe. His turn to violence is like a tap valve popping off. He doesn't need a reason.

Last year, when he asked for Cristóbal's help, Pepe said there'd be no turning back once they talked details. He required a full commitment. But Cristóbal knew right away that he would do it, and not just for his share of the money Pepe had accumulated by means Cristóbal has never asked about, or even because he missed life as a guerrilla soldier so very much and wanted any chance to recreate it. He'd do it because he and Pepe have a bond.

"One at a time, *por favor.*" Marta is hollering to be heard, something she's very good at. People must sense that tonight will be different. Attendance has tripled and everyone is clamouring to say their piece. "Please!" she repeats, then points to a raised hand several rows back. "You. Go."

A chair scrapes as a man in a too-big t-shirt and work pants stands. "*Compañeros y compañeras,* I fought in the war against the *imperialistas.*" Someone passes him a microphone attached to a long extension cord, itself plugged into one of only two outlets in the hall. "I worked in the refugee camps to keep our people positive." A hum of approval from the crowd. "I came back and helped rebuild this community when the government wished we would disappear." More approving sounds. "And since 1996 I have been fighting this mine."

Onstage Marta feels a creeping impatience. She doesn't like to interrupt speakers. The whole point here is to encourage community participation. But there is always one man who can drone on forever. "*Compa.* What is your comment tonight?"

"I have fought against this mine," the man reiterates, "and now I think we need to support our brother who has taken a step to close it down."

"Thank you, *Compa.* And what about the women here? We never hear enough from our sisters. Yes — you!"

A shy-looking woman seated nearer the back, directly under one of the tube lights that run the length of the hall's peaked tin roof, takes the mike. Several news crews, who've made the trip from the capital city for the first time in ages, crowd around her. Despite everything Marta knows about the media and their distortions, she is delighted. The Committee needs the coverage.

"*Compañeros y compañeras,* I don't support this abduction because

I think it will bring a negative image to the fight against the mine, and the message of *Jesus Cristo* and *Monseñor* Romero was to use violence only when there is no other choice, and today is not like that, even though the mine is poisoning our water and my cousin has skin rashes from it and some people think this is reason enough to resort to violence, but I think they're wrong, and we need to continue our work of closing the mine down, but we should not support violence, which is bad for the struggle."

"Good," says Marta, "Thank you." She paces her plywood stage. People tilt left and right to see her. Many stir the heavy air with paper fans. "So. We've heard many views tonight. Some of us are worried. Some of us want to fight. But brothers and sisters, we also have to think strategically, no? Whether or not we support the person who is demanding that the mine be shut down temporarily — and I repeat, temporarily — we still have an opportunity to use the media who are naturally being drawn to this case, as you see." She sweeps an arm towards the cameras. Lenses whir, tightening their focus.

"We've wanted to make a statement before the mine's expansion begins at El Pico. Here's our chance. How can we amplify our voice? You remember the bullhorns in the camps?" The crowd laughs as Marta mimics the comical overuse of this device by zealous guards in the Honduran refugee camps where many of those gathered survived the civil war. "Well, think how a tool can make you loud. That's what we need to be. We have a vision, a *cosmovisión* that involves this land and its people living harmoniously. How are we going to compete with *Los Estados* if we don't have clean water? Productive land for our children to live on? How, if we don't have real jobs? *Compañeros y compañeras, por favor!* We have tools. Mass demonstration is one of our best. We must make ourselves as loud as we've ever been. Louder!" Marta finds herself nearly shouting as she stomps a foot down. She inhales deeply. "Now, let's break into groups and discuss how we can best bring our *cosmovisión* into the world using this opportunity. Then we vote. *Vaya entonces.*"

A murmur as people rise, bumping into one another and laughing. Watching them order themselves into groups, Marta is impressed, as she so often has been, with the effectiveness of playing to people's democratic urge. She is also happy to remember how public speaking improves her mood — even when she's scared as hell.

Ever since she gave up waiting for the delegation at the market it has started to feel like old times. Threats. Intimidation. Fear. Before the abduction even hit the front page this morning, she got her first heavy-breathing phone call. Cancel your meeting, they said. Manuel Sobero and MaxSeguro have wasted no time. Or the police haven't. In Marta's experience, private security and law enforcement are often indistinguishable. The mine has also made a show of muscle, driving a bus full of MaxSeguro guards through Los Pampanos. This afternoon, a senior Committee member called to say he'd been approached to act as a spy for an anonymous party. Again: the police? The mine? It's hard to say. But cancel her meeting? No. *Jamás.* This is it. Marta's last shot at NorthOre.

She approaches a table where the discussion has stalled. "What's happening over here? Someone give me an idea — any idea," she says, taking a chair. From the corner of her eye she catches sight of a man she has not seen in a long time, except on the news. She throws herself into conversation, hoping he'll leave, but she soon feels a tap on her shoulder.

"Dying to talk to me, as always."

Marta leans away. "I'm busy." But the people at the table are becoming distracted. Carlos Reyes is still a hero to many in Los Pampanos, a guerrilla who pulled off some incredible feats. How many times will Marta have to remind them that his *famoso* helicopter attack was a group effort? That one of the snipers who took it down was a woman?

"*Comandante!*" one elderly gentleman says with pride, raising a raw wood cane. Marta has to resist rolling her eyes. This, for the man whose new party, the DAP, is trying to rob the legitimate ex-guerrilla party of its voter base.

Carlos smiles. "May I borrow your leader for a moment?"

Exaggerated gestures of approval all around. Marta gets up, resigned. "You should start correcting them. They should call you *El Presidente*. That's your long-term goal, isn't it? People are saying it is."

"How are you, Marta?"

"How do you think? The police have been to my house twice in two days asking loaded questions. The mine parades their hired guns around town. Your friend Mitchell Wall won't budge on the kidnapper's perfectly achievable demands — let alone ours that he take himself home. Business as usual. But not for you. You seem to be doing excessively well, now that your reports about the police are so generous."

"Marta," Carlos says, still smiling, shaking his head. "You are always spirited."

"I'm often angry, if that's what you mean. Why are you here?"

"Didn't they tell you? I wanted to see if I could address the crowd, let them know I'm monitoring the situation, that any police work related to this abduction will be closely watched."

Of course. An angle. Carlos Reyes always has one. "So you want to use this kidnapping, then, to get votes? Or win favour with the mine? Or both. Which is more important to you?" Marta is still figuring it out as she speaks.

"I use what's at my disposal. Just like you. Though you've also profited from the support of your foreign friends. The privileges of living abroad, yes?"

Marta glares at him, outraged. This man has not changed. Thirty years on, he is still the same shameless kid who tried to recruit her into a guerrilla cell at the university — into the sack, too. Both efforts dramatic failures. "I don't think you really want to get into a tit-for-tat about privilege."

"It's true. Five minutes of your supporters' time is all I ask."

"Impossible."

Carlos opens his mouth to challenge her, but he's engaged by another of the people at the table, who throws an arm around him and pleads for a war story. There's no denying Carlos can weave a good one. When those brown eyes focus on you, they seem so honest. If Marta hadn't been certain of her own mission back then, that her place was in San Salvador, organizing people, who knows? He might have convinced her to follow him to the mountains.

Carlos breaks from the conversation to address her again. "And this Reverte?" he says, casually. "From the forensic team. You know him."

Marta is taken aback. She was as surprised as anyone to read Alejandro Reverte's name in the papers — nearly as surprised as when she found out the kidnapper is asking for anything besides money. Marta has indeed known Reverte for years, but so do half the activists in Latin America. Reverte is a fixture, travelling everywhere and anywhere to dig up evidence of human rights violations. This hostage taker has done his research; if anyone can conduct a last-minute forensic dig on the grounds of a hostile mine, it's Reverte. But why does Carlos Reyes care? Is he looking for new information to pass along to his political cronies — Mitchell Wall, even? It has always been difficult, with Carlos, to know how your words will be used. He was that way in the war too, Marta knows, gained a reputation for creative interpretations of the rules. After '92 he carved out his plum position heading a police watchdog, a cozy spot to hatch his ambitions for office. Marta tries to formulate an answer about Reverte that Carlos won't be able to trade on.

But now the entire room starts to shake, fluorescent lights faltering, folding chairs screeching. No one panics. The mine has simply added an evening shift to their endless schedule of dynamiting. Hairline cracks through house walls, scattered livestock, the entire municipality covered in a thumb length of grey dust — those weren't enough for Mitchell Wall, apparently. He needs to shake people up some more. Everyone pauses until it stops.

"They never let us forget," Marta says, seeing Carlos put on a face like the blasts have nothing to do with him. But that's a lie. All those faithful men and women Carlos led into the mountains in the 1980s? A lot of them are still here. And without any other economic prospects, many have sold the very parcels of land they went to war over to NorthOre. MaxSeguro bullied and intimidated plenty more into doing the same. Marta has long believed that Carlos and others like him left the mountains too fast, dropping everything, the details of people's broken lives, tedious wrangling over the peace accords, for people like her to pick up, piece by piece, like restoring a thousand cracked eggs. "I'm sure MaxSeguro has security people planted here," she says, feeling her anger surge. "You know, to rattle us from the inside."

Carlos looks around a little more nervously than Marta expected. "It's possible," he says. "But come on. Who else can they think is asking for the mine to be closed but someone from Los Pampanos? From the uncompromising Committee for the Environment? It *is* quite a coincidence that these foreigners were here to visit you."

Marta will not to dignify the insinuation with a response. "I have to get back," she says, with finality.

"Good luck, Marta," Carlos turns away. A few steps on, reporters hurry to accost him.

Marta watches Carlos settle in, responding to all their questions, gesturing in his confident way. Then she gets it. He hasn't come to address this crowd, or even to prod her for information, as he's let her believe, but to be seen, to be documented as having attended, in case there's some gain to be got from it later.

Shortly afterwards, the people in the hall vote with raised hands. Those in favour of beginning a series of major demonstrations in the capital to demand that *Mil Sueños* close for the forensic exhumation carry the day.

March 12, 1980

Dear Neela,

I've made my first friend. This crazy Belgian priest who was in San Salvador doing religious training until last year. He got so inspired by the struggle he quit and came here to give Mass to the compas wherever he can find them. Also, I'm finally allowed to travel — with him! My chance to jump the totem pole! And I'll have someone to talk to (he doesn't even seem bothered by my atheism). When he describes this conflict, I remember why I came. These people need land. They're willing to die for it. They were already dying without it! In camp, you can forget that. The days are all the same. Same bored kids. Same tedium. Same war songs every night on the same homemade guitars.

I need a change of tune. ¡Viva El Salvador!

DB

TUESDAY
APRIL 5

11:30 AM (EST). *Toronto*

The camera pans the length of the conference table, pausing to name and title the speakers: Catharine Keil, Canadian Ambassador to El Salvador; Raul Schiffer, Salvadoran Attorney General; Antonio de la Riva Hernández, Captain, Anti-Kidnapping Unit, Salvadoran Civilian Police; and Xavier Barraza, Spokesperson, NorthOre Inc. Fronting each is a full glass of water and a skinny microphone. By the time the camera cuts to a wide shot of all of them, Aida knows she will learn nothing from these people. They're putting on a show, their faces balanced between hope and the possibility of tragedy. They'll say whatever it takes to buy time while they pray for this abduction to stop. Which isn't unreasonable. Danielle and her group have put these people's jobs on the line. It's just disappointing. Aida has missed work again on the slim hope that something here could change her mind.

André is beside her on the couch, fingers threaded together and resting against his thighs. Though Aida has so far avoided discussing it with him, he must sense the effect Danielle's letters are having on her. He approved of Aida's decision to take another day off, despite his general view that an entire day spent at home under any circumstances is a waste.

The camera comes in on the Attorney General. Raul Schiffer is a striking man with a near-bald head that makes Aida think of an eagle. She's surprised to see that he doesn't look at all Latino — far less than she herself does. The several flashes going off as he leans into his mic accentuate pale skin and blue eyes.

"Gracias por su presencia esta mañana." The network's simultaneous interpreter begins over him in English. Aida picks up the boxy remote, but the button is stuck. She longs for the apartment she shares with André, where everything functions. Staying at Danielle's house is probably a mistake. But Foreign Affairs says it's best, in case there's an attempt at contact. They've already sent someone to install a recording device on the phone. Aida digs with her nail until the volume goes up.

"We want to provide an update on the status of the investigation into the abduction of five Canadian citizens —" Reading from his paper, Schiffer lays out the essence of Danielle's predicament.

"Weird," Aida says, under her breath. It's a novel experience, having already absorbed — as much as possible — the news others are only now getting from the TV. André unknits his fingers to squeeze her elbow, but it comes off badly, like he's honking a horn. André is not good at pity.

The Attorney General, who turns out to be very boring, digresses into a discussion of his government's commitment to the War on Terror, which he says takes many forms, including zero tolerance of gangs, drug cartels and kidnappers, as well as the continuing presence of Salvadoran soldiers in Iraq.

"Too much politics," says André.

True, thinks Aida, nodding. André prizes the idea of self-care first, just like her. Aida has been trying to keep it up. She's been dressing especially nicely since finding out about Danielle. Today:

a wool skirt and the grey cashmere sweater André gave her for her birthday. Unlike her mother, Aida doesn't wallow or look for someone to blame for her problems. Personal choices matter. Dressing well makes her feel like she can cope.

Eventually, Schiffer passes the floor to the ambassador. "Thank you," says Catharine Keil, her voice unexpectedly husky. She's short, but has a grey pageboy that helps make up for it. Keil lauds the Salvadoran police and their professionalism then says that while her government doesn't negotiate with terrorists she is open to "reasoned dialogue." To Aida, this sounds like the same thing. "It is in the interest of all parties to take a calm, measured approach," Keil insists. She repositions the microphone and looks up, speaking directly to the camera. "I do not pretend to know what could motivate a crime like this. No past act can excuse it. However, there are options besides violence."

The ambassador, Aida realizes, is speaking to the person who took Danielle, the one who signed his ransom note "A humble Salvadoran peasant." Aida has read the note a dozen times, but its meanings still evade her. Why would someone wait so many years before looking for his family? How can he be so sure they're dead and buried where he says they are? Maybe Keil's got a plan. Maybe an ultimatum is coming that will guarantee Danielle's freedom — Aida's too.

"The Bishop of San Miguel has offered to act as a neutral third party. Meanwhile, I've taken the step of contacting the team of forensic specialists, led by Alejandro Reverte, named in the letter. Right now, this team is in Guatemala. It will be difficult to obtain their services in the restrictive time frame provided. My discussions with them can continue, but only if there is a clear demonstration of will from those who have imperiled these innocent lives. They must contact the Bishop's office immediately to work with us towards a peaceful resolution."

Keil pauses a moment, as if weighing something, whether to say more. Aida tenses. This woman must have something up her sleeve. Some leverage. But the ambassador puts a hand over her papers and passes the floor to NorthOre's spokesperson, the wide-faced Barraza. Aida feels herself deflate into the couch.

As Barraza plants his palms on the table, Danielle's phone rings. André gets up. He knows the drill: if it's a journalist, he's to say "Not interested" and hang up. If it's the kidnappers, he's to hand the receiver to Aida and use his cell to dial the number Foreign Affairs gave them. Aida cannot envision that moment, how it would be to talk about Danielle's capture — her life, the imminent threat against it — with some outlaw kidnapper who has a grudge against a gold mine.

"It's your mother's friend," André calls from the kitchen.

That means Neela. André knows her name, so it bothers Aida that even now he won't deign to pronounce it — as he tends to avoid saying Danielle's. Is it really so hard? Aida goes into the kitchen to take the call. The only house left in Toronto with a rotary phone bolted to the wall. And Danielle actually uses it.

"Can you believe this?" says Neela. "Keil says they don't negotiate with terrorists. They spend half their time cutting deals for leeches like NorthOre! But that's not terrorism. Oh, no."

Aida says nothing. Neela's moral outrage makes her want the couch and her sane, rude fiancé.

"Anyway, I won't keep you long. Just wanted to touch base. Have you thought more about tonight?"

Aida is still unable to see herself at the vigil Neela has organized. But she hopes it might work — like the press conference won't, apparently — to surprise her. She needs a jolt, a reason to reject the scheme forming in her mind. "I think I'll come, yes." She enjoys the brief pause that follows, Neela at a loss for words.

"Wonderful. I'll pick you up."

"I prefer if we meet you there." Aida hasn't broached the idea of the vigil with André yet. He's even more allergic to activists than she is. She strains around the corner, where André has returned to the television.

"Either way. Oh — did you see Mitch Wall in the papers?"

"I saw him." Aida actually spent some time with the photo of NorthOre's CEO. She scrutinized Mitch Wall, trying to determine what kind of man he is. Here was the one person with the power to get Danielle home. Logically, Aida should've been angry. Wall has completely rejected the kidnapper's demand for a shutdown at his mine. Instead, she found that he looked decent. Standing in front of a helicopter with another man, a Salvadoran, Wall looked genuinely proud of his business, his success. Probably he's just wishing the kidnapping would blow over before too much harm is done, much like the ambassador on TV. Like Aida.

"The statement he put out! He takes no responsibility for what he's done to that town. Self-serving prick." Neela is headed towards a rant.

Aida hopes to stave it off. "I read it. I get it. And I really do have to go —"

Neela drowns her out with angry rustling of the newspaper where Mitch Wall's picture and statement appear. "This guy is sucking the water table dry!" she shrieks. "Los Pampanos will be a dust bowl if this expansion at Pico goes ahead. And the river! You have no idea what's getting into the river. Do you know why he's really refusing these demands? Money, my dear. Wall can't afford a shutdown. He's scared, and he's blaming the victim."

That word. Victim. One of Neela's favourites. In her world, victims are always justified, as they are for Danielle — as they are, Aida realizes, for the kidnapper. For all of them there are no mines, no dust or damage. But life isn't like that. There's always damage. Aida feels her throat constrict. Neela deserves some of the blame here. Handing those letters back to Danielle after all these years has changed everything. "So?" she says.

"So? So we have a responsibility to fight the — ah, you know what, Aida? Forget it. I'm not going to get into it. The other reason I called is I want to respond to his bullshit. I'm going to put the names of the hostages up on the PJA website."

Aida grimaces. The government has made it clear they won't publicly release any names until all the families have been notified. Apparently, the parents of one hostage are out of the country and unreachable. But Neela, who runs the NGO that puts these delegations together every year, is in a position to override time-tested official policy out of pure spite. "That's a terrible idea."

"So I'll piss off the government. So what? What're they doing for us? I'm going to embed the names into an opinion piece. Just demolish Wall, point by point. The press'll pick it up, guaranteed. But I wanted to see how you felt about it first." Neela pauses. "Now I know."

Aida doesn't have the energy for a fight over publishing the names. She's exhausted, already. Since the news of her mother's disappearance, her feelings have become uncomfortably inter-mingled, like a ball of elastic bands she doesn't dare touch for fear one will snap. She only knows that she's lonely. And the people who could fix it are long dead, so far away she can barely make out their faces when she closes her eyes. She can see her grand-mother's smile. The shape of her grandfather's head. "Do what you want," she says.

Neela clicks her tongue sympathetically. "I know that what's happened to your mother is *beyond* hard for you. It is for me too. . . ."

She breaks off and Aida almost feels sorry for her. Neither Neela nor Danielle ever married. In a way they've become each other's next of kin — closer than Aida, for sure.

"She's going to be alright, you know," says Neela, recovering. But there's an air of cheerleading about it that Aida long ago learned to despise.

"She always is."

"I hate to hear you sound so angry. Danielle left you her letters so you could understand better. She can't change the past. It's been years. . . ."

"I'll see you tonight, Neela."

"Okay, Sweetie. Sure."

Aida hangs up loudly.

Back on the couch, the mining rep is finishing a live rendition of Mitch Wall's statement from the newspaper. ". . . amounts to trespassing and would result in multiple negative consequences, including a major disruption to our operations, a blow to employee morale, and possible endangerment of the safety of our own families. Obviously, these consequences are unacceptable to NorthOre."

Barraza nods gravely, and now it's the turn of Antonio de la Riva Hernández, head of El Salvador's anti-kidnapping unit. Below a brush of black hair, he has big eyes that hang low in their sockets, moving slowly from side to side, taking in the room. Aida catches a phrase of his slow, wheezy voice before the translator overlays it. "I am limited in what I can say, of course. But I feel I must clarify that it is the responsibility of my agency and no other, internal or external to El Salvador, to carry out this investigation. This is a crucial moment in our country. The criminal elements would like the upper hand. We will not let them have it."

Hernández has the mannerisms of a cowboy, which Aida finds comforting. She can see a man like him standing over the dead kidnapper, dual pistols still smoking. But Barraza doesn't speak of any such concrete plans. Just a few more vagaries about readiness and swift action before the camera switches to the anchor's desk in Toronto. Coverage of the press conference is over. Aida's window onto El Salvador slams shut.

She presses the off button over and over until the screen goes blank, then rests the remote on Danielle's coffee table. She and André sit side by side in a silence broken only by the refrigerator clattering in the kitchen.

"My mother fell in love there," Aida says. "Last time."

André turns towards her. Despite everything, under his square jaw, the olive skin on his neck looks inviting. The eyes, though, are wary. "Her letters?"

"Yes. I could read you one." Aida has half decided not to. André will probably find them corny.

"If you think it's important," he says.

Aida does. So much so that she ignores the tension in his voice. She begins.

April 16, 1980

Neela,

You know romance has been the last thing on my mind, right? I know you know that. Well, I met someone anyway. Here! In the middle of nowhere. I was out with my Belgian priest friend, Sosa. We were a day's walk from here, getting more quotes for that profile I've decided to do on him. We met up with some people and he was going to give Mass for them when a more senior-looking guerrilla showed up with some young recruits. The guerrilla and I made eye contact. It was intense.

Tonight, at supper Adrian — that's his name — sat with me and Sosa. The two of them told stories for hours. Stuff I couldn't believe about the violence happening in this country. One time they both had to hold their breath underwater in a river while soldiers fired bullets across the surface!!! I just sat there in awe.

Adrian walked me back to where I'm supposed to be sleeping (thank god for this flashlight) and wished me good night. Tomorrow, he's coming back to camp with us. That's lots of hours. I'll let you know how it goes with my very own Che (ha).

DB

Aida closes the letter.

"My Che?" says André.

"It was a joke. She was young. My age."

"Nothing like you."

"Anyway," says Aida, widening her eyes at him in annoyance. "I've never known any of this stuff about her."

"Maybe it was better."

"What? Barely having any idea what my own mother was like?"

"You have not expressed much interest in your mother's past, that's all," says André, bristling.

"I didn't think there was anything *to* know. Danielle went to a war zone, met someone, got pregnant, and later he died. That was it."

"And she left you. Now you know she was 'in love.' So."

"There's more."

André looks away and back. "If you want to read them, then read," he says, making it sound like it's a duty.

Aida knows he's being protective. He can tell the letters have rocked her, and he probably wishes she'd just put them away, stick to the problem at hand. But Aida can't. Because the problem didn't start with Danielle going missing. It started in those letters, the year before Aida was born.

The hostages are handed two bars of cheap-smelling soap — one for the men, one for the women — and marched to a creek. Probably, like the cigarettes, this is intended to manipulate them into feeling a little better, especially after the incident with Pierre. As soon as she touches the water, Danielle succumbs. She cups as much as she can onto her body and lets it trickle down. She wants to splash around like a child, throw herself into the pathetic, depleted creek and come out in her bathtub at home. Already she senses the mind-numbing boredom of being a hostage, and this is her first respite — manipulations be damned.

It won't last. Delmi, sulking on the bank above her, lifts the strap of her gun every so often, repositioning, while staring impatiently at Danielle and Tina. Stumpy, cross-eyed Delmi. Not very chatty. But her manner suggests a grating, self-satisfied enjoyment of the situation. Danielle has always been very private about her body, and she loathes this woman's shameless staring. Standing barefoot on the muddy edge, Tina also seems embarrassed, though her body looks perfect. Danielle remembers having a body like that. Maybe not so sculpted, but nice enough that she never gave it a thought. Age has altered things. Now she should pay attention, but she has never got a feel for working with her older self's appearance — to Aida's ongoing mortification. Danielle can't imagine getting involved in the kinds of maintenance most women undertake. Dyeing her hair? Pilates? Certainly not to please Aida. But then, who else? Danielle accepted some time ago that she will never settle down. She dates online when she wants sex. Otherwise, she prefers bouts of loneliness to the steady work of a man.

"Here," she says, keeping herself slightly turned away, passing Tina the bright pink bar.

Tina pulls it down one of her lean arms, her eyes averted.

Danielle wishes she'd had more time to get to know this girl. At breakfast at the hostel in San Salvador, while they were waiting for Martin, Danielle suggested that the others say something about their reasons for joining a human rights delegation. Tina was the only one who sounded a little jaded, and Danielle liked her for it. "The reserve where my mom's family's from has a program. You can go on trips like this, political stuff, and they'll pay. You have to give a talk to young people from the community afterwards. I'll go up there when I get back." Then she shrugged and stretched in her sensual way. Danielle felt a twinge of envy, but Tina's body language was not calculated. "I've been to Australia and Thailand through them," she went on. "It has to be somewhere that there's native people — which I didn't even know there were any in El Salvador, but Partners for Justice says there are. Called 'Lenca'?" Tina sounded like she only cared the minimum about the concerns of this obscure indigenous people, like a young woman who wanted to travel and had figured out a way to do it. She then flirted a bit with Pierre, who was sitting beside her. She seemed, in short, many things Danielle wished she'd been in her mid-twenties: charming, independent, politically weary, and childless.

Danielle recalls Tina's words to her family during the video taping. Something about her and her sibling being in the same boat — prison, probably. Checking over her shoulder and seeing that Delmi is distracted, she whispers: "Tina. I'm sorry about your brother. John."

Tina too has just her bra on, a pale thing that hugs her above the prominent rib cage. She's washing her hair. She nods under its shiny bulk.

"What's he in for — drugs?"

Tina pulls her hair back suddenly and checks Danielle's face, narrowing her eyes. "Not that it's your business, but he's an entrepreneur?"

Danielle's noticed that Tina is part of the generation of young people who end sentences on a high note, like a question.

"He made a few mistakes."

"I didn't mean to imply —" Danielle starts, but realizes what she has implied. "I just thought you looked sad about him. Yesterday."

"We shouldn't talk," says Tina, her eyes flicking towards Delmi and back. "They just get angry. Like with Pierre."

Danielle pictures Pierre as he must be at this very moment, somewhere not far off with the other men, surely freed of his restraints so he can wash. Since his outburst, Pepe has kept him bound at the hands and mouth. They didn't even remove the gag on last night's trek, which was as long and arduous as their first. Pierre was forced to gasp and salivate through the night. The message to the rest of them was clear: keep your mouths shut, or else. Still, Danielle feels compelled to try to explain herself to Tina. She isn't in the habit of making racist assumptions. "I just thought —"

A voice interrupts her. "Have these two been chatting like hens the whole time?" It's Rita. She has appeared beside Delmi. "Such *sucias* shouldn't even bother trying to get clean."

Tina, who hasn't understood the Spanish, still instinctively shakes her head no.

Delmi giggles nervously, something she does often, her jaw shaking under her mask. She moves back several steps, ceding power to Rita.

"No?" says Rita to Tina. "But I heard the old one yapping. She knows this is not allowed. *Qué lástima.* I'm going to have to cut things short. Get your clothes on."

Tina stands there confused, covered in suds, until Delmi swings her gun in the direction of the creek bank several times. For Danielle, the order is too outrageous.

"You too, *vieja*," says Rita, coming to stand over her. "And for talking, you'll put your same clothes on."

"But they're filthy!"

Rita picks up the soiled clothes, which are caked in dust, and thrusts them at Danielle so hard she has to step back into the water, soaking her left boot, to keep from falling. "I said do it." Rita's mouth is painted in thick, orange-red lipstick today, which, in combination with the balaclava, makes her look like a Mexican wrestler. Something flashes across her big brown eyes. "Did you learn Spanish when you were here before, *vieja?*"

Danielle takes the bundle of clothes. "I grew up in Central America," she answers flatly. She wants very badly to go and stand with Tina and Delmi.

"*En centroamérica?* That's *mierda*. You're a rich *blanca* with too much free time, travelling to poor countries, getting your passport stamped."

"I was born in Costa Rica." Should she explain that her father was an agronomist? Danielle doesn't want to. They have her documents. Hasn't Pepe let the rest see?

"*Perra,* you are a *desgraciada puta* liar," says Rita, shaking her head, but Danielle can't tell if she really thinks it was a lie. Rita seems to enjoy hearing herself swear. "In Canada, it's colder than in Miami all year, or just part of the year?" she asks, hauling on Danielle's arm to go up the bank, Danielle's boot going squish-squish.

Why does Rita care how cold it is in Canada? Unless that's where she's planning to end up — with a doctored version of Danielle's passport, maybe? Danielle runs through possible scenarios, including one in which Pepe is taking them north to the Honduran border where they will be shot, their bodies left to blister in the sun, their identities and clothes spirited north. But then why send Ramón off to the capital with that paper?

Rita spins on her heels and slaps Danielle in the face. *"Contéstame!"* she says, a casual look on her face, still expecting an answer to her question about the weather.

Danielle's paranoid notions depart, replaced by intense anger. "Only in the winter," she says, a tear wetting her lip. "It's cold in the winter." She can hear Tina crying further up the bank.

Rita assesses, then seems to accept as true, this description of the northern climate, and has gone back to holding Danielle's upper arm too tightly, pulling her upwards, when Pepe appears on the other side of the creek. "Go to your post," he says to Rita. "Take them with you."

Rita has no choice but to retreat, Delmi and Tina trailing behind, but she shoots Pepe a parting look that Danielle reads as hateful. A flutter of hope moves through her at the thought of a rift among her captors. But then Pepe takes several fast steps to cross the creek, the soles of his boots making a sucking sound where the ground is muddiest. Oh God, Danielle thinks. Her punishment is coming. For having been in El Salvador before. For having once been so foolish.

"You were an *internacionalista*. A journalist. You know these mountains."

Danielle hasn't heard the word *internacionalista* in more than twenty years and it's like a jack-in-the-box popping open in her face. "No," she says, frantically shaking her head. "I was young. I didn't know anything. I'm not a journalist — not now."

"Yet you've come back. Strange to know so little and care so much. Who are you writing for?"

"No — I'm not. Not here to write."

"Why did you come here, then? If you aren't going to write anything."

Danielle recalls the bundle of letters on her dining room table. Her own rash decision to take Neela's place on this trip after her friend surprised her with their old correspondence, calling it an intervention — the first startling pop-up from Danielle's past.

"Did you kill a lot of military in 1980?" Pepe continues. "Or do you own shares in the mine?"

"The gold mine? In Los Pampanos?" she says, surprised to hear mention of the object of the delegation's visit.

Something in Pepe's neck twitches. "Who did you know in the war?"

Danielle wants to answer, but she's busy going over everything Neela told her about local opposition to that mine.

"Who?" Pepe repeats, stepping in closer, his posture more aggressive.

"A lot of people — unimportant people. I knew some other foreigners. A priest. One commando. . ."

"Special Forces?"

"Yes."

"And did you yourself train as a Special Forces commando?" Pepe isn't laughing at this absurd suggestion. He displays very little emotion altogether, like he's fishing for what should worry him. It strikes Danielle that he might know something about interrogation.

"Of course not. How would I have done that?"

Pepe shouts: "I ask the questions!" He pauses, then adds more calmly, "I don't assume. That's how I survive."

Danielle suspects more than ever that Pepe was once in the Salvadoran military. She remembers all the stories of torture and disappearance that she ever heard in 1980, the mutilated bodies of civilians that she saw with her own eyes. Is this who she's dealing with? But what would somebody like that care about a gold mine?

Pepe reaches slowly into a pocket from which he pulls paper and a pen. "Write down the names of all the people you knew and what their role was."

"They were all assumed names."

"Do it."

Danielle looks down. She's still in her underwear. "I need to dress," she says, dying of shame. Pepe gives her a look like she's stripped off her clothes on purpose to cause a delay. "*Allá,*" he says, pointing to a tree.

Danielle picks up her fresh clothes — Rita can rot — and goes to change. Behind the tree she tugs on her pants and t-shirt quickly as mosquitoes bite her everywhere. She has mostly dried off, save that left foot, which is warm and wet, back in the boot, but now she starts to sweat all over again from the intense heat of the day. She tries to decide if there's anyone she should leave off the list. But why risk angering Pepe? It was all so long ago. He's unlikely to recognize anyone, even if he does have knowledge of the North-east guerrilla faction, with whom Danielle was placed. Most of the people she knew really were unimportant.

Back at the creek, Pepe foists the pen and paper back at her impatiently and Danielle bends down, laying the sheets across a thigh. She feels out of practice. At home, she runs an editing business, and her computer, pens and reams of paper are like extensions of herself. Here, writing and its instruments are alien. She begins to list the names with their occupations in brackets. Doing so forces more memories back to her with carnivalesque horror, memories she's hoped to revisit more slowly, on her own time.

"*Vaya,*" says Pepe. "It's not hard to make a list. Unless you're inventing."

"I'm not."

"We'll see."

They're quiet for some time, with just insects buzzing in Danielle's ears and getting under her collar as she puts down the names of all her main contacts from 1980, many of whom had more than one war-given nickname, something she always found confusing and, she believes, also led to confusion among the guerrillas. She sees their faces. Chepe, the young messenger she befriended, was also Enano, because he was so short. Gabi, one of the cooks, was La Gallina for being such a gossip. Freckle-faced Renaldo was Pecoso. Danielle herself was La Rojita, for her red hair, and sometimes Delgadita, for how thin she got when she had stomach bugs, which was often. Then she adds Sosa, her friend the priest.

Eventually Danielle has to decide what to do about Adrian. It seems conspicuous, somehow, to put him last. He was the most "important" person she knew. She squeezes his name into the middle of the list, a decision she immediately regrets. Why protect him? She remembers Adrian telling her that, at his rank, names could change depending on the importance of the mission. Sometimes the insurgency didn't even want members of a particular guerrilla unit to know the true identity of the person assigned to lead them. Secrecy was paramount. But Danielle can't recollect whether Adrian ever told her what his other name was. He was Adrian to her, so that's what she writes, followed by his occupation: commando, Special Forces.

Pepe holds out his hand. "Homework for later," he says, folding the paper back into his pocket. "Now. Something else."

Danielle feels the blood drain from her face: he's going to abuse her, rape her in this muddy place.

But Pepe makes no sudden moves. "If you are a journalist, you write well."

"I am not one." Danielle's hands remain in tight fists. "I work as an editor — by myself. Freelance."

"*Bien*," says Pepe, not conceding the difference. "You can write something for me. With you, I can document episodes of my life. So the people understand my motives."

"But who will read —?"

Another of Pepe's withering looks stops Danielle mid-question. "Go!" he says, standing behind her, waiting for her to move out.

3:00 PM. *Canadian embassy, San Salvador*

Mitch pauses at Catharine Keil's door, reminding himself to be nice. But Keil does not return the smile he offers when he walks in, or even bother getting up from her desk.

"Please," she says, indicating a chair facing hers.

Mitch sits, sinking lower into the seat than he expected. He lifts a foot over the opposite knee, trying to compensate. "I didn't know you guys were in this building," he says, still failing to get any height. "I actually ran into an acquaintance at the elevators — exploration guy. Small world!"

"I'm sure," says Catharine Keil, tucking a section of hair behind her ear. It's greyer than last time Mitch saw her in person, evenly silver. Has she dyed it that way, he wonders? She's not even that old.

"Do you need clarification on something in particular, Mr. Wall?"

"Okay. Let me first say that no one could've anticipated these demands." Out of the corner of his eye Mitch can still see Keil's assistant, who showed him in from reception. Mitch assumed he would leave before the meeting began, but the man has taken up a spot by the window. Mitch tries to ignore him while appealing to the ambassador's reason. "We've been blindsided — as you have."

Keil picks up her pen, stands it on her desk, then lays it down again. "These things happen. We have policies. Your insurers have probably briefed you before."

"About employee abductions? Oh, sure. But that's completely different. These tourists weren't my employees!" Mitch starts to laugh, looking towards the assistant, who is stony-faced.

"One interesting thing about those cases is that companies regularly pay a ransom rather than risking people's lives unnecessarily," says Keil.

Mitch remembers this smug attitude from last time he chatted with Keil, at some event for Canadian businesses abroad. In that gruff voice, everything is a lecture.

"Some would say it's the price of doing business in markets like this one, that are, otherwise, very cost-effective," she adds.

"We're launching a multi-million-dollar expansion," says Mitch, trying to put across the simple truth of what's at stake. "This month."

"The abduction has posed some extreme challenges for everyone," says Keil, stubbornly neutral. "And as the owner of the property, it's within your rights to refuse this exhumation. Regardless of consequences."

Mitch questions his decision to ask for this meeting. Keil is about as pliable as a brick. He searches for a new tack. "The reason I came by is I felt we should speak face to face about the police. I know Captain Hernández comes off a little strong. But I have it on good authority that the anti-kidnapping unit really is ready to end this at a moment's notice without any danger to anyone." The mention of Hernández seems to freeze Keil's facial muscles. With concern? "I know that's not your preferred option," Mitch says, guessing. "But there's no need to let a dangerous situation linger either —"

"No one in this embassy wants the abduction to last even one minute longer," says Keil, jumping on his last word. "Nor do we control how the local police react. As the Captain has made clear, it's his jurisdiction. But hasty action in cases like these is always risky, as past examples in this country have shown."

"But no risk, no reward, right?" says Mitch, smiling.

Keil furrows her brow. "Mr. Wall, are you aware that some of the families of the hostages are travelling to San Salvador because they want to show how important it is to resolve the abduction safely? Maybe you would consider meeting them, hearing their point of view about the exhumation."

Mitch tries to look regretful. "That would be great. But I've been advised by my legal team not to speak directly to anyone so close to the kidnapping. For my own safety." Mitch's PR people did get a couple of calls about the families, but Mitch has no interest in having parents bawling in his office over something he can't do anything about. He's not the one who took their kids hostage. "I sincerely hope everyone is reunited," he goes on, illustrating his hope by weaving together the fingers on both his hands. "At the same time, these families can't possibly keep perspective on the demands. They've been put in an impossible position. Your own office has a travel warning in place. People have to know what they're getting into when they leave Canada to fraternize with — well, we all know that group in Los Pampanos, that 'Committee,' is a fringe organization. Who's to say they didn't invite the delegation here expressly to stage this kidnapping? In the end, this is a police matter."

"I understand your point of view. And I will express it to Foreign Affairs as we go forward. But until we can come to a resolution, we need the police to stay in dialogue with all parties, rather than stepping in too soon," says Keil in a new tone, which sounds to Mitch like someone trowelling mortar, adding a layer to a tall wall. She rises with her hand extended.

Mitch stares at it from his low chair, his lips pressed together. Bad words are straining to get out. For the moment Keil can afford to look down at him, watching as he swallows them back.

They are nearly at the campsite — today, a dank, earthen cave. Danielle hurries towards it through the trees. Earlier, she recognized small piles of guano in that cave. When night falls, the bats will descend. Danielle doesn't want any delay in leaving for their night's walk before that happens. She gets close enough to hear Cristóbal's voice, starts towards it.

"No. Keep going."

Danielle stops to look back at Pepe, confused, but he just signals that she has to walk the other way, guiding her left and right with clipped orders until they reach a spot where Danielle assumes he slept earlier. A few of his effects are there. It smells like him too, of warm canvas and sweat — and something else. A sweet, lingering odor. Has Pepe masturbated here? Danielle doesn't want to dwell on the possibility, or worse, on thoughts of who else Pepe might be having sex with. Not Rita! Already, Danielle and the others have sensed a partnership between her and Cristóbal, extreme loyalty between the two men. But is Pepe making do with Delmi, then?

Pepe drags a large stone forward, gauging the dirt. He invites Danielle to use it as a seat, choosing for himself one of the tarps he seems to have in plentiful supply. He hands her the writing instruments and folded paper that he took back earlier. "Put down everything I say" is his only instruction.

He seems almost nervous as he shifts his rifle over his legs, which are crossed at the ankles of his heavy lace-up boots. He pulls a large beige object from his belt. Danielle has noticed it before. Now she identifies it as a telephone. Rectangular and bulky, probably works off a satellite. She has to work not to let her interest show in this device, which could bring a rescue team to them within hours — less! El Salvador is tiny. Pepe cradles the phone lightly in one hand, as if he enjoys the feel of it, before putting it down protectively by his side, exhibiting it, letting Danielle know she's more likely to get her hands on an actual satellite.

Then, as if the phone isn't there at all, he starts talking. Danielle resolves to put aside her discovery for a time when she can mull over the phone's potential. She focuses on the movement of Pepe's full lips in his mask. She tells herself that this mouth belongs to a normal face, that Pepe is just skin and bones, just a man. She guesses his age by his voice, putting it at forty-four.

The strangeness of her task amazes and frightens her, for though Danielle has been yearning to know the reason for her kidnapping, she hasn't wanted to feel anything about it, to know more than the facts. But as she responds to Pepe's firmly pointed finger, which insists that she get started, and her pen starts moving awkwardly across the page on her lap, she can't stop herself from feeling a heady mix of things: nostalgia, excitement, shame. Then two more sensations she has steeled herself against for a long, long time: sympathy and political outrage.

"Now, rewrite them," Pepe says when he has finished speaking, pointing at Danielle's notes. "Make a story. Like for the newspaper." She has forty-five minutes, he says. Then he picks up his phone and leaves.

Is it a trick? She has to run. But which way? How far will she get before she's hungry? Thirsty? Danielle tries to calm herself. Two nights now they've walked steadily uphill all night long. She's seen practically no signs of human life except a few rooftops in the distance, some thin smoke from a chimney. Pepe knows how to keep hidden — just as the faction did in 1980. There is nowhere to run. Danielle closes her eyes and listens to the world around her. Never-ending insects and birds and the breeze. She breathes deeply, opens her eyes again. The late afternoon sun is beautiful where it illuminates the nearest treed ridge, tingeing the foliage gold. She thinks of a trip she took last year with Aida to a beach town on Georgian Bay. One of her attempts to spend quality time with her daughter.

They sat side by side on lounge chairs the entire afternoon, two days in a row, not fighting at all. A record Danielle craves the chance to beat. She bends her head to the paper on her lap.

When Pepe reappears, Danielle is startled. She's become totally engrossed in her task, her hand aching with effort. Pepe sits back down loudly on his tarp, his short legs folded in front of him, and lights a cigarette, which creates a brief, terrible distraction for Danielle. If he offers her one, she won't say no. Cessation did not prepare her for captivity. The thought obviously doesn't cross Pepe's mind, however. He orders her to read aloud, in Spanish, everything she's written. Nervously, Danielle starts, her own voice sounding strange to her, tinny in the wide open air.

"My name is Danielle Byrd. You can verify that I am the author of this report by asking my daughter to confirm a birthmark I have behind my left ear. The person responsible for my detainment wants people to know he is not a terrorist. He has been subject to what he calls the 'tides of history.'

"'Enrique' was only twelve when his family was disappeared by the Salvadoran military. This is the reason behind his present actions.

"It was common then for the military to raid villages and abduct young men. In 1977 they came to Enrique's village. His family was killed and he was taken for basic training. This was at the time when the U.S. was advising the Salvadoran military. Enrique was among the first to learn from American specialists.

"He came to admire his trainer, Colonel Evans. Evans could be brutal. Many students were beaten. But he also gave them plenty of rewards. Enrique had the best food of his life during this time. American food. Meat and mashed potatoes every day.

"The Americans weren't supposed to take part in missions, but that didn't stop Evans. He said you couldn't trust a Salvadoran to do the job. He got the recruits to work highway checkpoints. Evans ordered them to humiliate any man who couldn't produce his documents fast enough. Enrique was surprised at how easy it was to make people do what you wanted.

"Then they started going into villages. They would arrive at nightfall and go house to house, looking for insurgents.

"Once they went to a hamlet that reminded Enrique of the one he grew up in. He'd heard a rumour that Jesuits were teaching countrywomen black magic and he got nervous. It felt like there was a bad spirit there.

"They entered a house that belonged to an older couple. The woman looked a bit like his mother, which paralyzed him. He stood by while his unit searched the place. They were just leaving when Evans walked in and came over to Enrique. He asked what they'd found.

"*Nada,* said Enrique.

"Evans laughed. *Nada?* He turned to the old man, addressing him as Papa, which sounded strange. His Spanish wasn't good. Tell this soldier where you are hiding the guns, *Papa.*

"The old man mumbled that there were no guns. He tried to laugh like Evans did. Evans smiled. *Papa!* Don't lie. We hate lies. Your son has joined the boys in the mountains. You're hiding their guns.

"This time the old woman said something about her son being gone to work on the *milpa,* and Evans got mad. He walked up to Enrique, grabbed him, and forced him across the room to her. Then he pulled the pistol out of Enrique's holster. He forced it into

Enrique's hand and pushed his finger onto the trigger until it fired. The woman slumped over.

"When Evans turned the other way, towards the husband, Enrique shook him off. He was his own.man. He pulled the trigger himself, aiming for the chest.

"Evans went to the only shelf in the house. He lifted the corner of an old blanket and pulled out a leaflet, holding it like you hold a dead mouse. He said to Enrique, This is not nothing. It was a promotion for a local farm cooperative. Pin it to the door and move on, Evans said.

"That night, Enrique remembers that he was more tired than he'd ever been in his life. But he didn't feel bad. He'd been in limbo since his family was killed. Now he wasn't. God had chosen a new life for him and he was relieved.

"From then on, it was possible to carry out his commanders' orders without much thought. He did many terrible things. Over time, he became suicidal, but his religious belief and a vision of his mother being worried about his soul kept him from going through with it.

"Later, he was glad he didn't die. His life changed again. He got out. That's not what he wants people to know about first, though. He wants to tell the other part, when he was responsible for hurting others. He says there's a difference between what he did then and what he's doing now. He says that what he's doing now is right."

Danielle looks up. Pepe's cigarette has been smoked to the nub.

"Leave the paper here," he says, putting it out against a stone. "Your food is waiting for you." As Danielle gets to her feet, he adds, "If you tell the others anything, I'll kill you. I'll say it was necessary, that you worked for the CIA during the war. They'll believe me."

Danielle returns to the cave alone. There, she faces the questioning eyes of her fellow hostages and of Rita, who looks like she will spit, taking in Danielle's clean clothes, which she had hoped to deny her. Danielle ignores her as best she can, but the others are harder to block out. They've all finished eating supper and have nothing else to distract them. Danielle seesaws between guilt and defensiveness. It's been exhilarating to rework Pepe's words. A sad irony, so many years after her journalistic ambitions were quashed in this very place. But she hasn't done anything more. She isn't telling secrets. If only she could explain.

Rita is busy scanning her like an x-ray over and over with ravenous eyes, waiting for any reason to pounce. And so Danielle picks up her plate of food. Beans, tortillas and a dollop of bright orange canned spaghetti. The kidnappers have a system for cooking that involves an underground fire and a tunnel to channel the smoke. This was a guerrilla technique during the war, a way to avoid attracting attention from military aircraft. But Danielle can't imagine that any of her abductors were ever part of the guerrilla army. The women are too young. Cristóbal seems too mellow to have been any kind of soldier. And Pepe, unless he's a seriously good liar, was on the other side. He did those "terrible things." What kinds of things? What could be worse than shooting defenseless old people? Danielle shivers as fantasies of torture and brutality mingle with the cooling air. A word comes to her: *capucha.* The name for the military's local form of torture: covering people's heads with a transparent bag and tying it. The person who controls her fate now could have techniques.

Danielle changes her mind. She wishes the bats in this cave would awaken early, fly to Pepe, tangle their leather wings in the material of his mask, and force him to run back with his guilty face exposed. She tears off a hunk of tortilla and begins to eat without pleasure.

They pull over on the north side of King Street, just west of Bay. Neela is there with her placards, a rolled-up banner and a bullhorn. Seeing this apparatus, Aida wants to go back, but Neela has already caught André's eye and beckons them.

NorthOrc's offices are in Vancouver, so Neela has chosen to protest the company where their shares are traded. Due to automation, there's little left of the physical stock exchange. Just an office tower that contains the exchange's head office and, at its base, a media centre. The location, Neela has decided, at least has symbolic value. The particular patch of sidewalk where she's setting up is becoming a scene. A few people have gathered, including a thin, middle-aged man in a jean jacket and a girl, younger than Aida, dressed in punk clothes.

There's a large TV screen set up inside the windows of the building across the street. It pours blue light over Aida and André as they approach. The screen shows an all-news channel, a fast-moving ticker under the news anchor providing updates of headlines, stock quotes, currency values and other information Aida is normally very interested in. She's wanted to work in business ever since she can remember. Using books her grandfather brought home from the university, baking cookies with her grandmother, she ran successful yard sales as a girl to supplement her allowance. Now she's a work term away from her MBA, and besides the few thousand dollars her grandparents left her, she's done that on her own too. She has anticipated that André's family, all business people, will help her get her first real job. That future has seemed so close! Stepping up onto a street corner in good heels and a trench, carrying her work papers in a leather satchel on her way to an important meeting — or to grab lunch with André. But it all seems laughably far-fetched tonight. Aida has already missed several days of work at her co-op placement. She can't see herself graduating in June, or even going back to her desk tomorrow, as she should. It's like the present has opened up and swallowed her whole.

Neela is handing out candles to a group of people who've just shown up. Aida reluctantly takes one in her gloved hand. Nearby, the banner she saw earlier unfurls, reading: *Bring the hostages home! And NorthOre too!*

André lights Aida's wick. "It's like church," he says, waving it. The shadows cast by the candlelight further chisel his sharp features.

Aida smiles. She's touched that he's come. They argued earlier, after André told her she should give the letters back to Neela so she'll quit obsessing over them.

"How long do we have to stay?"

"It should be short," Aida says, but she really has no idea how long protests last.

The punk teenager has a laptop, and presently she and Neela sit on the street corner, shivering happily in their jackets and tuques, taking their sweet time reading postings the teenager wants to show Neela, which have been written in response to the commentary Neela put up on the PJA website earlier. Neela claps with delight, impressed by the speed at which her words have travelled through the activist community. She's made a good bet: since publicizing the hostages' names, she's been asked to do a string of interviews. Aida turns away, preferring to watch traffic.

Suddenly, two TV news vans pull out of the flow of passing cars, each disgorging a camera crew. Neela gets up and orders people to take their positions for a chant, which she leads: "No tainted gold! No tainted gold! Bring the hostages home!" There are fewer than thirty demonstrators altogether, but when they all bunch up, as they do now, Aida realizes it will be enough to fill the small screen. Neela actually knows what she's doing.

Instinctively, Aida moves away. But as she does, each news crew, led by a well-dressed journalist, follows. A light goes on in Aida's face.

"What is your response to the hostage video, Ms. Byrd?"

Aida takes several more fast steps away. Video? Someone else is calling her name. "Aida!" yells Neela. "It's your mother!"

Aida stops, turns, her candle dropping. Neela is pointing to that big television screen, now half a block down. Aida doesn't recognize the person whose head and torso appear there: an old woman with unruly hair, a blank green expanse behind her. She starts walking back, ignoring the reporters and their cameras. By the time she's standing fully in the screen's blue glow she sees: that old woman is Danielle. Her shoulders bent inward. Graying red hair curling every which way. Dark circles under her eyes. Her lips are moving.

André, at Aida's side now, puts his arm around her shoulder and pulls her close. Neela comes up alongside. "They recorded them," she says, repeating what someone is telling her over her cell. "They sent a video out."

The punk girl trots up with her computer open. "It's streaming on the newspaper website." She holds the laptop out to Aida. "Here. Take it. I can get it back later."

Aida hates touching other people's electronics. So grimy. But she's grateful. She makes eye contact with this teen she would normally have no time for, then takes the computer.

"I'll come pick it up tomorrow," says Neela.

André helps Aida into the first taxi he can flag down, the news cameras still trailing them, unsatisfied.

"It means she's alive," Aida says, when the door shuts.

"Yes. She's alive."

Aida clicks "play" and there, full-screen, but more humanly proportioned now, is a man she's never seen before — attractive, young, in a loose shirt.

"My name is Antoine Thériault, of Québec. I am a member of the Partners for Justice in the Americas delegation to the municipality of Los Pampanos, El Salvador. I urge the government to do whatever is necessary to secure our release by Monday, April 11th. Otherwise, these people will start taking our lives."

He pauses, looking off camera. Aida faintly hears a voice speaking Spanish. Antoine continues again, switching to French to say something more, talking to his family. There's a sharp edit and his head is replaced by someone else's — a man, Martin, who crosses himself and cries. Then a pretty Native girl named Tina, followed by a thin, angry-looking man named Pierre. Each of them repeats the same statement. Each time, their words are followed by some Spanish from off camera.

And then, finally, Danielle. She does her own translation of the statement before switching back to English. "Aida, hi. I — I probably look worse than I am." Danielle pats her hair. Like it could be smoothed so easily. "I'm sorry it's happened now, in the middle of your placement. Please don't worry. Not that you will, but I'm alright. We have lots of food and water. And I can communicate. Tell Neela that I'm doing that, for the others, thanks to Mom and Dad. So I'm thinking of them. I'm thinking of you. But I'm not worried. I'm going to be fine."

The video ends on the word "fine" while Danielle's mouth is still open. Aida pulls the cursor back across the video and watches her mother move and talk again. "Please don't worry. Not that you will. . ."

"Is that all?" André asks.

That is all. Enough for Aida. She has heard the exact core of her relationship with her mother. The desire and restraint. The hope and disappointment. And she's heard a call. Not Danielle's, but her own. She's glad she booked her ticket before the vigil, because all she wants to do now is sleep.

May 20, 1980

Dear Neela,

Adrian is staying the whole week, overseeing that training I told
you about. Everything is different with him here. Time goes so fast.
People come to talk to him. Interesting people — unlike the usual
camp crowd.

On that note, I'd say the mood is finally improving. It's been two
months since Archbishop Romero was assassinated. For a long time,
a lot of people in camp would cry together every day and do these
elaborate prayer sessions. This week, all that stuff tapered off.
Sosa says Romero was El Salvador's Martin Luther King and
Malcolm X put together. Personally, I have trouble with the way
religion and revolution get mixed up. Sosa says I'm too much of
a lapsed Protestant to get liberation theology. Maybe he's right.
One more thing to make me feel like an outsider.

DB

WEDNESDAY
APRIL 6

2:30 PM. *28 KM east of previous campsite, Morazán*

Antoine is heavily into a game of Thirty-One with Martin, and Danielle is bored enough to keep up. Martin transfers his cigarette to his mouth for a drag, displays his cards. He has started accepting cigarettes from Delmi and smokes often, but like an amateur. His hand shows 27 points. "You'll take this round," Danielle says, because he hasn't won one yet. Despite Pepe's strict no-talking policy, she knows that when Cristóbal and Delmi are on duty, as they are now, a smattering of words won't get a rise out of them.

"I'm sorry, but no," says Antoine, smiling in his shy, self assured way. He puts down three sixes, giving him 30 ½, the second-best possible hand.

Martin starts gathering up the cards in a hurry, erasing the game. He's let his cigarette dangle too low from his lip and it tips out onto the tarp. Marlon Brando, he is not. He seems dejected, actually. The men were allowed to shave back at the creek, but it's left him with a nasty nick on his chin, which presently he picks at in a gross fashion. Such bad luck for a guy like this to have ended up here. Danielle tries to think something nice. Martin's blond hair does have a good wave to it, and it's becoming lighter, practically golden, despite the tree cover they are nearly always kept under. Maybe he's someone Aida could find attractive. Danielle generally finds the men Aida dates humourless and old before their time — or at least Danielle doesn't get their jokes. Like the latest, Mr. Moneybags, smirking his way through life. Supposedly they're engaged. Moving to Europe forever. Danielle will believe it when she sees it. Aida always falls so hard. Danielle has too, but at least she feels she's gone for edge and drama, not cash and cheekbones.

She keeps watching Martin as he shuffles the deck concertedly. She remembers the description he gave of himself at dinner the night they all landed in San Salvador. "Me? I'm in risk assessment — commodities sector, mostly base metals. I've been at Newton-Thomson two years. We basically advise people who buy stocks."

Pierre leveled a cool stare at him. "You encourage people to invest in companies like the gold mine we're going to visit."

Martin blinked. "No. Like I said, I do base metals. I don't know about precious metals. That's someone else's file."

Tina stepped in. "So why did you come on a delegation about a gold mine?" Unlike Pierre, her question wasn't loaded with judgment.

"I'm just interested, that's all," Martin said.

There must've been more to it, though. Danielle translated Martin's video message home. He said he knew God hadn't abandoned him, that everything happens for a reason. Did Martin come to El Salvador as penance? To see where all those profitable mining companies do their dirty work? If so, he must be pissed at his God! Maybe even experiencing religious doubt. Danielle can only hope. But it makes her wonder what useful doubt the situation might yield for her. She thinks none, except about having come here at all. Neela justified giving her the letters by saying Danielle was "sleepwalking through life" and letting her past control her. From this distance, that sleepy life looks nearly ideal.

Martin notices her staring and throws her a defensive look. Danielle turns away, towards Pierre and Tina, seated side by side across the abandoned shed — their latest hiding place. Pierre's arms are laid out straight in his lap, a position that shows off the long tattoo on his left forearm. Danielle is willing to bet he doesn't even know the meaning of its intricate Japanese script. She's never had time for body art, as her neighbour's son calls it. On this one point, at least, she and Aida are in full agreement, though for different reasons. To Aida, so immaculate, so into the purity of her body, tattoos are a desecration. To Danielle, they're just silly.

Pierre is gagged with that blue bandana, but somehow manages to flirt with Tina anyway, which irritates Danielle. How can he act like nothing's happened? His outburst during the tapings has put her in a worse position than the rest. Translator, and now ghostwriter. Danielle expected the others to feel at least a little bad for her, even if they don't know what Pepe took her away for. It could've been torture! But she gets the impression they're suspicious. Neither Martin nor Antoine asked if she wanted to join their game. Tina and Pierre have been huddling for hours, not once looking directly her way.

Danielle leans against splintered wood. Under her tarp, prickly, disintegrating hay is making her legs itch. This place is miserable, cramped, dim, bare, derelict. A hole. Danielle closes her eyes, craving all the small spaces she's ever enjoyed. It's 1980 and she's in the tiny office she occupied at the university student paper. The walls are covered in clippings, a production board, images of trendy revolutionaries. Sandino rubbing shoulders with Mao. She's considering a trip to El Salvador to prove her politics to herself and to her proto-hippie parents. In the fantasy, she decides against it. The next year, she begins an internship at the city daily. Her writing career takes off. She has a string of romances, but never marries. She doesn't age. Currently, she lives in New York, where she collects sculpture. She is very happy.

A flea bites her leg and Danielle scratches hard, drawing blood. Her fantasy oozes away.

"You want some water?" Tina says to Pierre, quite loudly. Everyone looks over. It's strange to hear any bold, full-volume voices besides those of the kidnappers.

Pierre nods and Tina gets Delmi's attention so she'll go over to pull up the bandana from Pierre's mouth. When Delmi does, Pierre lets out a long, loud sigh, sucking air and letting his eyes close with evident pleasure. At the end of his narrow nose the nostrils flare and collapse like tiny sacs. Tina gives him the canteen and he takes a big drink. *"Merci,"* he says, looking right at her.

Even from where she's sitting, Danielle can feel heat pass between them. Not like before — not only flirtation. It's friendship. Or maybe love. Who knows what emotions these young people are experiencing? Their inner lives are off limits.

The corners of Pierre's mouth have become chapped from his gag, and suddenly Danielle can't resist reaching for something. "Are you sore?" she asks. She's stupid. A fool. She's promised herself never to appear desperate with these kids. But the terror of being ostracized has taken hold of her voice box.

Pierre shakes his head lightly.

"I haven't done anything, you know," Danielle blurts out, not loudly, but wanting them all to hear. Someone has to be the link between the group and the kidnappers. It may as well be her. "He's making me take down his —"

"Daniela," says Cristóbal, picking up on the emotion in her voice, and maybe feeling that something more is being discussed besides Pierre's water drinking. He and Delmi seem to know no English.

Pierre looks at Danielle angrily, communicating that he thinks she's a liar. As soon as he empties the canteen, Delmi goes over and puts his gag back on. Tightly.

Eventually, Rita comes in and Delmi, in moping mode (the counter to her giggling), shuffles out. Danielle has memorized the kidnappers' routines. They get about six hours of sleep per day, though they split it up. The women manage a bit more. Rita and Delmi are allowed to nap alongside the hostages in the middle of the night, when they always stop the walk from campsite to campsite for a long rest, while either Pepe or Cristóbal keeps watch and the other disappears — to act as lookout, Danielle assumes. The only part she hasn't figured out is what Pepe does during these late afternoons when he isn't around. She feels certain he doesn't only sleep. She's had visions of him hiking out to meet secret collaborators. He sent that video to the media somehow. And now there's the story she wrote for him. He couldn't have planned for that, and so whatever arrangement he has must be flexible, an open line to someone. Danielle decides Pepe is using his satellite phone. If only she could snatch it from him. She craves those buttons against her fingertips. But Pepe keeps it nearly always on his belt loop.

On his way off shift, Cristóbal lingers a moment, standing outside the door of the shed speaking quietly to Rita, who looks almost human as she leans gently towards him. Danielle notices that when they're together, Rita acts differently, less mean. They seem married, but how could that be? How could Cristóbal, Danielle's favourite, who seems utterly lacking in cruelty despite everything, with his gangly limbs, his caved-in chest and his goofy hat-over-ski-mask ensemble, choose Rita as a wife? Danielle wonders if there's more to this compact woman than she's letting them see.

As soon as Cristóbal leaves, though, the Rita Danielle has come to abhor returns. Steely. Hungry for conflict. It takes her five minutes to figure out how to start one of her games. The painted mouth in her ski mask turns up in a leer. She pulls a small MP3 player from her pocket, tucks the earbuds under the mask and turns up the volume so loud it's audible throughout the shed. Danielle doesn't recognize the tune — she rarely listens to music — but when she looks over, Martin is glaring at Rita, his mouth forming the words *"One love. One love."* Now Danielle remembers him handing the player over after they were yanked from the bus. The kidnappers took everything. Music, watches, nail clippers, keys. Access to these possessions is controlled by Pepe, who decides when they need everything from fresh underwear to a hairbrush.

Martin clearly wants his music back. He puts yet another cigarette in his mouth, unlit. Rita pretends not to notice. She bobs her head and hums out of tune like a teenager alone in her bedroom. Two songs in, when she must feel she's sufficiently agitated them, she puts the player away. She stands and saunters in her loosely tied boots over to Pierre and Tina, taking a seat on the far side of Pierre, dispersing hay dust. She knows a little English. More, anyway, than Danielle thought, because she starts talking to Pierre, keeping her voice at a whisper so that he has to lean in. This is meant to scare the rest of them, and it works.

When she's finished, Rita nods seriously at Pierre, who looks back intently, as if confirming something. Then she returns to the far wall, laying her rifle across her lap. "Stop looking at me, all of you," she says in Spanish. Danielle doesn't need to translate. Everyone tries to find somewhere else to put their eyes. "And tell Pierre he's allowed to choose one person to whisper to," Rita adds.

"Pierre," says Danielle.

He nods without looking up.

"She says you can whisper what she said to one person."

That gets his attention. Pierre shoots Danielle a questioning look then turns to Rita to verify. When she eggs him on with a nod, Pierre makes the obvious choice. Antoine, who's still holding his cards, puts them down slowly, like he thinks it's a set-up and he doesn't want to bite. Rita rolls her eyes. *"Vaya!"* she says, pointing to Pierre. Slowly, Antoine walks over to his friend. Looking a bit hurt, Tina trades places with him, sinking into his spot and twirling her hair around one finger, as she tends to do. Then Antoine pulls off Pierre's gag again and listens while his friend whispers in his ear. Afterwards, the gag back on, they sit staring at one another, exchanging secret meanings.

This is not funny. Something has happened. Danielle has nothing to go on except her profound distrust of Rita. Can she be involving these two in some plot? A product of her deranged mind? Pierre might be susceptible to someone who would make him feel like the heroic young man of his dreams. Danielle was that way once too, so she knows how you can get taken in. Rita will use him. To mutiny? She tries to read Rita's eyes.

In response, Rita produces a feral grin.

Danielle switches to silently begging Pierre not to take anything this woman says seriously, explaining to him with her eyes that Pepe really will kill anyone who disobeys, while telling herself that Antoine is measured, reasonable. A bike mechanic. A good kid. Not someone to scheme or partake in risky plans, even for his oldest friend.

Pepe appears in the door. Everyone jumps like he's the dad and they've all been naughty. "*Daniela*," he says, looking around suspiciously. He signals for her to come out.

Danielle's heart sinks. She wants to stay, to be like the others, not a conspirator. But she gets up, feeling all their faces turn, their eyes burrowing into her, but especially Pierre's, which, when she looks back, seem to be doing some very scary math.

2:40 PM. *Outskirts, Los Pampanos, Morazán*

Julia Rendita is in her church clothes when her husband is pushed through her door by two strangers and hits the dirt floor with a thud. Babbling and slobbering, he tries to prop himself up on his single arm but fails. As the strangers step over him, Julia registers that he's not the one they're after. She picks up her baby from the *cochón* and thrusts him into the arms of her second youngest, Ufemia, then advances to meet the men, giving her daughter her best chance to get out.

Each takes one of Julia's arms and pulls.

"*Perdóname!*" her husband calls, crying now, whimpering, as they drag her past him. "*Perdóname!*"

The stark afternoon light hurts Julia's eyes. The strangers shove her into the front of a truck. One of them has square shoulders like a rack, the other a thick beard. She screams and wiggles furiously, but they're too strong and pay her no attention. Julia's face ends up pressed into the dashboard beside a sticker with an image of a chunky fist holding a lock. Below it in block letters, a word: MAXSEGURO.

Some neighbours have come out to watch. What else can they do? Julia wishes desperately that she'd never been approached by that woman who offered her the money, that she had never agreed to go up the old trail.

The men get in and the truck starts up, driving for a long time. When it stops, one of them sticks a gun to Julia's belly and tells her she's going to lead them to the place where she met the kidnappers. Then she can go back to her children. Thinking of her baby threatens to make Julia's breasts leak, so she shakes the image of him away, concentrating on staying alive. She tells the men the truth: she never saw anyone. The men pull her roughly from the truck and make her walk anyway. Julia remembers her childhood in the refugee camp, how people tried to reason with the guards. Those soldiers never listened either.

Outside the vehicle, there is nothing in sight except trees. But as she steadies herself, Julia distinguishes a familiar hilly landscape to her left. She points her feet instinctively towards them.

When, nearly four hours later, Julia reaches the bottom of the shelf of rock she rose to that day, she mumbles that this is it — where they left the envelope. The men snap at her to shut up, forcing her into a crouch. One keeps Julia there, a hand cupped over her mouth, as the other moves ahead. Eventually, he returns, looking frustrated. Obviously, whoever left the package for her to pick up is long gone. She could've told them that.

The men make a joke about Julia being a stupid *campesina* and push her back and forth like a ball until she falls. Their game is unnerving and demeaning. Julia considers the excitement she felt retrieving the envelope, counting out the money, and the thrill of travelling to the capital to leave the tiny memory card at the newspaper office the woman had given her directions to. Except for the refugee camp, Julia has rarely left Los Pampanos. Now she wonders if she'll die for those experiences.

One of the men takes her by the waist, pressing one of her arms to her side. The other, with the big shoulders, takes her free arm and forces it back until Julia hears a crack. Her knees buckle. Her mouth fills with saliva. "Now you match your husband," the man says, matter-of-factly, and in Julia's mind, the pain blossoms into a clear image of these two men entering the bar where her husband always goes to meet his old war buddies on the days she travels to town to pray. He bragged to them, made a spectacle of himself. If only she'd been able to hide the money.

The one with the beard steps off to make a call on a heavy-looking phone. Julia doesn't care who he's calling or why, but the other shoves her out of earshot at gunpoint, telling her they'll be back to cut off her breasts and kill her children if she tells anyone about where she's been. For good measure, he fires a shot near her feet.

Julia cradles her injured arm. She moves so fast her lungs seize and it becomes difficult to breathe. But she presses on, trees streaming by, night eventually overtaking the sky. Julia runs so long and hard that she enters a terrain of memories from her early life, before the war, when she collected herbs in this area with her grandmother, so that when she gets back onto the familiar trail, free to return home, she feels almost happy.

—

"We're close, *Jefe*," says the man, wind creating sucking noises around him.

"How close?" Sobero shifts the receiver to his other hand.

"We'll find them. Soon."

Sobero is in his office, facing a bank of security cameras. On one black-and-white screen, he can see Mitch Wall moving along a corridor followed by that public relations flack, Barraza. Both men are agitated, talking with their hands. Finally, Wall is beginning to show signs of genuine concern. He's understanding that this incident will not be wished away.

"I chose you because I know your skills, but you have achieved nothing," Sobero says into the phone. "I am only so patient."

"*Sí, Jefe*. We'll find them."

Sobero hangs up angrily. It's boring to have to threaten such negligible elements, but so far they are the only weapons in his arsenal. He remains seated a moment longer, watching Wall. Sobero knows his employer has tended to see this abduction only in the narrowest terms. Wall isn't aware of its broader implications, either politically or for Sobero's own status. Sobero experiences a sharp prick of irritation at this: he must always consider Wall's interests, while Wall will never consider his. The irritation passes, though. Sobero decided long ago that ultimately Wall's ignorance is advantageous. He picks up his phone again. If his trackers are moving this slowly, he will need to explore other avenues.

4:45 PM. *Morazán*

When Danielle has taken down all his words, and Pepe has given her, as he did last night, about an hour to turn them into a coherent text, he comes back. Danielle is still scribbling, but Pepe swipes the paper from under the pen. He ignores her dirty look and sits across from her to read silently.

At that time, most people in the countryside were hungry. They never were. Enrique's father was on good terms with the local patrón, *so the* guardia *didn't bother them. For these reasons, his family was considered well off.*

His mother was religious. She's the one who'd gone to meetings organized by the priests who were teaching people to use the Bible to think about oppression.

Someone found out about it and made a list. That's what Enrique thinks happened. The military came into town a few times to scare people. After that, like some other men, his father took the family to sleep every night in the bush above Ixtán, on the slopes of El Pico, to avoid a night raid.

But there were a lot of spies then. People needed the money. The military played on old rivalries. Someone must have told.

One night, Enrique had to go to the bathroom. He didn't wake anyone up and went off by himself, making a game of it, pretending to explore the mountain. He felt grown up. There was no moon and he got a bit lost. He'd just sighted the outline of that big tree when he heard the noise. People were coming.

His mother yelled. Enrique stayed where he was, behind a rock that was nearly as tall as him, trying to figure out a way to save her — all of them. He had a younger sister, Liliana. She was fat and funny and stronger than a boy, and they were always together. But he was so scared. If he stood up on his toes and looked over the rock, he could see figures moving in and out of flashlight beams.

For the next hour he listened to the soldiers taunt his father, saying he was a subversive, that his wife and daughters were whores. They must've done something else too because Enrique heard his mother scream in pain. Enrique started running towards her, but an arm grabbed him by the waist. A second soldier put a gun to his chest and laughed, said he'd caught one. One to keep.

Enrique howled for his family. And his mother yelled back until the men stuffed something into his mouth and took him away. That's when he started his life as a soldier.

But his family didn't go anywhere. To this day, he believes they're still at El Pico. Exactly how they fell when they were shot, probably in a shallow hole. He knows because this is how the military did it in those days, how he was trained to do it.

Since then, no one has ever agreed to acknowledge them. After the Ixtán evictions, the mine controlled the land and it was impossible to —

That is as far as Danielle managed to get. When Pepe finishes reading, he looks up.

"*Lo siento,*" she says. I'm sorry.

Pepe points sharply towards the campsite, which is just out of view. He doesn't even bother leading Danielle there because he knows she won't run. She leaves him on his rock staring at the papers in his hands.

Before making her last turn though, she glances back. Pepe still hasn't moved. He looks frozen. What must it be like to read the story of your past, of the loss of your family? Danielle thinks of her own parents, of her mother's illness, and then of Aida, reading her letters from the 1980s. Was it fair to leave, to force Aida to interpret them alone?

An unnatural sound interrupts these thoughts. A vibration. Very faint. So faint Danielle thinks she's dreaming it. Pepe is reaching for something — his phone. He puts its boxy form to his ear, answering. Danielle wants to scream for joy — for help. Someone is calling! But no. Whoever it is will be on Pepe's side. She should go. But her curiosity is physical. She takes a step off the path and into the bushes to watch.

How the same, and yet how different Pepe looks. Moments ago he was stiff with what Danielle read as pain and memory. Now she sees only need. Pepe barely moves as he receives whatever information is coming over his precious line out. She should be back with the group by now. She's pushed it too far. Also, she needs to piss. But Danielle feels that she has no choice but to keep standing where she is. She presses her legs together and waits.

Pepe shifts. He reaches into a pocket of his fatigues and pulls out folded paper, holds it up. It's her story! The first or this latest one? Impossible to tell. Pepe starts reading into the phone. He's sending one of her stories to the newspapers — or TV, the internet. Whatever. Part of Danielle is amazed that Pepe can bear to repeat those words about his life. Part of her can't help picturing her name attached to them.

Then Pepe touches a button and the call is over. Danielle wants to go, but something's wrong. Pepe seems perplexed and then flinches — with anger, Danielle thinks. He looks directly over at the spot where she stands. She doesn't breathe, makes herself as small as she possibly can, praying to each branch, each leaf between her and him to do its job as camouflage. Has she been seen? If so, Pepe will kill her, murder her while the others eat their dinners. But he just looks back at his phone. Danielle is about to get away when Pepe reaches into a different pocket in his pants. This time he pulls out the Swiss Army knife Danielle has seen him use before. Cursing under his breath, he flicks out one of its implements and presses the tip into the seam where the front and back components of the phone come together. He applies enough pressure that his mask bends at the mouth, the hole closing outwards. He keeps at it until *schwwiiick!* The front plastic cover pops off abruptly, landing among the leaves at his feet. To Danielle, this is tragedy. Why would Pepe ruin his perfectly good phone? He puts on his flashlight and scrutinizes the inner parts. After a moment, all of his body seems to relax. Pepe retrieves the cover and snaps it into place.

Danielle senses that he will get up at any moment, and so she moves, letting tree branches pull against her as soundlessly as she can, returning towards the shed. She tells herself that Pepe will not hear or even think of her. As she goes, she plays back everything she's seen. Why check inside the phone? And then she knows — for no reason except years of watching police procedurals: he thought it was bugged, that someone was tracing him, someone he doesn't trust. Who? Rita? Danielle cannot imagine Rita trying such a sophisticated ploy. Who else? Pepe's contact out there in the world — the one calling him? But that makes no sense at all. The contact is almost certainly someone like the delegation's bus driver, Ramón, obviously paid to lead them into a trap. Or like the spies who sold out Pepe's family. People in need of money.

Unable to determine the object of Pepe's distrust, Danielle is left with a strange feeling that takes her some time to identify. It's pity. She pities the man who has taken her captive. His aloneness, his history. She wills the feeling away. She doesn't need Stockholm syndrome on top of everything else. But Danielle also knows firsthand how distrust can make you crazy.

By the time Pepe returns to the shed, Danielle is sitting down, having already wolfed down half the food on her plate. He looks around for her, finding her as she knows she is: pale and sweaty, sick with fear, about to piss her pants. But he must assume this is a consequence of what she's just heard about his life. Pepe's eyes only rest on her a moment before he snarls at the others, then goes back out. Ten minutes later, Delmi comes in. That didn't take long. Everyone knows they're sleeping together. No one cares. Danielle finally gets permission to urinate. Returning, she sits down to share the silent anxiety of the group over the walk they know begins momentarily. Will it be harder? Rockier? What happens if someone breaks an ankle?

Finally, Pepe reappears. The sex must be working for him because he's looser. He walks directly over to Pierre, tears off his gag unceremoniously and cuts his wrist bindings. "*Vamos,*" he says, and everyone tries to overcome their surprise to scramble into line, retying boots and hauling on their packs. Pierre is last to get going. Danielle turns back and sees him running a hand delightedly over his lips like they're brand new.

June 14, 1980

HAPPY BIRTHDAY NEELA!!

Do you believe it? A quarter century! Who knows, maybe I was
already too old to take this trip on. I'm bored, Neela. The faction
controls my entire life. I need permission to go anywhere, do anything.
But they're so disorganized, nothing ever happens when it's supposed
to! I end up sitting around reading. If it wasn't for that American
journalist I told you about, who left me some paperbacks, I'd be
reduced to reading canned food labels.

The other day I was cutting my toenails, eating a banana, thinking:
aside from the food, the diarrhea and the bugs, I could be anywhere.
What am I doing here?? I'm still gathering material, sure. But it's
like being allowed to add one piece to a puzzle per week. And can
I just add that a lot of people in this faction are quasi-literate at
best? I hear you cringing. I guess I thought it would be idealists and
visionaries all around. But I've only got Sosa and Adrian to talk to,
and Adrian's not here right now, as you'll have guessed by my mood.

DB

THURSDAY
APRIL 7

12:50 PM. *San Salvador*

Aida is riding in the backseat of an overly air-conditioned car between Ralph Joseph and Sylvie Duchamp. Having watched the kidnapper's video an unhealthy number of times, Aida notices that Ralph has the same jaw and the same high forehead as his niece, the hostage named Tina, while Sylvie, so tall and freckled, bears only a passing resemblance to her son, Antoine — unlike Sylvie's husband Benoît, seated in the front, who's a dead ringer for Antoine.

Ralph clears his throat loudly. "Bad drivers," he says, shaking his head at traffic.

Aida agrees. She's already seen two motorcycles riding on the sidewalk, one with an entire family arranged on it. And there are endless run-down buses spewing black clouds of diesel fumes, grinding their gears. Every so often she also spots a luxury vehicle, and even one candy yellow Hummer rolling calmly forward in a far lane, which, to Aida, is even more jarring.

"They need some truck inspectors around here," Ralph adds.

Aida has overheard him say that this is what he does for a

living — truck driving. Ralph wears large, dark sunglasses and a shirt with a soft collar. He smells strongly of cologne. He seems as uncomfortable to be here as Aida is, like he would prefer to be alone, or at least to be the one driving. The man currently behind the wheel is named Pedro. Marta Ramos said he's trustworthy. She claims he was once a guerrilla commando and can respond to any problem, traffic-induced or otherwise. Seems far-fetched. Pedro is slight, dressed in a faded denim jacket, jeans and a baseball cap. His teeth aren't good. Not the picture of a fierce guerrilla — although Aida admits to herself that she's not the expert on what Salvadoran guerrillas looked like, on people like that man her mother fell for, Adrian.

"There's a lack of respect for life," says Sylvie, looking at Aida, but responding to Ralph's comment about truck safety. "In poor countries, that's the way it is. You were so brave to come, Aida." Sylvie pats Aida's knee. "Foreign Affairs, they don't want us here, you know. *Espèces de bureaucrates.*" She says this like a bureaucrat is the worst thing a person can be.

"They *don't* want us here," says Benoît, repeating his wife's view exactly, as he has already done more than once. He twists in his seat, wide-eyed. "They know we're going to cause trouble. Put pressure. We're going to fight until they shut that *maudite* mine down for an excavation."

"Exhumation, *chérie,*" says Sylvie, trying to smile.

"People need to be buried properly," says Ralph, without turning from his window. He and Antoine's parents rarely communicate directly. Aida wonders if this has to do with Ralph being Native. She has no experience with Native men — not much with Quebeckers either. She's curious about what the other families make of her.

"Isn't it *ironique,*" says Sylvie, casting the word like a stone, "that someone who says he wants to find his family would threaten other people's families?" She is truly stuck on this irony and has closed a well-manicured hand over her mouth as if to keep from crying over the contradiction. Aida gently points out to her that she has lost one of her earrings, but Sylvie just shakes her head. Up front, Benoît gives his wife a sympathetic look, then returns to staring at a composite photo of the hostages, made up of stills from the kidnappers' video. It's been printed on the front page of a local newspaper that's folded on his lap. He turns to Pedro. "He's our only son," he says in French-sounding Spanish.

Aida looks away. She doesn't like Benoît's pleading or the stills. Her mother looks so awful in those shots, so haggard. By now, everyone in Toronto will have seen the video. And those who also know Aida's background, how little Danielle participated in her upbringing, have probably found reason to further pity her. Aida wishes she could avoid all this press.

Which would be very difficult right now, with Benoît thumping the newspaper, trying to force a reaction from Pedro, who finally concedes with a friendly sniff. Benoît still doesn't seem satisfied, which Aida finds sad. She can see how helpless he feels. They're all helpless. But Aida knows she's even more so, because she can't say for sure that a reunion with Danielle will make her or her mother happy. Aida is here on a meagre hope. To meet a different Danielle, to be a different kind of daughter, to talk in person about the letters and move past them. Excavating their authentic selves and all that. It's a long shot.

She stares out the window. Heaps of garbage appear every so often by the side of the road. When the car is stopped by a haphazard-looking roadwork crew digging a huge, muddy hole in the middle of the street, Aida glances up an embankment and sees a group of five children in school uniforms but no shoes leaning out the doorway of a tin and wood shack. Further on, a tree glitters, bits of debris hooked among its sparse branches.

Though she has no sense yet of the geography of the city, Aida guesses they must be nearing its centre when the road suddenly curls around and is squeezed into a single lane between the walls of buildings blackened with soot. Every inch of the sidewalks they pass is suddenly covered with goods for sale. Pirated DVDs, Mayan-themed plastic and wooden jewelry, massive stacks of newspapers (her mother's face on many of them, she marvels), sweets, hair products, TV antennae, religious icons. People cross in front of the car frequently. Each time, Sylvie says, *"Dieu Seigneur!"* Ralph shakes his head and Pedro brakes. They turn another corner and Aida's eyes go wider. The view has opened up. Across a large, busy plaza that includes a garden and an equestrian statue is a white building with two narrow bell towers. The cathedral.

Pedro moves the car gently to the side, careful not to kill anyone, which Aida can see is a challenge. They stop. Sylvie immediately grabs the door handle, but Pedro says quite firmly in decent English, "Please. Wait." Sylvie throws Aida a look that says she's not pleased to be told what to do by this man, but they all remain seated until another man, who looks a little like Pedro, short and unremarkably dressed, appears at the driver's side door. Pedro gets out, keeping a hand up to indicate that his passengers should hold on a moment longer. He looks around for whatever or whoever could be a threat, Aida supposes, and the other man takes his place behind the wheel.

"Okay," Pedro says, and waves them all out. Aida has her first inkling that she might have underestimated him.

When Ralph, beside her, opens his door, the acrid smell of the city and the noise of buses and people yelling out prices for their wares floods over Aida. It must be thirty degrees. The strangeness of everything is suddenly palpable — this place, this event. Marta Ramos is the one who proposed that Aida come. She said it might cheer her up. Aida, who wasn't keen on being left alone at a stranger's house, didn't feel she had much choice. Marta has only made brief appearances so far, picking Aida up at the airport, dropping her off at home and telling her to make herself comfortable before Pedro escorted her off again to some meeting Marta claimed she couldn't get out of. This morning was the same. Aida and Marta shared a hasty breakfast during which Marta received call after call on her cell. From what Aida can tell, she's always busy, always thinking of ten different things, informal in her manner, laughing easily and boldly. Aida already feels swept into her world.

The others, confident that their own participation here is mandatory, seem unfazed by the heat or foreignness of the scene. They're hurrying onto the opposite sidewalk ahead of Pedro so as not to be hit by any red, coughing city buses. Aida follows, but as soon as she steps up, she's accosted by two men walking backwards ahead of her, each holding a velvet-covered oblong with a series of watches strapped to it. "*Relojes? Relojes?*" they ask, rapid-fire, in unison.

Aida momentarily forgets her Spanish. "No thanks."

One of the men considers this response then says, without inflection, "I want to eat your pussy."

Aida nearly stops walking, but Pedro, suddenly behind her, puts a hand lightly to her elbow and keeps her going. She feels relieved, like she might've run back to the car and begged to return to the airport otherwise. She turns briefly to look towards the safety of the vehicle, but it's gone. Pedro's associate has already driven it away.

They enter the plaza, which is surrounded on all sides by large buildings with elaborately framed windows and immense wooden doors. Aida recalls her single trip to Cuba with André last year, the colonial architecture of Old Havana, which she found equal parts romantic and tragic. She generally prefers new design, or at least older buildings that have been properly restored. Here, like in Cuba, each structure sags more than the last under faded stucco. And yet, together, the buildings are oddly lovely, forming an appropriate backdrop for this sun, these big flocks of cooing pigeons, the old men they pass, who sit together on chipped benches, smoking.

Pedro leads them along a pebbled pathway that cuts through the garden where all the trees are painted white on the bottoms (to fight off some tropical infestation, Aida thinks, concerned). They emerge just across the street from the cathedral. On its steps, a small group of about fifteen is milling about, holding placards. Among them, Aida spots Marta Ramos.

"Aida!" Marta yells, seeing her. She hurries over and hugs Aida forcefully and fast, same as at the airport and again after breakfast. Aida can see why Marta and Neela are friends. Both gleefully ignore personal boundaries.

"No problems getting here?" Marta asks. She's wearing sneakers, khakis and a short-sleeved blouse that accentuates her flabby arms. She smells strongly of baby powder — like her bathroom at home.

"*No, gracias. Todo bien,*" Aida says. "*Muy bien,*" she tries again, looking for the right sound in her "*-ien.*" She's still finding her feet with the language she knows so well from the classroom but that, in truth, she's rarely used in a real-life setting besides her grandparents' home and on that one trip to Cuba. The language limitation is going to drive her crazy, she knows. Aida prides herself on speaking correctly.

She begins to ask Marta if there's been any more news about the exhumation. Worrying rumours have been circulating that the forensic specialist Alejandro Reverte is too committed to a long-term project with a Mayan group in Guatemala to come to El Salvador, a prospect Aida needs ruled out by someone in the know. But Marta has already moved on and is introducing her-self to Sylvie, Benoît and Ralph. The abrupt shift in her attention confirms Aida's growing sense that Marta juggles too much, that her focus on any particular person is mediocre, a problem Aida has noticed in many people too into their "cause."

"*Ahora,*" Marta says, clapping her hands sharply. "Who wants to speak at the demonstration?"

Aida stumbles as she translates for the others. No one has said anything about speaking.

"Isn't that illegal?" asks Benoît.

Marta laughs. "You Canadians! Very law-abiding."

Aida finds the comment patronizing, but Marta doesn't even pause.

"You think they are going to come and pull you out in police cars? No. Bad for publicity." Marta has small eyes, and they nearly disappear as her cheeks stretch into a wide smile.

"I'll go up," says Ralph.

Aida turns to him in surprise.

"I don't mind," he adds. "But I can only do it in English."

"*Qué bien,*" says Marta, and she immediately drags Ralph to-wards one of the other organizers, slotting him into the schedule. "And Aida can translate," she says, dashing back.

Aida glares at her. "My Spanish is —"

"*Imperfecto,*" Marta says, and everyone laughs a little. "It's okay. Listen to my English. *Horible!* And I lived in your country. You will be great. Good for your mother."

For the next half hour Aida sits on the steps of the cathedral trying to make the reality of her situation more tangible: she's at a rally in a foreign country for her kidnapped mother, whom she's never gotten along with, about to do live English-to-Spanish in-terpreting in front of activists she's never met, which could get her arrested (no matter what anyone says) by police that she's been told used to kill Salvadorans for attending things like this. And she's paid for all of these wonderful experiences with earnings from her (now jeopardized) MBA work placement. Money she was saving for her life in France, with André.

But as the minutes pass and people start to gather, the mood becomes noticeably more upbeat. The event feels nothing like Neela's small, forced vigil in Toronto. There are some relaxed-looking priests and nuns, a group wearing workers' overalls, and several students dressed like the kinds of bandana-wearing anti-globalization types that used to occasionally get in Aida's way at the university. Marta hugs practically every one of these people. What a contrast between this big personality and the cramped house where Marta lives.

Aida was so disheartened walking into that house behind Pedro yesterday. Everything in sight was hideous. Old, random furniture, dark blankets over the couch and recliner, a TV on an empty, overturned box, glaring fluorescent lights pouring over it all. It looked like a poor person's house, which confused Aida, because Marta doesn't seem poor. In the evening, while Marta was out at her meeting, Aida spent time looking at the dusty photographs covering one of the living room walls. Many were of Marta's adult children — no husband that Aida could see. Some showed Marta in other countries with dignitaries, farmers, women's groups. Lots of photos of her holding up signs opposing the *Mil Sueños* mine. Definitely Neela's kind of lady. Which explains why Neela practically forced Aida to stay with her.

Now Marta goes up the steps to fiddle with a portable microphone and amp. "*Compañeros y compañeras, les pide su atención, por favor.* My name is Marta Ramos and I am co-founder of the Committee for the Environment, based in the municipality of Los Pampanos, where we're fighting for the rights of *campesinos* to clean air, water and land. We began this series of demonstrations yesterday and we will continue until we see action on the part of NorthOre. As someone who's been directly affected by violence, I do not support the forced detention of the Canadian hostages. I don't support violence at all. However, I also know that the *Mil Sueños* mine has carried out great violence already. When we have sought peaceful, legal means to resolve these problems through our justice system, we've been met with nothing but obstacles, lies and closed doors. Here, they call this The Law. But it is violence. The threats I have received this week, telling me not to speak so loudly, these too are violence. Do we accept these forms of violence?"

The crowd yells back, "No!" So does Benoît, sitting beside Aida on the church steps, clapping.

"And do we forgive when justice has not been done, and when impunity is granted to the American and Salvadoran masterminds who supported the killing of thousands of innocent civilians during twelve years of war?"

"No!"

Marta keeps at it until everyone else besides Aida is calling out the answers she demands. Even Sylvie and Ralph, to whom Aida tries to provide a running translation, seem to brighten. Aida claps so that she won't look out of place, but she doesn't think it's right to equate NorthOre with the kidnappers. They don't belong in the same breath.

Before long Marta mentions that some of the families of the kidnapped foreigners have made the long trip to El Salvador in a show of solidarity. And then she's introducing Ralph Joseph and Aida Byrd, and Aida realizes that's her, that she's supposed to get up. Ralph goes first, striding confidently along one of the steps towards Marta on his big legs. Prodded by Sylvie and Benoît, Aida follows. Several news crews, which Aida didn't notice before, come in closer. She resents their intrusiveness.

"*Ho*-la," says Ralph, and many of those assembled smile. "My name's Ralph Joseph. I'm a counsellor with the Wikwemikong Unceded First Nation. I belong to the Ojibway Nation first and foremost. So when the Canadian government tells me I shouldn't be here, I don't listen too much."

Ralph turns to Aida, and she knows she's supposed to say this in Spanish, but she's stuck. This is too much weirdness. She fears an out-of-body experience. Slowly, she reaches for the mic. It's warm from Marta's hand, then Ralph's. Aida holds it away from herself. All the brown faces assembled look at her expectantly. She tries to find someone in particular to focus on, which she once learned from a debating coach is the best way to communicate to a crowd. At the very back she finds him: good-looking, late forties or maybe fifty. Zeroing in on his face, Aida begins, stumbling several times. But everyone seems to understand. She gets a lot of nods.

Ralph goes on to talk about his niece, Tina, and what she means to him, how exemplary of her people she is, and Aida keeps up, looking at the man in the crowd all the while. He's the only person she can see who's wearing a full business suit. There's something familiar about him, too. And he's staring back. Almost to the point where Aida thinks she should be uncomfortable. Does she know this person? From the airplane, maybe?

By the time they're finished, Ralph is in tears, his shoulders heaving with emotion. Aida walks back across the step with him and they sit. She looks through the crowd again for the man in the suit, but he's gone. It's strangely dispiriting, as is Ralph's powerful connection to Tina, so unlike hers with Danielle. What would Aida say if she were the one speaking? Her decision to come here has been impetuous. It's the exception in a life of wanting to get as far away from her mother as possible. Applause would be thin.

Marta has returned to the mic to wrap up. She pleads with everyone to return tomorrow and every day until NorthOre agrees to shut down, permit the exhumation and deliver the remains of the kidnapper's family to the authorities. People disperse. The car has reappeared and the families all ride together back out of the old city centre. Pedro drops the others at their whitewashed guesthouse before making his way to Marta's.

"That went well," Marta says, stepping inside and tossing her purse onto her exhausted-looking recliner. "Tomorrow, we'll have some unions. A full bus from Los Pampanos. It will work out well," she says, like that's the obvious outcome. Then she's gone, hastening to the kitchen to put up coffee.

At first Aida half agrees, but as she walks into her tiny bedroom it occurs to her that no amount of cheering and rallying tomorrow, the next day, or the day after that is going to change NorthOre's stance. Mitch Wall will need to be convinced some other way — by someone from his world, not Marta's. Otherwise one hostage will be dead by Monday. That could be the real outcome.

Aida returns to the living room, where she follows instructions Marta has taped to the phone for dialing the international operator. In an act of sainthood, André has agreed to stay on at Danielle's, just in case, and Aida is hugely relieved when he answers on the first ring. She launches into a detailed description of her strange first day in El Salvador, keeping her voice down so that Marta won't hear. The house is so puny. Only an archway of chipped drywall divides the living room from the kitchen.

When Aida gets to the part about translating for Ralph, she remembers: that man in the crowd — he was in the newspaper, beside Mitch Wall at the *Mil Sueños* mine. She asks André to pull up the photo online. He doesn't understand why Aida cares so much about one stranger, but he does as she asks, reading her the photo caption. It includes the man's name: Carlos Mendoza Reyes.

July 5, 1980

Neela,

Very bad day. The buzz of military planes is making me crazy. Last week, they got way too close. We had to get into the bunker nearly every afternoon. I spent hours in there, glued to guerrilla radio. They had reports of entire villages being wiped out.

At last, a couple days ago things calmed down enough for us to leave camp. They wanted me to document a process the faction has started where people elect a 'poder popular' in the communities — like town council (which is a totally new concept around here). When we got there, the locals were like zombies. The military had just been there. Some houses were still burning, all the crops destroyed. I saw bodies, Neela.

These three skinny kids wandered over to us, practically naked, with cuts and blood all over them. They'd lost their parents (kidnapped? killed?). The children had hidden in a shed behind their house until the soldiers left. It was filled with bats — those giant, evil ones I told you about. The oldest got on the shoulders of one of the guerrillas and came with us, back to camp.

When I came to El Salvador I thought it was going to help me, as a journalist. Like if I published really good stories, I'd get somewhere. But I'm having trouble with that idea now. There are so many stories like those kids. Publishing in Canada — what will that do for them? I wish I was the kind of person who could pick up a gun and fight. But I know I'm not and won't ever be. I don't like the way they're running this war. I don't like the lower status the women have. Everything is done ass-backwards.

I've tried to talk to Adrian about the problems I see, but he's always distracted. Always has some important mission to plan. Why won't he make more time for me? I intend to corner him about this next time he's here.

DB

FRIDAY
APRIL 8

9:00 AM. Mil Sueños *mine*

"Namaste."

"Namaste," Mitch replies, then separates his palms and lifts them over his head before bowing and bringing them to the floor to begin his sun salutations.

"Remember to constrict the throat," the instructor continues. "Build the fire."

Mitch does the loud Ashtanga nose breathing, immediately breaking into a sweat. But five minutes later, after arching into an upward dog, he lets himself down onto his stomach while the video plays on.

"Extend. . . breathe!"

Mitch promised his wife he'd keep up his practice until his next trip home, but it's no fun without her. And this room is making it impossible to relax. He's never minded sleeping at the mine when the two-hour drive back to his apartment in San Salvador feels like too much. But the stress of this abduction is making him long for basic comforts. This portable has none. He sits up.

"Try to feel the energy of the earth rising through your sit bones, your heels. . . ."

Mitch wonders exactly what kind of "energy" he's receiving from the land beneath his trailer — bad karma? Initially, Mitch didn't give much thought to the hostages. He genuinely feels that they came to El Salvador with their eyes open and must live with the consequences. But this morning he woke up with Carlos's voice in his head, an echo of something he said over the phone last night. "I don't see this person shifting their deadline," he told Mitch. "By Sunday, you'll have to decide what's best for you and your business." All doom and gloom. Mitch wonders if he's setting himself up for cosmic retribution if he doesn't agree to an exhumation. It's a morbid thought, but Mitch lets it drift into his consciousness without judgment, then out again, the way the thin male instructor on the video always tells him to. Mitch sees the Canadian hostages sitting around a campfire somewhere at the crack of dawn, Monday morning. One of them is called to stand and bang-bang! Shot at point blank range. Because of him.

The image is alarming enough that Mitch stands and begins to pace. This is crazy. In his heart, he knows that if Catharine Keil would just mind her own business, the police would deal with the kidnappers long before that scenario plays out. Why the hell is the Attorney General listening to her over his own police? And what is that woman's problem? Keil is unnecessarily rude, first of all. And now Mitch hears she's brought in some senior bureaucrats from Ottawa to lobby Schiffer even harder into keeping Hernández and the anti-kidnapping unit leashed. Meanwhile, she tries to put the blame on him? As if Mitch made those fools come here on their sham "delegation"! It's not going to be Keil's face on the news if the kidnapping goes south.

Mitch feels his heart accelerating. He's not practicing his

letting-go. He closes his eyes, sits back down, crosses his legs and promises himself to just be.

A knock at the door.

Sometimes when his director of operations or the geologists know he's staying on site, they come by for advice. But Mitch isn't even dressed. Just the Lululemon shorts and tank top set his wife bought him. "Busy here," he yells.

"You asked for the update as soon as I had it, *Señor* Wall."

Sobero. Mitch grabs a t-shirt from his single chair and throws it on. He answers the door to find his Chief of Security looking cool in the brilliant morning.

"The newspapers," says Sobero, handing Mitch a stack of Salvadoran dailies.

Above the fold of the top copy is a blaring headline that reads, "Kidnapper received high-level military training, admits to previous violence." Mitch scans the article. What kind of warped. . . ? The hostages are writing on behalf of the kidnapper now? "Christ," he says, rereading the byline: Danielle Byrd. The old one — delegation "leader." A total loser, from what he's read in the Canadian papers.

"It is not unusual in El Salvador for men to have some formal training," says Sobero, as if the fact that they're dealing with a professional killer who's talked one of his hostages into publicly making his case is an insignificant detail. "Also, it seems they'll have a few extra today. In the capital." Mitch isn't sure he can take more bad news. "How many?" he asks, reluctantly.

"Not so many."

"Like how many?"

"Two hundred, two hundred and fifty."

"What —" Mitch cannot understand why people are attending those demonstrations in San Salvador, or why the papers in Canada are making such a big deal of them. "We should've reached out to those families before that Committee for the fucking Environment did. They got them onside while they were easy pickings."

Sobero looks disappointed in this outburst. "Families are of no use to this mine. We are going to start putting people on the ground at the cathedral. Eyes and ears. I am also working on some meetings that could assist us."

Mitch nods, knowing Sobero will say nothing more about his security strategy. "Thank you, Manuel. I'll shower and talk to you when I get settled."

Mitch closes the door and goes to shut off his video. The shot has changed to a close-up of the instructor in a twisted seated position, his left elbow hooked around his right knee, looking behind him at the camera. "Keep your eyes going further right, extend the stretch. Hold here. Five. Slow. Breaths."

The microphone squeaks. Marta taps it. "*Sí?*"

Several people nod. She's being heard.

"*Bueno. Gracias a todos y todas que están aquí con nosotros. Qué bien!*" She claps for the crowd. Their swelled numbers do impress her. She predicted to Pedro that the story in the morning papers about the kidnapper's life would strike a chord. It has. "Thank you to the Archdiocese of San Salvador for permitting us, again, to be here, on their doorstep." Marta keeps her eyes on two heavily armed police who are strutting back and forth across the roof of one of the buildings on the west side of the plaza. The cops have also seen the story, apparently. Despite the violence described in it, some people are taking Enrique's side. The police are on alert. And worried police are always dangerous. Maybe, Marta thinks, it's the same all over, the way talk of the past makes them trigger-happy. But in Central America, the past is also recent. Its residue is everywhere. "And thanks too to the police and to our government," she says, "for extending to us such *full* protection today — to all of us citizens, who have come here in the name of our country's historical memory and a future in which our environment flourishes."

Laughter and applause from the maybe three hundred people on hand. Now Marta shifts her focus to their faces, looking for anyone that might be a plant. She's still being threatened. More phone calls. One distorted voice that grunted at her, "If you like your life, stop the demonstrations!" then hung up.

She ploughs ahead, trying to forget those words. "We have all read in the newspapers today an account of the life of the man who carried out this abduction. This letter has affected me deeply. Maybe, like me, these words have caused you pain, and you are wondering why we should continue to be here in support of demands by a man like this. But hear me out. The crimes he describes committing are heinous, unfeeling. But I challenge anyone here to tell me that *Mil Sueños,* with its *famoso* expansion at El Pico, is not carrying out crimes today that parallel those of the military during our war. What else can we call the dynamiting that has destroyed the land around Los Pampanos except unfeeling? Have the people who've made millions selling this gold internationally given a single thought to the families who live downstream from the mine? To the value of their lives? Their children's lives? I challenge anyone to deny the crucial role the people of Los Pampanos played in dismantling El Salvador's military. They faced terror, death squads, mutilation. And yet they succeeded because they knew the regime was criminal. So tell me why we shouldn't do the same to *Mil Sueños* now? What you read today about 'Enrique' is a crime of the past. He has owned up to it. *Mil Sueños* and the El Pico expansion are crimes of our time. Of this very day. No one wants to admit to those. But we can prevent more tragedies. We must write a new ending for El Salvador."

Just as Marta feels her face flushing with emotion and she's begun leading the crowd in a cheer of *"El pueblo unido, jamás será vencido!"* she looks out and her eyes fall on the person she's least expected to see again so soon: Carlos Reyes. She watches, confounded, as he actively ignores her, shaking hands with people, moving forward, stealing away one vote at a time for his new political party. Why should this surprise her? Men like Carlos always sniff out opportunities for political gain. It takes an effort for Marta to keep on with her cheer and look like a leader for those gathered and the several news crews that have come out to cover the event.

Then Carlos stops. He has come to stand behind Marta's young guest, Aida Byrd.

Aida feels a hand on her shoulder.

"Miss Byrd?" says a deep voice.

She turns to see a middle-aged man with a lazy smile and a thick head of curly hair extending his other hand towards her to shake.

"Carlos Reyes."

It's him. The man in the suit. Mitch Wall's friend. Aida blushes. "I know."

"Ah?"

"You were in the papers. With the helicopter."

Benoît, overhearing from nearby, practically leaps towards them. "You're with the mine! I think that you need to leave 'ere," he says to Carlos, looking like he'll either hit him or fall down crying. Benoît has found a real live human who sides with the company that's condemning his son to death. Aida is embarrassed for him. Benoît and Sylvie are disintegrating by the hour. Ralph, meanwhile, looks and seems the same. Not particularly friendly towards anyone. He keeps a calm eye on the confrontation between Benoît and Carlos. Sylvie just shakes her head.

"Please. I am only here to acknowledge the situation you are all in," Carlos says, continuing in excellent English. "I offer my support. I am not 'with the mine.' I work as an independent investigator of the police. My office is close by. I thought I would introduce myself. I believe there is still room to negotiate the —"

As he talks, Aida feels that Carlos is addressing her more than the others, often turning to look her in her eyes. She can't decide if he's being flirtatious or just acknowledging that they've seen one another before. She loses track of his words.

Eventually Benoît interrupts. "I don't think we should trust any man that walk off the street with a business card." He eyes the one Carlos has just handed to him.

"Benoît!" Aida chides, taking one for herself. As she does, her hand comes into the briefest contact with Carlos's. His palm is dry and warm, unlike her own, which is unpleasantly sweaty. If anything, the city air is denser and more pungent than yesterday. "I don't think the people who are trying to hurt us would come here — to this demonstration." Her defense emerges before she's had time to think it through, and Aida searches Carlos's eyes, looking for proof that he deserves it.

"I hope I will not cause you any trouble at all," he says earnestly. "I came by to see if any of you would consider discussing with me what interactions you've had so far with the police."

He's old. But still good-looking. Authoritative, though Aida can't figure out what makes him seem that way. The voice? The hair? She hears her mother telling her she should be more wary of older men. What Danielle has never understood is that it's exactly wariness that repels Aida from men her own age. She filters out inexperience and game-playing. Older men are direct — even when they intend to use you. Still, as an offering to her invisible mother, Aida decides to reserve judgment on Carlos. For now.

"I want to ensure that you are treated with respect," Carlos continues, but he doesn't get any further because Marta Ramos has appeared.

"Here you are," she says, her face unusually severe. "Again." Aida looks between her and Carlos: these two know each other?

"Marta. I came in support of the spirit of your event. And to offer my assistance to these Canadians."

But Marta doesn't seem to be listening, which reignites Aida's protective urge towards her new acquaintance.

"As you know, I have a greater chance of controlling the police than you," Carlos adds.

"Coddle, yes. Control. . . ?"

Carlos's smile fades. "You're being unfair, Marta. I only —"

"Okay!" Marta says over him, reverting to her poor English.

"Everyone, Pedro is ready. Maybe you go home a leetle bit early today."

Aida watches the others nod obediently, preparing to leave in the direction Marta is pointing, back across the plaza. Like lambs. Aida stands her ground. As of this morning, it appears that her mother is writing on behalf of the kidnappers, a fact that, in truth, Aida doesn't doubt. The kidnappers are toying with the press. But from the tone of the piece, Danielle is more than their middleman. Like Neela, she's prone to seeing the world through the lens of victimhood. Her mother has always been susceptible to thinking she feels other people's pain. It's easier for her to deal with than her own, or Aida's. Since reading about that horrible man, Aida has been struggling all morning to keep a positive frame of mind, and she doesn't need Marta robbing her of the one personal contact she's enjoyed all day.

But to her surprise, Carlos is giving in like the rest. He bows, excuses himself politely and waves goodbye.

Aida trails the others to the car, where Marta issues a warning that Aida is forced to translate. "Carlos Mendoza Reyes is a man our country owes a debt to for his bravery in our civil war. But he has important political ambitions and a lot to gain by ingratiating himself with many different people, even while he remains close to Mitchell Wall."

Benoît crosses his arms and whistles, Sylvie shakes her hair, and Ralph sighs, all of them united in judgment. Aida's face remains neutral. As soon as she can, she jumps into the car and stares straight out her window all the way home.

The hostages are spending the day in an actual house. Just a one-room adobe shanty, but it has an owner, which makes it ten million times better than that rotting shed, as exciting as theatre. He was sitting in a corner on his haunches when they arrived. Looked about seventy, with the palest beige button-down, through which Danielle could see a patch of grey chest hair. He had exceptionally long arms that ended in a pair of skeletal hands. It was only through sheer discipline that Danielle tore her eyes from him and put down her tarp for sleep, worried that he might leave before she woke up. The others obviously felt the same, arranging themselves in nearly a line so that they could look until their eyes drooped closed. This man might be capable of something — a great performance, of telling them their ordeal is nearly over, that his house is their last stop. But when Danielle awoke around noon, he was still squatting in exactly the same place, smoking the cigarettes Cristóbal gave him and saying nothing.

Now Danielle feels the hope she and the others have shared — of an ally or a show or a miracle — thinning, blowing away with the man's languorously exhaled smoke. He's only changed positions once since lunch, to go out and piss. They all overheard the stubbornly healthy-sounding stream.

Pepe only reappears after his usual absence, just before supper. He nods briefly at the man, who responds with a single, slow bat of his turtle-like eyelids. Danielle is busy trying to figure out how the two might know one another — from their home village? the war? — when Pepe turns to address her. "*Venga*," he says, calling her away as he has each time before.

Danielle's heart rises and drops simultaneously. She actually wants to go, break up the monotony. But as she gets up, she hears at least one tongue click among the others, and she is miserable at the idea of whatever supply of goodwill is left being squandered through more suspicion.

Pepe walks Danielle past the man's small farmyard, in which bony, nearly featherless chickens dart around, straining their pink necks towards invisible specks of food. At a certain distance he tells her to sit down on the bare ground, under tree cover, as always.

"When you take me away, they think I'm collaborating," she says.

"Be quiet."

Danielle reddens. What's coming is inevitable. More horrific stories. More scribbling. There's no arguing it away. But instead of pulling out pen and paper, Pepe reaches back and tugs out his phone — the one he so inexplicably pulled apart and put back together. Stunned, Danielle lets herself imagine that Pepe is about to give it to her. A reward for her help. He's going to let her call home. She'll be a hero to the group. She hears Aida answering: "Danielle?" (Aida only ever calls her by her first name.) "Is it really you?" But Pepe puts the phone down in front of him and stares at it wordlessly. His gaze is impatient. This is what he looked like that other time, too. He's only waiting for a call from whoever out there works with him — for him. Out, Danielle thinks with sudden despair, in the world of people who move freely, who do whatever they want, eat and sleep what and where they want. And so the phone takes on a sinister aspect. It will lead nowhere except to more help for Pepe.

"We'll hear it ring soon," Pepe says, speaking quietly. "I will listen first. Then you will talk. You will say you have a report. You will read this." He shoves some papers towards her. Danielle is momentarily confused, then realizes this is the second report she wrote, that what she saw before was Pepe delivering the first one. Is it already published, then? She can't know. Doesn't want to. Doesn't want any part of Pepe's justifications to the outside world. The others are right to be suspicious. She's becoming as much of an accessory to this kidnapping as whoever's about to call. She shakes her head.

"Yes, you will," Pepe says and spits loudly to one side. "Or I will shoot one of them."

"You wouldn't —"

Pepe grabs Danielle's wrist, wrenching it painfully. "Tell the caller to take down your report, that it should be signed in your name. They should deliver it to the media tonight." Then he throws her wrist back at her like it's contagious.

To keep calm, Danielle tells herself his behaviour is the result of mental illness. First he thinks his phone's bugged. Now he doesn't want to use his own voice, making her his stand-in. It's schizophrenia. Bi-polar disorder. Looney Tunes.

But Pepe appears unsatisfyingly sane as they sit in a strained silence. Only after an excruciatingly long time does the phone finally begin to vibrate. Who can it be? The only image that fits is a stock character from a film noir, standing in a tipped fedora at a payphone on a foggy LA street corner. Pepe answers and turns away.

Danielle waits, noting the construction of his head in profile, his eyelashes long enough to reach past the edges of the eyeholes in his ski mask, parting and closing at a furious pace, registering the intake of information like telegraph needles — a sign of bad news? Confirmation that things are going well? His hand presses the phone to his ear as if it's a seashell and inside the secrets of the world are swishing around. Suddenly, he pushes the phone at her. "*Ahora*," he says, and Danielle takes it, feeling its heft, the moisture where Pepe's palm has just been.

She wants to let it drop. He's crazy. But Pepe tenses threateningly, and Danielle puts it to her ear. She hears a voice speaking Spanish. ". . . I am going to hang up now."

"No. No. *Tengo un informe,*" she croaks back across the line. I have a report.

Her interlocutor, a man, sucks in his breath. Obviously it's as unexpected to him as it is to her to be connected this way. What a tight operation her captor is running, everyone working on a need-to-know basis. Danielle receives no verbal reply, only breathing. She has an odd sensation she can't identify, something not right about the moment, about the person on the other end of the line. It makes her free hand tighten into a fist. Anxiety. The madness catching. She launches into her text.

By the time she finishes, she's crying all over again at the story of Pepe's family's murder and at her knowledge that this report is going to be read by a lot of people, including Aida. She'll be hurt. Her deadbeat mom's name attached to such words. Danielle can't do anything about it.

Then the line goes dead and Pepe grabs back all his communications links — the phone, its invisible satellite, the papers full of her own words — leaving Danielle utterly empty-handed.

August 30, 1980

Dear Neela,

Adrian and I are through. I'm going to tell him next time he's in camp. I'm sure it bores you to hear about him all the time. It bores me. I didn't come here to go gaga over some guy. But I can't seem to focus on anything else anymore. We're always saying goodbye. I end up feeling so desperate. I'm not going to do it anymore.

Sometimes I just want to leave. Then what would he do? Come back here and find that I decided to get out early, that I followed one of those groups leaving for Honduras. He'd never see me again.

To be honest, it would be a relief. People in the camps are so crude. They don't seem to know it's not normal to live this badly. It's hard not to feel like they're being used. It's confusing though, because they seem to believe in the war more than anyone. I swear, we're from different planets. I am sick to death of theirs.

DB

SATURDAY
APRIL 9

12:45 PM. *San Salvador*

Aida is wandering around. There isn't much else to do at this time of day after Pedro drops them at the usual spot and before the demonstration gets going. It's her third afternoon in a row at the cathedral, and both the fear and the novelty have worn off. She's pretty sure she won't come again.

The other families are trying to keep up their enthusiasm. Aida can see them a few feet off, Benoît and Sylvie huddled in serious discussion, likely parsing the minutiae of the news surrounding the kidnapping, Ralph beside them with a hand in his pocket, listening in, his dark sunglasses making it hard to judge what he makes of their chatter. Aida sighs. These are her people — for now. She bends to fix the strap on one of her sandals.

"Hello again," says a voice behind her, in English. Just like last time. Carlos Reyes.

Aida bolts upright, surprised and excited. "Hello," she says, then remembers her resolution to remain on her guard. "Hello," she repeats, more seriously, and turns towards the others, as if to join them.

"Would you be free to have a coffee?" Carlos asks, stepping closer.

A coffee. The most interesting person Aida's met since arriving in El Salvador wants to take her for coffee. But there are the others to consider. Aida promised herself in the morning to be extra nice. Though no one's said anything, she can tell they're upset by Danielle's bizarre involvement with the kidnapper, this writing she's done for "Enrique." Aida has to work against the possibility that she'll be excluded by the other families over questions about Danielle's loyalties — or her sanity — if any more articles show up.

"It's going to start soon," she says, smiling apologetically. She glances towards the steps of the cathedral. Marta should be up there somewhere by now. She's not going to approve of more interactions with Carlos either.

"There's a place just across the plaza. It will calm you," he says.

Aida looks towards Sylvie, Benoît and Ralph, who have just been accosted by a reporter. Benoît immediately starts in about his son, but the reporter tries to steer the tape recorder towards the other two, eventually gluing it to Ralph's nose. "They'll want to interview you next," Carlos says, taking Aida gently by the arm. "Come."

He leads her through the crowd and around the far side of the plaza. "There are so many people," Aida says as they go, feeling like she has to fill the quiet between her and this near stranger. But it's also true. She and the other families were amazed, on arriving, to see that the crowd is at least twice as big as yesterday. Aida assumed the opposite would happen, that reading Danielle's stories about the kidnapper in the newspaper would turn people against "Enrique." He's a murderer, isn't he?

At the first side street Carlos veers right, and she follows without much thought. Normally, Aida analyzes her options in great detail before coming to a decision. Or she lets André make one for her. But the analytic rules of home have stopped making so much sense. She's on some kind of adventure, almost like she's left her normal self behind in Toronto and become someone else since reading Danielle's letters.

They make several more quick turns and end up in an uncharacteristically quiet lane where only foot traffic can pass, and where the vendors gathered on the sidewalks are less aggressive. "Here we are," says Carlos, as they enter through a tall, colonial-style doorway. Inside, it might be the 1950s. High old windows let in the sun, which lands in diffuse streaks over a dark wood counter that runs the length of the narrow café. Below a mishmash of framed photos and artwork, two baristas with mustaches and short-sleeved white shirts slam grounds out of hand cranks while their espresso machines steam and sputter. It smells like roasted beans and cigarettes and Aida is transported back to Havana. She's shocked to find anything like it in El Salvador, which, outside the central plaza, seems to be populated by greasy food stands and chain stores.

"*Lindo*," she says, amazed, walking along the bar. She gets smiles from the mostly older, male clientele, their newspapers laid out ahead of them. Aida wonders if anyone will recognize her from the photos that have appeared in the press.

Carlos is gracious. He chooses seats at the bar and orders two coffees, pulling a napkin from a dispenser for her. He tugs at his cufflinks several times, alternating left and right, looking straight ahead at nothing in particular. Aida wonders why he's brought her here if not for the reasons Marta has implied — for his career, or because he thinks she's young and stupid enough to sleep with any middle-aged man who shows her some attention.

The barista brings their order.

"You speak good Spanish," Carlos says to her, sliding a cup her way.

"My grandparents lived in Central America. They wanted me to learn." Aida enjoys invoking her grandparents.

"You're from a close family."

"Close to them, yes. They're gone now."

"I'm sorry."

Aida doesn't like the loaded pause that follows. "I have three languages, actually. French too. In Canada, the French is nothing special. Mine's not as good as it should be if I'm going to live in Europe."

"You live in Europe?"

"No no." Aida decides to switch to Spanish. She's eager, suddenly, to show off her skills. "Not yet. I'm likely to move to France soon."

"Ah! A very special country."

"You've been?"

"Of course. France, Spain, North Africa. I've travelled a lot — less now." He smiles. "I hate to fly."

Aida is puzzled. She can't see how a guerrilla who lived in the mountains during a long war, as Marta says Carlos did, could be so cosmopolitan. When did he do all this travelling? She continues to struggle with the concept of what a "guerrilla" was. Carlos and Pedro, Marta's driver, are such opposites, yet supposedly they fulfilled similar functions in the war. Aida has nothing to help her judge their sameness or difference. Could Carlos be making up it up? She gives him a look that says she's impressed, while retaining a private doubt.

"So. Have any of you had any problems yet — with the police, for example? Or your embassy? From anyone?"

Aida, who's sipping her coffee, stops abruptly.

"Marta has spoken to you about me," Carlos says, resting his face on one palm, like Marta's cautionary tales tire him out. "She has told you to distrust me."

Aida blushes. She doesn't want Carlos to think she adopts Marta's views wholesale. But how can she ignore the warnings?

Why does Carlos care about her embassy? It's becoming more difficult by the minute to know what to believe. Aida becomes flustered
trying to decide what to say. "She just told us it would be good for
your election plans to get us on your side."

Carlos looks her square in the face. Above them, the clock
strikes 1 PM. The demonstration is starting. The others will be
worried.

"Marta doesn't believe in what our new political party is trying
to do." Carlos's face has changed. Something hard has come into
his eyes. "But we are not looking to sell El Salvador out. I am not
looking to sell you out."

"I'm not that interested in politics, actually."

He seems relieved to hear her say this, and Aida relaxes. She's
already decided that Marta's preoccupation with this man's agenda
is just another version of Neela's tirades against the corporate
world. Marta might even be worse. She's paranoid, especially about
the police. She literally scoffed when she heard that Hernández
and the anti-kidnapping unit got the delegation's bus driver to
confess to being involved in the abduction. Like that's so meaning-
less. And this morning Marta barely glanced at the police sketch
in the newspapers showing the woman whom the driver claims
hired him to betray Danielle and her group. For Aida, these developments are the only signs of hope so far. Marta was far more
interested in Danielle's stories in the newspaper. "In these situations, the person will use whatever they can to get their message
out," she said, hugging Aida. Marta is all about the message.

The conversation shifts to Aida's MBA, then to which global
markets are predicted to grow in the near future. The coffee is
delicious and comes with a small cookie that Aida enjoys. Odd
for her, as she rarely permits herself sweets. She's having a good
time, she realizes. Her first really good time since arriving in El
Salvador — maybe longer. She can practically forget the worry

she's causing the others, or even, for a minute, that her mother is being held against her will somewhere within these borders.

"Our party sees the Central American republics as a lesson in unrealized economic potential, especially El Salvador," says Carlos, referring to Aida's claim that the European Union is a model for growth and integration. Aida isn't sure why, but she hasn't mentioned André as part of her possible future there.

"But this country is so small. It seems like it doesn't have what it would take to compete these days," she says. "There are so many producers geared towards agricultural export — what would its niche be?"

Carlos smiles wearily. "The World Bank talks a lot about niches, doesn't it? With good reason, I suppose. But growth is much more complicated than that in countries on the isthmus. Not every place can follow the same formula."

Aida is annoyed, suddenly. "I haven't studied Latin America specifically. That's not my purpose in being here." It's like Carlos thinks she's too immature to try her on specifics. He can't know how hard it is to even be admitted to an MBA these days, let alone finish. She dabs her mouth and refolds her napkin in her lap.

"Of course," says Carlos. "You're here for your mother."

"For her and for myself."

"*Cierto. Cierto,*" he says, reassuringly.

But Carlos doesn't probe into what Aida is getting from the trip. Part of her wishes he would. She's had so few people to tell, to help her decide whether she might also be experiencing a period of growth.

"I was sorry to read that whoever has done this forced your mother into writing those terrible articles." Carlos goes on, his voice concerned. "It is not her fault, you know."

Aida nods, but her alarm bells are going off again: Carlos seems to know exactly what she needs to hear. Reading the second story by Danielle really was awful. And not just because of the possibility of being rejected by the other families. The reports are giving Aida vertigo. Her emotions, which formed such a tight ball in Toronto, are becoming brittle, snapping regularly and painfully now. One moment she's raging against Danielle for helping the kidnappers. The next she despises "Enrique," convinced that every word of the articles is made up. That feeling is nearly always followed by intense foreboding: there's just today and tomorrow, after all, before Enrique has promised to kill a hostage if Mil Sueños doesn't close. He could easily decide that Danielle knows too much, that she will be the first to die. The prospect that Danielle truly hasn't had a choice about whether to write for him lifts Aida's spirits so much she suspects Carlos of trying to manipulate her. "Why do you even care about this case at all?" she asks, and she's surprised to hear in her voice some of the bitterness she's accustomed to experiencing around Danielle. She sips her coffee and feels childish. Down the way, one of the baristas lines up several tall glasses, pours foamed milk into them, drops smaller amounts of dark espresso into the middles, and takes them to three men at a small table near the doorway.

"I am interested —" Carlos begins, but he hesitates, as if he's waiting for an answer to come to him, "— for my work. As I've told you. Despite what Marta thinks, I have not decided to become a candidate for office yet. I still have a job monitoring the police. How they respond to a kidnapping with foreign hostages is directly relevant to my mandate."

Aida listens as Carlos describes the particulars of the *Consejo Policial*, which he helped establish after the war. He doesn't go any further back in time than that, which only makes Aida more curious. Who was Carlos before? Marta said El Salvador owes him a debt. For what? What kind of soldier was he? Did the person sitting across from her actually kill people? What kind of people? Aida doesn't dare ask. "Do you have kids?" she says instead.

Carlos looks startled, like the question is off-putting. "I — yes. I have five. All grown now." Grown. Like her, he means. In this man's eyes, she is a child playing dress-up. Aida straightens her shirt and without quite meaning to, stands and puts her napkin on the bar. "I have to get back," she says, feeling rattled and, ridiculously, jealous of these children of a man who's made so much of his life. She is also ashamed, suddenly, of her suspicions of Carlos, realizing they have more to do with the vacuum of knowledge surrounding the man Danielle mentioned in her letters to Neela: Adrian. Aida is eager to return to Ralph, Sylvie and Benoît, to get back to her old self, to her role as the daughter of a hostage. She says her goodbyes.

"*Sí, sí, sí,*" says Carlos, confused. He passes some money to the barista and hurries out after her, insisting on accompanying her back. On the way, he stops to speak to the most senior-looking policeman in sight, pulling him aside and making a show, Aida thinks, of speaking to him. She assumes Carlos is telling him to avoid any problems with the families. It's a bit much. Maybe the others are right to avoid someone who performs helpfulness so often for others.

Then, just as they're parting, Aida changes her mind. She is sorry to leave him and feels herself reach out for a hug. Carlos hugs her back. The moment is exciting, surprisingly emotional. But it's brief. Looking up, Aida spots Marta on the top of the cathedral steps, glaring at her. In the space of mere seconds, her host's face switches from panic to relief to anger. Aida sees Marta signal to Ralph, who is also above the crowd, with Sylvie and Benoît. They all look over and, Aida can see, breathe a collective sigh of relief to find her there, but it's mixed with disapproval. Aida doesn't wave. She says goodbye to Carlos before winding through the crowd towards them.

They've been walking five hours when Danielle hears her new favourite sound in the world: Pepe stopping and turning, the regular pace of his footsteps interrupted, becoming noisier, resounding against the rough ground, bringing his boot heels across some pebbles, the whistle of his breath changing, indicating annoyance and clout, coming closer. And then the crackling of brush. This is the beautiful sequence, the signal that they can rest, and the hostages know it as well as they've ever known the sound of a school bell signalling lunchtime, or the scrap of theme song that says the commercials are over and their favourite TV show is back. In her excitement to begin the break — tonight they've done their hardest hike yet — Danielle nearly trips over Delmi. "Sorry," she says.

Delmi turns and shoves her indignantly anyway. Danielle tells herself to let it go. The smaller injustices are not worth her time. But the shove sours the happiest moment of her night.

They all gather in a small group until Cristóbal takes the painfully long, suspicious look around that he always takes, while they stand on their sore legs wanting to collapse. When he gets back he motions for them to move again about twenty feet more, under some trees where there's less moonlight. Even there, Danielle is surprised at how brightly it shines. It reminds her of nights in Algonquin Park, where she lived for a time with an entomologist she thought was the answer to all her problems — he turned out to prefer the company of Ontario's multiple species of beetle. That was her last summer away from Aida. Before Danielle's parents died.

As she locates a spot to lay her tarp, Martin approaches, sighing loudly, but not unhappily. Although he is still a bad smoker and slow walker, mostly taking up the rear on these hikes just ahead of Danielle, he seems stronger and is generally more at ease, while for Danielle, the night walks remain extended tours of misery. Pepe always seems to be taking them uphill. Danielle remembers that back in 1980 it would take four to five days to walk from the south to the north end of this province. This is their seventh nighttime walk. Pepe must be forcing them into some kind of zigzag, or even backtracking, keeping them hidden. But Danielle is also convinced they're moving progressively north. Every day, she notes that same set of taller mountains, the ones she crossed over into Honduras on foot in 1980, and not even the miserable places Pepe keeps them, with their bad sightlines, can stop her from knowing: those mountains are getting closer. Her creeping sense that Pepe is literally walking them in circles so near an exit from the country, wasting what little energy she has left, makes Danielle want to lie down and weep.

Tina crouches on Danielle's left. She's recently caught some kind of bug and has developed diarrhea. Danielle watches Tina's moonlit outline as she ritually lays out her own tarp. Pierre and Antoine move to occupy a place to Danielle's right, and Martin gets down on the ground directly behind her head so that when she turns onto her stomach Danielle can see the soles of his boots. Cristóbal takes a place a little further off, adjusts his hat and puts his gun across his knees, while Pepe walks off. It's Cristóbal's night to keep watch, Danielle knows, and Pepe will play scout. He won't be back for at least an hour.

Martin lifts his head, which appears to float above his feet. He gives Danielle a faint, open-mouthed smile that, while not exactly friendly, meets the minimum requirement of human communion: two captives acknowledging one another's existence. His teeth pick up the moonlight and shine light blue. Danielle considers how, for the last two days, things have been both more harmonious and also more distant within their tiny group. Pierre has been somewhat less on edge since his punishment ended. Not that he smiles or even looks Danielle's way. That would be too much to expect. But earlier in the day, as he smoked a cigarette, clearly enjoying the partial freedom of being unbound, she didn't feel like he was projecting anything particularly negative her way either. Progress.

Tina, meanwhile, is too sick to keep up much in the way of anger. She and Danielle even talked a little, when Danielle grabbed an opportunity to ask if she could help somehow with the diarrhea, maybe get the kidnappers to add something to her water — sugar or salt — to keep her from dehydrating. Tina agreed and when Cristóbal brought over a half-canteen of sweetened water, she smiled at Danielle. After a while, under her breath, she said, "About my brother. Why he's in jail? He was part owner of a club in Hamilton. Got into trouble because someone else — not him — was selling at his bar. It's the bikers. You can't stop them." Danielle was amazed to receive such personal information, amazed, too, at the capacity some people have to get over a slight. Tina was offering intimacy. Danielle shook her head, showing she was worthy of it, indicating her strong disappointment at her brother's unjust treatment. Tina shrugged, reaching the limit of her willingness to share. "We're not that close," she said. But Danielle saw that the girl was lying.

Now Tina is fast asleep, like the others. Danielle watches her back rise and fall sharply with her breath. Danielle wants the same. The first few nights, she managed to fantasize herself to sleep going over benign aspects of her home life that have come to seem supremely luxurious. Grocery shopping. Showers. Outings with friends. But since taking down Pepe's reports, she's run into a problem: for some undefined period before fatigue snatches her consciousness away and leads her into a dreamless slumber, she's wide awake and unable to stop a flood of much more upsettingly real situations from the past from flooding her thoughts.

She stares at the backs of Tina's ribs, which show through her dirty shirt, and tries to see herself in her home office, working on a client document. But slowly, onto this peaceful image, an image of herself at Aida's age is superimposed. The constant sound of insects begins to recede. There she is, young Danielle, waking from a nap near a fire on which a very large *comal* has been placed. Nearby are a series of wooden stumps topped by big curved stones, the *metates*. At each of these stations a woman is bent over, pulverizing corn with another stone shaped like a rolling pin. They are the *molinderas,* an exclusively female rank of guerrillas who make tortillas, the staple food, for everyone in camp. Danielle can hear bits and pieces of these women's jokes, their gossip and complaints. Some are quite old, with cracked hands and stick-thin arms. It doesn't matter. They prepare thousands of tortillas a day, their palms producing uniformly perfect, soft spheres to flatten and cook over the fire. Danielle finds the *molinderas* tedious and resents that she's been placed with them for an entire month, supposedly in service of her journalistic work. She's taken to napping because she's been sick a lot, but also because she's bored. The women don't like it. A *molindera* named Sara starts asking questions, prodding Danielle until she discovers that Danielle has no children. The other women laugh behind their hands. It's absurd, from their point of view, for a twentysomething-year-old woman to be childless. And absurd things, as well as embarrassing and contentious things, make the *molinderas* giggle — like Delmi, Danielle realizes, briefly returning to the present and propping herself up on her side. Where is Delmi? Danielle spots her, not far from Rita, on the other side of Pierre. She lies back down and returns to watching Tina's breathing.

Soon, she sees only her young self again. Sara's questions about her marital status anger Danielle as much as her own inability to produce a good tortilla. Why should she have to justify herself to a bunch of pre-feminist throwbacks? Danielle decides to provoke them. "I won't be having any children," she says. "I will become a writer." Sara looks at her as Danielle has rarely been looked at by anyone in the guerrilla camps. "That's okay," Sara says. "But you cannot be a good writer if you are not a good woman." She slaps a round of raw tortilla dough hard onto the *comal* like a gavel.

The funny thing, Danielle thinks, shaking herself fully awake, is that Sara was right: she didn't become a writer after all; never really became a mother, either; and in some ways she can't say what kind of woman she is, good or bad. Danielle flips onto her stomach again, feeling the uneven earth beneath her, and watches Martin's feet. Slowly, she feels herself sink deeper into her tarp as another memory appears. She is sharing a meal of nothing but tortillas and salt with Adrian. This is early in their acquaintance, before the *molinderas*, when Danielle can still enjoy a tortilla without thinking about female hands having pounded it out. She takes a big bite. "You're adjusting, I see. Nearly Salvadoran," Adrian says. "When you publish your stories about us in Canada, you must provide a caveat: I am biased towards their food. And their men." Danielle laughs, and they exchange a glance that says whatever has begun between them is not nearly over.

Danielle rubs her eyes, miserably awake. Everyone else is breathing heavily. The air is quite chilly. She gets on her back and stares at the swirl of stars above. What a selfish bitch she was! She loved the idea of revolution and people like Adrian, who could talk passionately about it, but never the ones making it happen, one tortilla at a time. Danielle experiences a mounting regret over this basic fact. But she's interrupted as Cristóbal rises from where he's sitting, a few feet behind Tina, presumably to piss. As he walks away, another noise comes from somewhere to her right.

"Hey!" someone calls. "Heeeey!"

Danielle's skin crawls: Rita.

"*Pi-hair*," Rita says.

Danielle feels her breath go out of her with relief. She thought Rita was talking to her. But Pierre — why him? And then she remembers: that day in the shed, Rita whispering her secret into Pierre's ear. Danielle lets her head turn very slowly their way, not letting on that she's awake.

"Pierre," Rita repeats, getting up and hurrying to kneel beside him. Danielle sees Pierre stir.

"*No mucho* time," says Rita, in English. "*El teléfono.* I use it. You make noise."

"*Quoi?*" Pierre sounds groggy.

"Pepe! *El teléfono!* You make noise — *distráelo.* I take. I calling San Salvador. Talking to *embajadora.*"

Danielle sees Pierre trying not to move, afraid of Cristóbal coming back, afraid of those restraints being tied back on, but wanting to find out more. "*Quand* — *cuándo?*" he says, searching for his non-existent Spanish.

"*Pronto.*" Rita flashes her even teeth. For a moment that's all there is of her — those teeth and the bluish whites of her eyes. A Cheshire cat. "*Dile a él,*" she says.

Pierre shakes his head, unsure. Rita sighs loudly and nudges Antoine. "*El!*" she repeats, shaking him.

A twig snaps. Cristóbal is returning.

Antoine makes a sound, like, "Hunh?" and Pierre says something to him very fast in French. "*Quoi?*" says Antoine, just the way Pierre did a moment ago, taking in the message as Pierre shakes his head wildly to prevent him from speaking more.

Cristóbal senses the commotion anyway. He whistles a neutral reprimand as he sits back down. "*Hay que dormir.*"

Both young men close their eyes with purpose. Rita, of course, is already back in her lair, playing dead. Danielle remains completely still, but her heart beats so hard she thinks Cristóbal, or even Pepe, however far off he is, will hear.

Minutes later, however, despite everything, Danielle is aware of herself drifting back in time again.

These nightly breaks normally last about two hours. At the one-hour mark, when everyone's asleep, Pepe walks down from the higher ground and comes near enough to flash his LED at Cristóbal. Cristóbal knows the flashes mean two things: all is well above, and it's time to wake up Delmi.

Cristóbal goes over to shake her shoulder. She mumbles and tries to turn away. "Delmi!" he says again. His sister-in-law is never easy to rouse. He gives her another firm shake. He has yet to see the resemblance between her and Rita and has actually concluded that they must have different fathers. Delmi makes an ugly face under her mask, rises and walks off.

By the time she's reached Pepe, following the LED flashes, Delmi is fully awake. She pulls up the mask, takes off her pants and lies down.

As Pepe gets on top of her, Delmi starts to giggle. "Rita's going to do something."

He stops. "*Qué?*" Pepe's breathing has changed. He pulls out of her and grabs the handgun from his pants, which are half off, puts it under her chin. "*Qué?*" he repeats.

Suddenly, Delmi isn't sure she wants to say. "I don't know." Rita never tells her anything. But Delmi just overhead her talking to Pierre, so she feigned sleep to listen in. Stupid Cristóbal didn't even notice. "I think she wants to steal your phone with that one — the thin one."

"Pierre," says Pepe. He eases away the gun.

Delmi rolls her balaclava down over her face and starts to get up.

"No." Pepe puts a hand to her stomach. "If you say a word —"

"I won't. But I want fifty more. Every time." It's only fair. She holds out her palm for the money. "And you can't tell Rita."

The sex seems to take forever. Pepe is unfocused. When he's finally done, Delmi goes back to lie down beside her sister, whom she's hated for a very long time. She has suspected that Rita would find a way to double-cross her, taking both their shares of what Pepe's paying and leaving for the U.S. without her. Delmi has foreseen waiting for her turn to leave, but no word coming from Rita. She's imagined herself stuck with some of Rita's children on top of her own. Delmi has decided she can do a little better than Rita. If this kidnapping succeeds and Rita doesn't, who knows? Maybe she'll get Rita's share. It will be her in Miami, her wearing nice clothes.

Watching her sister, who's either asleep or pretending to be, Delmi feels clever. Within minutes she is snoring loudly.

⬛

Tina wakes with a start not long afterwards. She's missed it, she's certain. She turns over, her tarp crinkling, and moans. Her stomach is being squeezed by an invisible vice. She presses her nails into her palms, fearing that Cristóbal will hear if she cries out in pain. But when she looks, he's smoking, turned the other way.

Here's Danielle, fast asleep, her breath whistling slowly. Tina feels sorry for her. She knows Danielle suffers from all this walking. If only she were more likeable. She treats them all like dim-witted teens. And she's obviously Pepe's darling. At first Tina figured they were sleeping together. So gross. But now that she knows he's sleeping with Delmi, she can't really see him wanting Danielle too, who's even older and reminds Tina of an unsexy Susan Sarandon. Danielle is doing something else for him, then. Probably letting Pepe know about their daily interactions. Who's trying to get away with what. Who's feeling good. Who's losing it. Danielle might be a rat. Until now, Tina hasn't seen much worth tattling about, except that whispering thing between Rita and Pierre. What *was* that? The dearth of gossip only makes Danielle's arrangement more pathetic. Tina has no time for rats.

Trying not to disturb her neighbour, she slowly maneuvers her arm up without making too much racket and pulls Martin's pant leg, which she can just reach. She has to keep at it for some time before he bends his head forward and up so that they see one another. Tina reaches down and yanks the bottom of her shirt, which she purposely tangled on a thorny bush earlier in the night. It's ripped enough that she can work it now, pulling a whole piece of the shirt clean away. The entire time, she keeps her eye on Cristóbal. He puts out his cigarette and stands, but takes some slow steps away from them, obviously bored and eager for the walk to get going again. As he turns his back, Tina steels herself, reaches up and quickly hands the torn piece of cloth to Martin before resuming her position.

It took just a few words, exchanged over a game of chess, to conceive their plan. (The kidnappers let Tina take out her travel set when she asks, thank God.) She felt that she had to do something, especially after the whispering between Rita and Pierre, from which she was excluded. Pierre is smart, but he's no team player. Now that Tina is getting sicker, she has to ally herself with someone. Martin seems game. After all, how many more days before the kidnappers get serious? There has to be a time limit. Isn't the whole idea of a kidnapping that if you don't get what you're asking for, someone dies? Pepe hasn't even told them what his demand is and shows no sign that anyone's granting it.

A moment later, Martin reaches back and Tina has the long, soft piece of material in her hand, part of his shirt tied to hers. She waves her free arm until she has Cristóbal's attention. "I have to shit," she says when he walks up. "*Mierda,*" she adds, remembering the word.

He goes with her a little ways off and makes her wait while he clears branches and digs a small latrine hole. Then he retreats and turns his back as she undoes her pants. Cristóbal isn't so bad. Tina almost feels guilty deceiving him. At least she doesn't have to fake the shitting. She's been trying not to focus on her sickness. She can't afford to be seen as weak, even if she's starting to feel that way.

She ties the material to a low branch of the furthest tree she can reach, then does her best to pull other branches in front of it. She uses leaves to clean herself and buries her mess, as they're expected to do. "Done," she says, her pulse increasing as Cristóbal inspects the job. She wills him not to look around anymore carefully than absolutely necessary.

"Okay," says Cristóbal. He follows her back towards the others.

Now she's on the ground again, trying to sleep a few minutes more. She lulls herself with the image of someone good — someone clever and careful — picking through this entire area, searching for them. Tina sees this person, who takes the form of her brother John, pulling up the piece of cloth and recognizing it. Then she sees herself back at home, leading her yoga class, standing on just her head and forearms, strong and calm.

September 16, 1980

I'll start with the good news: I finished the feature about the medical team. Definitely my best so far. These people will inspire you. That makes seven full-lengths in the can, by the way. See? I haven't been totally useless here.

The bad news is the doctors had to refill my medication. I'm sick again, and it's bad this time. I haven't kept much down for the past two weeks. You should see me. I'm like a scarecrow. Two new holes poked in my belt.

More bad news: the war feels like it's getting further from a resolution, rather closer to one. The head doctor of the medical team, a Cuban, told me about a man she treated recently who was tortured by the military. The way she described his wounds. . . I had to debate how much to include in the article so Canadians could handle it.

It feels like anyone here could end up tortured now. Or dead. Even me. I had a dream last night that I took my stories, rolled them up, put an elastic around them and floated out of camp. It was such a great feeling, looking down, knowing I was free of all this ugliness (not to mention laziness and backwardness).

But I woke up beside Adrian and I knew I couldn't leave. They need reporters here. He needs me.

DB

PS — We're shifting camp to stay clear of the fighting. We move tonight, so I'll only write when we end up wherever we're headed.

SUNDAY
APRIL 10

11:40 AM. *Multiplaza Mall, San Salvador*

They meet in the food court. He buys two heaping plates of Chinese food and Cokes and carries them on an orange plastic tray to an out-of-the-way table. Aida can't stop smiling. "I didn't tell anyone about our call."

Carlos seems concerned. "You lied?"

"Not exactly. I do need a shirt. Something for when my mother gets back."

"You believe that. That your mother will be back," he says, his tone not very distinct, not making the words into a question or a doubt.

"Of course," says Aida, surprised. "They've got a name to go with the police sketch now, right? Rita something."

Carlos does not react to this news. He seems to be in a daze. Dark circles rim his pretty eyes. "You look a bit tired," Aida says, smiling shyly.

"I sometimes have trouble sleeping. An old disturbance for me."

"Well, that woman, Rita, and her sister dumped their kids with relatives and said they were going away for a couple of weeks," says

Aida. "The embassy considers it a huge break. They'll probably just give up now. Or the police will do a rescue."

This time Carlos hears, but his face is grim. He looks unmoved by these scenarios. Maybe, Aida thinks, her enthusiasm does go a bit overboard. Marta has already given her ten reasons for doubting the success of a rescue. "I could take you to the graves of several hostages who would be alive today if the police had just waited," she said, shaking her head. But how long can they wait this time? The kidnappers' deadline is coming up fast. Something has to give! Carlos is in a position to at least hint at whether the police will intervene. It occurs to Aida that the reason Carlos looks so unhappy is that he might think she's using him, asking for more than he can give — a conflict of interest with his job. "Or," she ventures, changing channels, "I guess if it doesn't go that way, do you think maybe Mr. Wall might still decide by tomorrow to close his mine? Buy everyone some time."

"It's not so simple, Aida."

There's a finality in this statement that makes Aida redden. Like he's slapped her — lightly, but on purpose. "Marta said you wouldn't help me," she mumbles, hurt by it.

Carlos looks around. He seems edgy, like he thinks he'll find Marta in line at the KFC. "I thought you said no one knew you were coming."

"They don't. She said that before. Forget it."

Aida and Carlos descend into tense silence, glazed Chinese food cooling on their plates, untouched. Aida has hoped for a confidence boost. Or some help. Or some warmth. So far, she has nothing, which makes the silence feel endless.

Finally, Carlos seems to shake away the cloud that's been hovering over him. He reaches out and puts his hand over Aida's. A long scar she didn't notice last time runs across the back of it, up to his wrist. "I'm sorry," he says. "It's a stressful week. I'm glad you came."

The scar is intriguing — from the war? Aida won't ask. Too personal. But its rough edges seem to validate Carlos's gesture. He's been through so much, and yet he really seems to care.

"How have you been?" he asks.

"Those stories. In the papers? They're still hard," says Aida, disarmed, dying, she realizes, to talk. "It was weird to see the video of my mother, but these are on another level. They sound like her. She's making this guy's stories her own. Danielle never believes in herself, or in me, but she believes what this guy's telling her about his family, his past." Aida crosses and uncrosses her legs, pushes away the little tears she can't hold back. "Sorry."

"Are you angry with your mother?"

Aida checks Carlos's face to see if he's being cruel. "There've been so many articles about our families in the press."

"I haven't been following so closely."

That's strange. Didn't Carlos say it was part of his job to follow her mother's case? "Danielle didn't exactly raise me. She was there, sort of. She lived with us on and off, me and my grandparents. But it wasn't her I looked up to. I didn't have a father. Never knew him. He was Salvadoran. He died. My mother, she —" Aida stops. "I found out some things recently."

Carlos's hand comes off hers. "About?"

"She left me some letters." Aida pulls a folded envelope from her bag.

Carlos stares at it uncomprehendingly.

"It's all way in the past, but I just — can I read you something?"

Carlos looks unsure. Aida is too. She really didn't come here to tell him about Danielle's letters. They made no plan over the phone except to spend more time together. But Aida feels the same impulse that made her hug Carlos after coffee — she does want to share something intimate with him. "It's this one letter. From the end of her time here, with the guerrillas. She was involved with a man. He was an important person. She was lonely when he wasn't around. Like, she makes it sound like the war was an obstacle to her 'love'. . . but, anyway, while he was away, she went somewhere to write a story. Oh, and she was also sick, so the people she was hiking with sent her into a village with a guide so she could rest and get better."

Carlos gives a slight, confused nod that reminds Aida of her boyfriend André's resistance to finding out more about Danielle. "You're not interested. It's okay —"

Carlos places his hand back over hers. His scar is so long and faded. Definitely from the war. "I am," he says.

Aida takes a breath.

When I woke up I got disoriented. Guns were firing outside. People were yelling slogans I'd heard before in the faction. Isidrio said it sounded like an 'incursión.' That means the faction goes into a town, makes a big commotion and tries to convince young people to join. (I know because I interviewed someone just last week who was saying they're doing it more now, with Ronald Reagan in power. The Americans are probably going to beef up the Salvadoran military.) Isidrio told me it's a punishable offense to interfere with this kind of operation. We had to get out. He said he'd hike up and try to get behind the unit, tell someone they had a sick foreigner down below. Then he took off.

So I was alone. It was dark. I was petrified. Super sick. I promised myself that when I got home, I'd give up on politics. Just live my life. I don't care about other people's battles. I know you won't want to hear that, but it's true.

I crawled to the door and ran out, following the noise. I ended up on a kind of bump overlooking the village plaza. Young guerrillas were everywhere. But the real shocker was who was addressing the villagers: ADRIAN!!!

My first instinct was to run to him, but something told me not to. He went on about the people's struggle, 'la lucha,' and everyone cheered, until this kid stepped out. He was fifteen, maybe sixteen. I was too far away to hear, but he was obviously disagreeing, and he wouldn't give up. Adrian reacted really badly, tried to turn the crowd against him.

This went on until Adrian gave an order and two compas pulled the kid out of the crowd. They forced him down on his knees. There was more arguing. And then Adrian shot him.

Neela, he pulled out a gun and shot a kid. Just like that. Dead.

Carlos has his lips pressed together tightly when Aida looks up. "What?" she asks. "It sounds made up, right?"

"No. It doesn't sound made up." Carlos begins attacking his food, putting an entire chicken ball in his mouth. "Continue," he manages to say, chewing rapidly.

"That's all, actually," says Aida, folding the letter back up. "I don't even know why I read it."

"It's very upsetting."

"You were a guerrilla fighter too, right?" Aida asks, tentatively, the scribble of his scar still facing her as Carlos picks up a forkful of fried rice. "Is that why you can't sleep?"

Carlos flinches, a few grains falling to his plate. "No." He doesn't elaborate. He uses his napkin to wipe his mouth. "It was a hard life. I am glad it's over. We should all be glad."

"I think it sounds terrible. People did terrible things."

Carlos lifts his eyebrows, creating confused ridges along his forehead. "We were fighting because we thought that conditions were extremely unjust." He points down at her bag, where Aida has put her letter. "That incident was an isolated case." He goes back to eating for a long moment, then says without looking up from his plate, "Your mother, she wrote more about what she saw in that village?"

Aida shakes her head. "This was her last letter home. She left your country not long afterwards, chickened out of publishing the news articles she'd written — which pretty much wrecked her idea of becoming a journalist. . . that and the pregnancy."

"The man, in the village. He got away with murder, you think."

"I guess."

"Was he a person who knew your father?"

Aida looks out the windows at a full parking lot below, its gleaming rows of cars absorbing the intense afternoon sun.

"Aida, in the war, people did things that they thought were necessary."

"Don't say it wasn't his fault. He had options. He didn't have to do what he did."

"Our war was not optional. And, in a way, you came out of those difficult circumstances."

"Me? No. Biologically, maybe. But I have nothing to do with that. My grandparents raised me. My grandfather worked until the morning he died. Studying. Writing. My mother, meanwhile, she barely works to this day. She blames your war and me for everything that happened to her! It's seriously sad. People should move on. You did! The people at this mall did!"

"They have, in some ways. In other ways, they live with the past."

"Well, I'm trying to move on, okay? Obviously, it sounds looks like this killer was my father. But that doesn't mean anything about me. Only about Danielle. She couldn't resist a tough case. It's like catnip for her. Marta and the Committee are just another example of that. They don't let anything go. They've made a big political issue out of the mine and the kidnappers are using that rift. Meanwhile, they haven't seen the possibilities. The Committee should have worked with Mr. Wall. The way you do."

"Negotiations are always possible," says Carlos, and something seems to cross his mind. "But, even so, you shouldn't be so hard on Marta."

Aida nods uncertainly. Why should Carlos care what she thinks of Marta? Those two seem to repel one another.

"Marta lost a great deal in the war," Carlos goes on. "Her parents were early activists. They were harassed, beaten. And then her husband was disappeared. Her life was threatened. She had to leave her country."

Aida remembers the photos on Marta's wall, how there's no husband anywhere. "Disappeared? For good?"

Carlos touches her hand again. She pulls it back, ashamed.

"If you talk to her about it, you'll see that she's quite understanding. She's always been that way. With everyone except me."

Aida smiles, though she is perplexed. Do Marta and Carlos share so much history? If so, why does Carlos still trust Marta when Marta doesn't trust him back?

"You should eat," Carlos says, pointing at Aida's nearly untouched plate.

"I'm not hungry."

Carlos smiles more widely. "Eat anyway."

Aida finishes about half her food. Then Carlos suggests they take a walk. They stroll past electronics and shoe stores, a children's clothing store and then a jewelry shop, where reams of cheap gold necklaces and earrings cascade down the forms of necks and ears. Aida still refuses to see the blood that Neela and Marta want people to imagine is inseparable from the production of this precious metal. André gave Aida an 18k gold bracelet last year. Thin, with a simple turn of the metal to make it pop. She wouldn't give it up for anything.

When they get to one end of the mall, they stare out over the thoroughfare that passes the main entrance below. Traffic is thick and smog gives the scene an otherworldly sheen. Then they turn and walk all the way back. The entire time they say nothing, but it's a good silence, like when they're not talking she and Carlos understand one another better. Aida lets thoughts of blood and killers and mines slip away.

As they pass a women's clothing store, Carlos stops. "You said you have some things to buy. And I must get back to work. I will leave you."

Aida is crestfallen. She's imagined this meeting lasting longer, turning into the afternoon together.

"I will come see you at the demonstration tomorrow," says Carlos. "If you're attending."

"Okay, yes. I will. It's just I thought we would. . . I shouldn't have read that letter. It was stupid."

Carlos smiles. "It was courageous."

Aida feels a wave of heat reach her ears: he thinks she's got courage. "I will see you at the demonstration tomorrow. Yes?"

"Yes." She makes a mental note to tell Marta she's changed her mind.

"Good. *Hasta mañana, tonces.*" Carlos looks at her long enough that Aida starts to wonder whether he intends to kiss her, or simply communicate something profound that she's missed. But a moment later he steps onto the downward escalator, blending with the rest of the shoppers as he glides to the lower level.

The men keep their eyes down, scanning the earth and stones and grasses. Every so many steps one of them pauses to survey three hundred and sixty degrees at eye level, tilting his head to scrutinize tree branches, trunks and the spaces between them. They've been walking since before dawn and both ache with fatigue. One man takes out a bandana, ties it around his head, scratches his substantial beard, itchy from layers of perspiration. Their movements are more or less in sync. For this reason, they spot them almost simultaneously — small cuts aligned and angled on a single tree. The man with wide, square shoulders puts two fingertips into one of the cuts, pulls them out, rubs them against a practised thumb. He nods to his companion.

Keeping silent, each crouches and pulls up his weapon. The man with the beard gives the signal to split up and walk deeper into the bushes, one this way, one that way, silent footfalls, leaves grazing their large forearms. Ten minutes later, the bearded man calls out, "*Nada.*" His companion yells back the same.

They meet by the tree and look again at the machete marks. They know these could be traces of passing herdsmen or anyone else. A few nicks don't make a lead. Then, just as they're about to walk on, feeling deflated after three long days of trudging through heat and insects with nothing significant to report to the *Jefe,* one of the men looks into a thickness of bushes and finds something much, much more promising: two strips of coloured cloth tied together to a branch with a crude knot, near which the men also locate human feces — fresh, watery, carefully buried, though not quite carefully enough. The man with the beard, who feels himself to be in charge, pulls out his phone triumphantly.

Sobero answers on the first ring and takes in the update with a faint click of his tongue. There are loud traffic sounds behind him.

"Unless you are eager to stand there sniffing their shit all night, hang up and keep moving," he says.

The men obey, continuing on. The mountains cast longer shadows over the land. In the early evening, the two trackers take rest. Just enough. Just what they will need to keep moving through the night, under Sobero's orders, closer and closer to their targets.

Mitch imagines facing all the people whose cars are parked outside. This is not the kind of notoriety he has spent his life building toward. He takes a deep breath and repeats to himself what Carlos told him: now, more than ever, he has to seem relaxed. A week ago, that would've been as effortless as breathing. But as the maitre d' leads him through the arched brick entrance and into the restaurant, Mitch has to fake it.

Two tables on, a refined-looking gentleman stands, startling him. He takes Mitch's hand and shakes it thoroughly. "We are so, so very sorry for what you're going through," he says, in good English. "*Gracias, Señor*," says Mitch, taken aback. The maitre d' smiles and urges Mitch on to his table, where he sits and checks his messages. Every so often, he glances around and sees someone smiling and nodding at him.

Carlos enters not long afterwards, a newspaper under his arm. He shakes hands with several people along the way, elicits whispers from others. When he's settled, Mitch recounts his own entrance, but Carlos shows no surprise. "People here, this kind of people, they take your presence as a sign of strength," he says. "They are like you — and they will like you."

Mitch smiles, but receives this explanation with a twinge of annoyance. He has never once thought of any Salvadoran as being "like him." No matter how well-dressed and mannered the people are here, he'll be hard pressed to start now. None of them know what it feels like to have a deadline looming like the one haunting his mine. Neither does Carlos, for that matter, who is looking less than inspirational on the eve of it. Unshaven. White crust in one corner of his mouth. When he unbuttons his suit jacket, there's a large, reddish stain on his shirt. "You feeling alright?" Mitch asks, trying to sound casual before turning to accept a taste from the bottle of red he's ordered. He nods to the waiter that it's fine, though he's had better.

"I am working very long hours right now," says Carlos without looking up from his menu.

So this dinner is a waste of his time? It was Carlos's idea to meet up! Mitch stares at his companion, trying to reinterpret the comment, but he can't read his blank expression. Carlos is a foreigner, any way you slice it. Fundamentally different from him. The whole country is. Mitch taps his BlackBerry, which is resting on the table. The image he uses as his wallpaper appears: his twin daughters huddled into the jogging stroller. He works to mentally transport himself to their safe world of naps and tickling, to his own house in Vancouver, good BC wine, the everyday Canadian things he loves. But the voices from the table nearby, speaking a mile a minute in Spanish, and the Latin music being pumped into the room keep nudging him back. The screen on his device goes black, into power-save mode. How did he get here? Mitch never intended to work abroad as much as he has. But the government makes it practically impossible to turn a profit at home. Red tape and treaty negotiations over supposedly traditional lands are a uniquely Canadian kind of bullshit. Catharine Keil is the long arm of that nonsense. "They're betting against me," he hears himself say.

Carlos looks up. He's placed his newspaper atop his menu and has become absorbed in it. "Who?"

"Keil and your Attorney General. Schiffer. They're betting I'll give in."

Carlos sighs deeply, his whole upper body lifting and falling. The waiter takes their order and leaves. "Whatever happens now, Mitch," he says, "at this time, I see damage for you. You've lost some investors, I expect."

"A handful," says Mitch, his back up. That's no one's problem but his own. "But if the police went in right now, we'd pull up our nose."

"*If* they find them in time. *If* they free the hostages. Those are not certainties. Maybe there are problems. Casualties. Then people ask why you didn't save these lives by just opening your gate. All you had to do: unlock a single gate to the mine."

"We've been over this."

"That was before. Today, you are in a different position. How will your name remain separate from the murder of these tourists after tomorrow?"

Mitch is about to say that he doesn't have a fucking clue how, but Carlos reaches across the table and touches his arm to hush him while casting around the room, as if checking that it's safe to go on.

"There might be another way."

All of Mitch's senses open towards Carlos. These are the words he's been waiting for all week. "What way?"

"I have received some information." Carlos curls his index downward to tap the photo that appears on the newspaper. It's a grainy black-and-white image of a haggard-looking woman with light-coloured, ratty hair. The caption reads: "Rita Guadalupe Canales de Santos, identified by police as a person of interest in the abduction of five Canadian tourists."

"You know where she is," says Mitch, guessing. He pictures the police bursting through a door and finding this woman and some man named Enrique sleeping it off while the hostages sit bound at the hands, like in the movies. He sees the police cutting their bindings, sees himself at the mine, receiving the call that everyone is home safe, sees his top investors at the next meeting in Vancouver reviewing the strong numbers from Pico, and him and Carlos, toasting success together at this very restaurant.

Carlos shakes his head impatiently. "No. I don't know anything about her."

Punctured, Mitch's hopeful vision dissipates.

"I'm talking about the deadline the newspapers have made so much of. The one you cannot evade. The information I have could make it irrelevant. But it absolutely requires you to close the mine."

Mitch rubs his forehead, feeling that a conflict could be coming between he and his friend. "You've wanted that all along, haven't you? Are you afraid to be associated with someone who's crashing and burning? Is that it? You turning yellow in your old age?"

"Mitch, listen to me."

"Thinking of your goddamn election, then? Can't afford to be pulled down by a drowning man!"

"Listen, Mitch —"

"You want to be the hero again. Like the old days. Blowing up helicopters, right? Well, guess what? Your war's long —"

Carlos reaches over, grabs Mitch's BlackBerry and pulls it out of his reach. "Calm yourself," he says.

"What are you doing? Give me that!"

The waiter approaches. Carlos nonchalantly hides Mitch's phone under the table as the server places a nicely arranged plate of salad before each of them: octopus for Mitch, tomato for Carlos.

As soon as the man withdraws, Mitch leans in. "Give me back my phone." He feels surprisingly violated by Carlos's move.

But Carlos just shakes his head. "You don't understand. I need your attention. You are no longer in control. Not on the outside looking in. I have heard of evidence linking a certain member of the Committee for the Environment to this abduction. The police can get this evidence. Tonight. But things will still take time to sort out. The police will need to get there. This person will need to say where the hostages are. In the meantime, you must meet the kidnappers' deadline and take away their incentive to do harm to any of these Canadians or it will be perceived as your fault when they're dead. Close your mine. Right now. Let the exhumation team onto the property. Nothing will come of it. Twenty-four hours from now, it's over."

Mitch lets his fork and knife down slowly onto the plate. There's a lull in the restaurant and a line from a song wafts from the sound system: "*Cielos adentro, cielos adentro.*" For a moment he hears the lyric as *cielo abierto* — the Spanish for open pit mine — and he wants desperately for this to be the sign that, no, he should never let the shutdown happen or anyone else tell him what to do with his mine, that he should punch this man in the chin for yanking away his phone. But Mitch isn't superstitious, or much prone to physical violence. "*Adentro*" means within. The sky within? That makes no sense. There are no signs.

Carlos doesn't let up. "Everyone will see the news of your decision in the press. To your backers, it makes you gallant, the good guy. The Committee will be under suspicion. And politically, Mitch, this will count. Because there will always be more investors, but those tests they've done of the river water are not going away." He pauses. "I have the number for the Attorney General's private line. If you speak to him, man to man, he will listen."

Mitch watches as Carlos returns the BlackBerry to the tabletop. He uses the keypad to punch in the digits and pushes it across the table until it touches Mitch's fingertips.

The hostages eat off the floor. Two spoonfuls of watery, oversalted beans each, served with lumpy, rubbery tortillas and odourless coffee, extra sweet.

They're in another house, a dimly lit hut erected on a slanting piece of scrubby land at high altitude. The owners are a young couple with five children and a grandmother. The ceiling is low, patched here and there with black plastic, but imperfectly, so that earlier in the day when the light was strongest, it splashed bright gold pools on the floor, making Danielle wonder how much water falls directly into the house during the rainy season.

The cooking and heating facilities are equally limited. Just one large plaster wood-burning oven with a single bare branch stuck into it to burn. Danielle recognizes this kind of stove as typical of rural Central American households of the past, but she's mostly seen them built into a separate alcove. Here the stove is in a corner of the main living area and its smoke lingers, chokingly low and dense. The children all have red eyes and snotty noses, and Danielle is glad to be sitting on her tarp at floor level, rather than in one of two hammocks, both soiled and torn, that are slung higher up across the length of the hut. Cristóbal has been in one of them for some hours, lying with his gun at his side, unbothered by the pungent smoke hanging around his nostrils.

The grandmother appeared sometime in the afternoon with a few eggs tied into a kerchief, which she went to store protectively in a frayed basket. She eased herself onto a plywood shelf supported by two wooden stumps and fell asleep, then woke up and left again. The children, three boys and two girls, all under age ten, sit practically on top of one another right on the ground and alternate between whispering and staring nervously at the strangers.

Danielle, who woke up earlier than the others, spent some of the sweltering afternoon hours exchanging looks and a few smiles with them. When the tallest approached to show her a shapely stone he'd been scraping the earthen floor with, and which he obviously treasured, his mother sucked her teeth, shooing him back towards his siblings. This woman has attempted no conversation with the hostages, or even with the kidnappers as they've come and gone on their watch duty, and from this Danielle guesses that the arrangement to have foreign hostages staying in her house was made by the woman's husband, who left at sunrise, also without a word, swinging his machete, followed by his bag-of-bones dog.

Danielle hasn't witnessed such grim poverty since her last time in El Salvador and it discourages her. She feels guilty for taking part of these people's meager supper. She knows, though, that if she refuses it, there won't be anything else, and she can't afford hunger. She makes herself swallow bite after unpleasant bite.

After the last of her food is down, there's nothing left to do except wait for Pepe to tell them it's time to walk. She returns to the line of thinking that has been dominating her time for more than a day. Danielle dreads these thoughts because they relate to Rita, whom she knows is due to switch shifts with Cristóbal shortly. Every time Danielle looks around at the other hostages, who are all doing as she just has, eating their meals because they have no choice, she knows Rita has become like a cancer that will spread to them all if she doesn't do something. But Danielle has no idea what. No one around her offers clues. Not the mother, with her eyes turned away, her faded red skirt brightened somewhat in the light from one of two lanterns that keep the household from total darkness; certainly not Pierre, stony and sullen as he rips a chunk from his tortilla with his straight teeth; not the children, who seem so uncomprehending about the drama unfolding around them that it makes Danielle's heart break.

Eventually, the mother comes by and takes away the hostages' plates, still without looking anyone in the eye. Pepe will be here anytime. Danielle needs to think fast. To act. But she has no plan, and time grinds to a halt against this lack. Silently, dejectedly, she swats flies. By now, they are used to bites of all kinds, from *moscas, arañas, pulgas*. These creatures are nearly as relentless as thoughts of Rita, which buzz ceaselessly in her mind. Danielle tries to emulate the mother's studied detachment, to ignore the pests, real and internal, and wait for a strategy to pop, fully formed, into her head. It is only very slowly, then, almost imperceptibly, that something finally surfaces into her awareness.

Everyone was worried last night about Tina's ability to keep up on the walk, so the kidnappers have finally begun to administer some antibiotics. The drugs haven't worked yet. If anything, Tina's moans are getting louder. She's lying on Martin's lap, stuck there by a heavy gravity. The pain must be pretty bad, because presently Tina lets out a loud groan.

"What's the matter?" says Cristóbal, climbing from his hammock.

Danielle feels herself becoming alert. She is approaching a juncture, an opportunity. "She's got cramps. She needs to be taken out," she says. Cristóbal hesitates, but Tina's need is obvious. He looks over at Delmi and each takes one of the young woman's twig-like arms and puts them around their neck. As they lift her to a standing position, Tina's stomach rumbles audibly and she pukes, spraying their pant legs, Antoine's arm and beyond with half-digested beans and corn. Her brow instantly un-creases with relief, and Danielle nearly smiles: Tina is pleased to have thrown up on her captors. In the corner the children gape and one points at the vomit, fascinated.

Martin, on the floor, seems stricken. He and Tina look hard at one another. They have formed some new bond Danielle can't interpret. Meanwhile, Delmi and Cristóbal do exactly as Danielle has hoped: they haul Tina outside and towards the area where they've all been ordered to shit for the day. Cristóbal yells back for the group to "Stay where you are and keep your mouths shut," but it's half-hearted. After so many days of obedience, and with the family there to warn the kidnappers of anything unusual, he can't really believe they'll do anything stupid.

As soon as he's out of sight, Danielle proves him wrong. She startles Pierre by crawling quickly towards him and Antoine. "You can't do it — whatever it is Rita's suggesting. She just wants to get to the States. She isn't trying to help. Give it up." Danielle takes a breath and glances over at the mother, who's by the stove. Her dirty apron sags at the chest. Her whole demeanor says she doesn't want to get involved. "Rita told me so herself, that she wants to leave," says Danielle, pressing on. "And Pepe doesn't trust her. I saw them get angry with one another — Tina was there. You can check with her. I know he'll be watching for anything strange. He's a violent man. He'll hurt us."

Pierre, who has developed a heat blister on his upper lip, stares at Danielle a moment while Antoine and Martin look on. Martin doesn't understand the context, Danielle knows. He was sleeping when Rita approached the francophones. Pierre leans forward very quickly towards Danielle and says in an angry, choppy whisper, "You have all the information, enh? From your special meetings. But we don't. We hate relying on you. You have no *authorité*." Even as he utters the last word, Pierre is straightening back up because someone is coming.

Delmi. She walks back through the hut's door in her heavy way. Danielle freezes, but Delmi, who's still rubbing vomit from the front of her pants, doesn't seem to notice that she has changed spots. Danielle looks to Antoine and then to Martin for support. Surely they'll listen. They'll believe her. She whispers to Antoine,

"Don't do anything."

Fear crosses his face, but he masks it almost immediately, tightening his own chapped lips and lifting his chin in what looks like patriotic resolve, a commitment to his old friend Pierre. Bits of grass are stuck in his hair. "We have to try," he mouths.

"I'm not biased towards Pepe! I've only been taking down his stories. I —"

"*Da — nie — la*," says Delmi, in an annoying sing-song that makes light of her total control over them. "*Silencio.*"

Danielle ignores her. "I'm warning you about her because I care what happens to each and every one of you."

Her statement is met with dispassionate looks, Pierre's tinged with satisfaction, Antoine's with guilt. Martin is still perplexed and holds out the palms of his hands like he wants to know what they're going on about. It's too late to inform him, though, because through the door now comes Rita, awkwardly assisting Tina back inside and ordering Danielle and Martin to help the girl to a lying-down position.

"She's a leaky tank, that one," says Rita. "I wonder what will happen if she can't walk. Hopefully, this won't last much longer," she says, her eyes going wide, waiting for Danielle to translate her innuendo. Danielle does, but stares at Rita angrily. She's become very good at reading Rita's face, despite its mask. It's all she feels she's been looking at for a week. Rita's resentments. Rita's pettinesses. Rita's glimmers of humanity in the presence of Cristóbal and how quickly they vanish. What she sees now is Rita communicating with Pierre and Antoine. She's waiting for something from the men: an answer. And waiting to make Danielle suffer.

Rita laughs. "What's the matter, *Daniela?* Feeling sick too?" She turns to the woman of the house. "*Mujer!* More tortillas to take with us. We leave soon. And clean up this mess."

Rita goes to put her foot up on the lone folding plastic chair whose legs are caked in reddish dust. There she oversees the woman, who takes an old brush and pan and sweeps the vomit from the floor. Despite her ridiculous hair, Rita looks almost stately among the shadows. Her tidy waist, the white cable of Martin's MP3 player hanging like a sash across her torso, her small breasts very high under her shirt, and those shoulders square as blocks. Danielle wonders what's gone into the making of a woman like Rita, what has twisted her life into this ugly knot. Whatever it is, Rita wants it undone. She wants an entirely new stretch of life to knot up, and this is her time to grab it. Danielle can empathize, can practically bring herself to find Rita a sympathetic character in the story of her own abduction if she thinks about it objectively. But she cannot sustain that thinking at all.

MONDAY
APRIL 11

10:30 AM. *Media room, San Salvador Conference Centre*

Catharine Keil enters with Raul Schiffer through a side door and walks to the podium. She comes to stand ever so slightly ahead of Schiffer and unfolds her single page of notes. "Thank you for coming on short notice. We are pleased to announce that we received word last evening from representatives of NorthOre Incorporated's Salvadoran subsidiary, *OrNorte,* that the company will allow a team of forensic specialists onto their property at *Mil Sueños* beginning today, and that this will entail a stop-work order at the mine, effective this morning and lasting until Thursday night."

A murmur passes through the room. Reporters pull out their cell phones to inform senior editors.

"This step signals good faith on the part of the mine and demonstrates the tremendous efforts made by both the Salvadoran and Canadian governments, and by the *Policía Civil,* who have worked with us all week towards a peaceful resolution." Cameras flash, lighting her face. "In a moment, I will hand over to the Attorney General, who will describe another major breakthrough in this case. In the meantime, to the people responsible for this crime I must emphasize that we need to see immediate action." As she did last time, Keil presents the cameras with a stern countenance. "Your first step will be to hold to your promise of releasing one of the hostages within twenty-four hours, now that your initial requirement has been fulfilled. But we ask you to consider your options at this stage and release all five members of the delegation. You have exhausted the goodwill shown by all parties. The police, as you will hear shortly, have uncovered important evidence that will soon lead to an end to this situation. If you surrender now, your reasonable actions will lead to further reasonable actions on the part of security forces. And now I pass the floor to Mr. Schiffer."

Raul Schiffer smiles and edges forward, approaching the mic. "I want to speak for the Commissioner of Police and those overseeing this investigation, particularly *Capitán* Hernández and his Special Anti-Kidnapping Unit," he says, "to inform the public that we have two critical developments in this case. First, the *Policía Civil* have made an arrest in connection with this abduction. This person is associated with the Committee for the Environment, a group based in Los Pampanos." Another brief sound of surprise emerges from the scrum of reporters. "We cannot release the name of the suspect this morning, as it might undermine our efforts to bring the hostages home safely.

"What we can tell you is that, in response to our increased offer of a reward for information that would lead to an arrest, we received last night, at approximately 22:00, an anonymous tip indicating that there was evidence linking the suspect to the abduction. We assigned our best officers to investigate, and, at 2:30 this morning, they confirmed that they had the evidence in hand. This evidence was sent to headquarters for preliminary analysis, and subsequently an arrest warrant was issued. I have no other comments to make now except that this tip represents a willingness on the part of regular Salvadorans to see the criminals brought to justice.

"The second development involves new information stemming from the publication of a police sketch earlier this week, later identified as the likeness of Rita Guadalupe Canales de Santos, age 34. On Thursday, we announced that she and her sister, Delmi Luisa Canales Muñoz, age 28, both of San Miguel, were persons of interest in this case. Now, we have added two more individuals to this list, and if I can call your attention to the screen, we've now been provided by informants with photos of all four persons. On the left is Cristóbal Santos Molina, age 40, husband of Rita de Santos, who is to his right. Below *Señor* de Santos is her sister, *Señora* Muñoz, and beside her is the second man, José Molina Domingo, age 41. Both the men are also of San Miguel. We are making the photos public in the hopes that these individuals will come forward with any information they might have in connection with this case. Now I have a few minutes to take your questions. One at a time, please."

12:00 PM. *San Salvador*

Aida is shaken. Getting into the front passenger seat, she can still feel the warmth where Marta was sitting. She crosses a knee over her hands to keep from biting her nails — a disgusting habit from her teens that she rarely indulges. Pedro pulls back onto the road, lunchtime commuters all around them going about their normal, traffic-crazy day. Behind Aida, Benoît, Ralph and Sylvie all seem to be talking at once. Finally Pedro yells *"Por favor!"* and holds his cell away from his ear to make them understand that he needs quiet. After that, they whisper. Aida turns in her seat.

"How could this happen?" says Sylvie, painted fingernails set dramatically against both cheeks. "Marta has nothing to do with what has happened to my son."

"How do we know?" Aida says. She glances at Pedro to see if he's understood, but he's busy with his calls. She wants to be proven wrong, but on her own, Aida can't say anymore that Marta is not responsible in some way for the abduction. She has staked everything on getting rid of the mine.

"We know because she's been good to us this whole time. You especially," says Ralph, then looks away, out his window. "I'm not gonna believe a pair of handcuffs over that."

The mood darkens. Everyone is quiet, recalling how the police car appeared just minutes ago out of nowhere, forcing Pedro to pull over, how the officers took Marta away. The entire sequence, from the siren and flashing lights behind them to the nauseating click of the cuffs binding her wrists was too brief, too real. Aida has never been anywhere near an arrest, and she was amazed by Marta's calm reaction, how she went without a word, stepping from the car as if to put money in a meter. Had she expected it?

Benoît pipes up. "Whatever they need to do to investigate this case, I give them my support. *Honnêtement là,* if Marta has a good lawyer who can get her out, then it's still a good day for us. The mine is closing. One of our family members is going to be home tomorrow. I pray, with respect, that it is Antoine."

The rest nod, Ralph somewhat reluctantly. Aida knows it bugs him the way Benoît and Sylvie act like Antoine deserves special status simply because they love him so much. "What about the Thursday deadline the mine has tacked on?" Ralph says, clearing his throat like he seems to do when he's agitated. "How's that team from Guatemala going to find anything by then?"

"Those are details," says Benoît, dismissing the concern. Aida agrees. The kidnapper wanted a shutdown at the mine and he has it. Period.

They drive on, silent again. Aida thinks they're nearing the cathedral, but Pedro turns in a direction that seems wrong. "Where are we going?" she asks, disconcerted.

Pedro keeps his eyes on the road. "Marta will not want you at the demonstration. I'm taking you back. Please. Tell them they should stay together in their rooms. A friend of ours will watch over them."

Aida starts to argue, but something about Pedro's demeanour tells her it will be useless. He's stepping into Marta's shoes, playing boss. Carlos will wait at the cathedral for nothing. Aida knows she's being selfish, that she should be focused on Marta's well-being, but it's so unfair that she can't meet him there now.

An hour later Aida tries Carlos's cell phone for the twentieth time. No luck. He never did give her his home number, so, getting up her courage, she dials the office phone printed on his business card, asking, in her most formal Spanish, to speak to him, only to be told he's been out for some time. Aida wants to scream. Probably he's still at the demonstration. But if so, why hasn't he answered his cell? A man in his position will have heard of Marta's arrest by now.

Aida tries the first number once more, then finally gives up, slamming down Marta's receiver. Paco, the minder Pedro has called to stay with her, turns from where he stands, near Marta's windows. "What are you looking out for, anyway?" Aida asks him angrily.

Paco smiles. "Just being safe." He pulls back Marta's drooping brown curtains a bit further.

Until today, Aida has not seriously believed her own safety could be in danger. From whom? The kidnappers? It doesn't make sense for them to go after the families too. And if it's true that Marta or anyone with her Committee had something to do with the abduction, however tangentially, the kidnappers will be staying as far away from her place as possible. Then again, if Marta had something to do with this, what is Aida still doing here? Paco works for Marta. He's the one who takes the car from the cathedral every day. Aida looks him over, trying to see evidence that he's about to turn on her. But it's too stupid. She remembers how ashamed she was of herself yesterday, finding out about Marta's late husband. If Carlos and Ralph are right and she should put her trust in Marta, someone else is responsible for the abduction. Maybe someone totally unknown to the police. If so, can they be found before it's too late?

Aida can't seem to piece together a judgment — what she should think, where she should be. She finds herself wandering into her room and back several times before collapsing onto her bed and staring at a dog-eared poster of a young Ricky Martin. Leftover from one of Marta's children, she assumes. What was it like for those kids to have their father "disappear" — vanish, like Danielle has? He never returned. This must be at the heart of Marta's obsession with *Mil Sueños*. She must be looking for payback.

The phone rings. Aida rushes back out to the living room, but it's only Neela.

"Aida? Oh, god. I've been so worried. I couldn't get through."

"I was making some calls."

"I'm glad you're safe. If we ever needed proof of how twisted the Salvadoran police are, we've got it now. They've just arrested the one sane voice in this whole case."

"Neela, do you think we could talk later? I'm actually trying to get through to André." This isn't a total lie. Aida has been planning to call him as soon as she speaks to Carlos, though she's also come to dread her phone calls to Danielle's house. André has gone from relatively supportive to angry with her absence to fearful that something bad is going to happen to her. She misses her self-assured boyfriend like she misses her clear-headed self. "He'll be waiting."

"Oh. Sure. I just can't imagine what it was like to see what you saw today. You're probably in shock. Try not to worry about Marta. PJA's got a great legal team and I'm getting someone to pitch in on the case. There's still the chance Danielle or one of the others could be released, too. We have to hold onto that hope."

"It's not a hope. The mine's closing, just like the kidnapper asked."

"Yes. It's just that Mitch Wall has imposed a deadline for the exhumation. A very short one."

Aida puts a fingernail in her mouth but forces herself to remove it, unbitten. "We know. It's still better than nothing."

"Well, apparently, he only did it after the exhumation team arrived in San Salvador from Guatemala early this morning. I know quite a bit about Reverte's team, and let me tell you, they never would've agreed to come if they'd known what kind of tricks Wall was going to play. The ambassador must be pissed. She's the one who's been working on getting Reverte here from Guatemala."

"Like I said, better than nothing."

"Absolutely," says Neela, carefully. "So, just — just hang in. I want you all back here, safe and sound."

"Thanks, Neela," says Aida, ending the call. She means it. But she's filled with sudden foreboding. She realizes she doesn't want to leave for Toronto so soon if it means never speaking to Carlos Reyes again — a thought that makes her dizzy, because she so fervently *does* want the abduction to end.

A moment later, the phone rings again. Aida assumes Neela's forgotten something. "Yes?" Aida says in English, picking up.

"*Hola?*" says a man's voice. It's Carlos.

"Oh, *hola,*" Aida says, switching to Spanish effortlessly now, she's noticed, just a week into her stay. "I tried to call you."

"I'm sorry. I was busy. I didn't even get to the demonstration."

"You didn't?" Carlos specifically said he would be there.

"It's been a difficult day."

"Me too."

"Yes. About Marta, I am very sorry —"

"Why should you be sorry?" Aida brings the phone, on its cord, as far away from Paco as she can and sits on the floor near the entrance to the kitchen. "It's not your fault."

Carlos says nothing.

"Maybe it's not Marta. But maybe other members of her committee are involved somehow. It could've been them who hired those four 'persons of interest.' Anyway, it could all come together now. Especially since NorthOre changed its mind."

"With a Thursday deadline." Carlos sounds hoarse, like he's underslept again.

Aida feels a strong urge to cheer him. "I was thinking that maybe you were the one who. . . that maybe the things we discussed yesterday got you to talk to Mitch Wall."

Carlos makes a strange sound, like a simultaneous sigh and cough. "I'm afraid you think I'm someone I'm not."

Aida smiles. "I don't even know you yet."

"I feel that I do know you," says Carlos, so quietly Aida can barely make it out.

She flushes. "So do I," she hears herself say, despite the contradiction.

"Aida. Did you have time, before the — the arrest, to ask Marta about her husband?"

Aida doesn't answer. She'd intended to, but everything got so crazy. Now, with the arrest, she doesn't know when she'll see Marta again, or how long she can stand to stay at the house. "I ran out of time," she admits. "But Marta really has done everything to turn the mine into a moral campaign. It's like she's looking for revenge or — "

"You put your trust in things you shouldn't, and you are suspicious of the things you should trust!" says Carlos with force, cutting her off.

Aida reddens further. "I'm doing my best."

"This is not a school competition. No one will pat you on the head for doing your best. I have to leave," he says and hangs up.

Aida listens to the foreign-sounding dial tone, staring over at Paco's wide back as he keeps an eye out for dangers she doesn't want to guess at.

Sitting on his haunches, Cristóbal is unsure how to feel about taking the telephone call. He has been grateful to know just enough about Pepe's plans. He has felt capable of doing a good job. So, while he's happy to have his cousin's trust, he's afraid of the phone that rests about a foot in front of him on a flat, lichen-covered rock. This object includes him in knowledge Cristóbal would prefer to skip.

When it starts vibrating, Pepe picks up, as he said he would. Immediately, his face transforms. He looks intensely curious. Whatever this person is calling to tell him, Pepe needs to know it. Little by little, the curiosity is replaced by assent, Pepe nodding meaningfully. Must be good news. But now, abruptly, alarm. Something dark overtakes Pepe's face. His eyes rush back and forth as he takes in the voice of his contact. Those eyes are frightened. But Cristóbal can't dwell on why. It's his turn. He doesn't question the reason he will be Pepe's mouthpiece, or who's going to hear him. Pepe figures it's necessary and that's good enough. Cristóbal takes the phone, surprised by its unfamiliar weight. The line is open.

"Tell him to check his mailbox," says Pepe, his voice tight. "I've asked an associate to drop off a map and instructions for the exhumation team. These should be faxed to the Canadian embassy. The press too. There should also be a note signed by 'Enrique' that says —" Cristóbal hastens to keep up, but feels pressured by Pepe's increasing agitation "— that because of the mine's actions this morning, I cannot release a hostage."

Cristóbal stops cold. Releasing a hostage was always the plan.

Pepe scowls. "I have been left with no choice. Even if the mine is closed, if they do not lift this deadline of Thursday for the exhumation, on that same day I will kill a hostage instead. Tell them that!" Pepe nearly yells. "And tell them I've already decided which it will be."

Cristóbal searches Pepe's eyes to determine whether he really wants him to repeat these threats, but Pepe is already getting up, like his decision is final. Cristóbal says the words and hangs up the way Pepe showed him earlier, resting the phone back on the flat rock. The cousins are quiet. Above them, birds caw, and Cristóbal, who loves animals, listens in, picking out a *torogoz*. "*Primo*. Will they do it?" He poses the question as quietly as he can so as not to upset his cousin, doing nothing to pop the lid on his temper.

"They have to." Pepe's breathing has sped up. His exposed face is pinched with strain.

"Was there anything else about the police? Do they have our names?" Cristóbal has a bad feeling suddenly.

"They need to know how serious we are."

This doesn't sound like an answer. Cristóbal watches his cousin pace around, picking up speed, as if the thoughts in his mind are powering his legs.

Then he stops. "You need to talk to Rita," he says. "I know she's trying something."

"She isn't." Cristóbal is as forceful as he can be with just these two words, stepping over Pepe's last statement.

The abruptness startles his cousin. "Delmi told me," says Pepe, each word very precise.

"Delmi lies."

"I waited because I wanted to be reasonable, but if you can't handle her, I will."

Cristóbal knows he's putting a lot on the line, but he refuses to distrust his wife.

"I'm asking you to talk to her," Pepe says, nearly pleading. "To tell her to —"

"I won't," says Cristóbal. "And you stay away from her." Though his words are a direct threat, he tries to make them sound conciliatory.

Pepe rolls his mask back over his face then comes close and reaches out his hand. At first, Cristóbal thinks his cousin wants to help him up or to shake on it, but Pepe just wants his phone back. When Cristóbal passes it, Pepe pulls the object roughly away, turns and walks off, back towards where the others are.

Cristóbal resists following right away and stays defiantly seated, tearing at some nearby leaves and letting the pieces sprinkle over the lichen, listening for that calling *torogoz,* before getting up and making his way to the campsite, which is just a space like a corridor between two high rock faces over which Cristóbal has placed a layer of cut boughs. There, he sits with Rita and rests his back against the cool, damp rock.

The year after he launched his mine Mitch hired an efficiency consultant to assess his entire operation. Unlike a lot of people in his industry, he wasn't afraid of an outsider's perspective. The consultant provided excellent feedback, including the strong suggestion that Mitch delegate more, which he did, hiring more staff, cutting back on his time in Peru, where he co-owned another site. He focused all his energy on the project he cared about most: *Mil Sueños*. He stopped fooling around, remarried, had his twins. He aimed for balance, let his wife talk him into the Ashtanga classes.

All that was before. So what's different about El Pico, he wonders, as he hurries, quite late, through the main entrance. Why has it made him feel like a kid from the outskirts of Squamish again? He was on edge even before this kidnapping screwed everything up. Mitch knows it has something to do with the relentless criticism he's faced over *Mil Sueños*. All the talk has put him on the defensive. Not that he believes any of it. Mitch knows his opponents would hum a different tune if they had to run his business for a year — a month, even. If they were suddenly responsible for this much money, this many investors, they'd get how complicated it is.

Still, they've taken something from him. A trust or a faith, Mitch can feel it. He remembers those high school French tests he was forced to do against his will. Seeing his guards escort that forensic team and all their equipment past his gates was a lot like that. Mitch's hands were tied. But it awakened in him a new insight: in tough times, balance is a luxury. This is not a test. He cannot fail. Mitch is happy to go along with Carlos's plan, but he also has to cap his losses, like Sobero said. Thursday is plenty of time for those assholes to dig around their sandbox for old bones. Then they're gone. No one can say Mitch didn't give them a chance.

Mitch is held up at the front entrance for ten minutes, where he's gently frisked, and a tough-looking female officer with a double chin calls to verify that he is expected. He has no problem with the screening. Mitch is actually pleased at the level of professionalism on display in this modern, rather nice-looking cop shop.

Finally he's led up an elevator and down a hall to a door with a small reinforced Plexiglas window. The guard puts her pass card to a panel, the light flashes green and the door clicks open. Inside, Sobero is sitting on one of several folding chairs, looking very much at home. It takes Mitch a moment to pinpoint what else looks different about him. Then he realizes: Sobero has removed the suit jacket he nearly always wears at *Mil Sueños,* and his shirtsleeves are rolled up to reveal nearly hairless forearms. Despite a sign posted high on the wall behind him that says smoking is prohibited, Sobero exhales from a cigarette stuck into the corner of his mouth.

As the door opens further Mitch sees that another man is standing with his back to them. He's facing the kind of one-way mirror Mitch has only ever seen on TV. In the adjacent room is Marta Ramos. Mitch has expected her to be handcuffed, but she's seated on a chair with her elbows on a desk, palms apart. Across from her is a man in a casual shirt with his legs stretched out to the side and crossed at the ankles. Neither of them appears to be talking.

Though Mitch has craved this sight and more than once imagined himself in the position of inquisitor, judge and executioner in fantasies of revenge against members of that Committee, of Greenpeace, MiningWatch, Rights Action and many other organizations that have enjoyed kicking him in the balls, the stark contours of the interrogation room make him queasy.

"Sit, *Señor* Wall," says Antonio de la Riva Hernández, without turning.

Sobero lifts his eyebrows and Mitch moves to take the chair beside him.

"Manuel says you want to watch."

"I — yes. Well, no. It's not really about watching, *per se*. Manuel said this meeting could be fruitful. I just want this whole situation resolved."

"Resolved," Hernández repeats. In the semi-transparent glass, Mitch can see the reflection of the man he knows from the news. "Okay," says the captain, slapping one thigh in a startling manner then turning suddenly to face Mitch. His hair is dyed a depthless black. "We resolve this 'situation.' For you." Hernández is not ugly, as he seemed on TV. His big nose suits his face. But his large round eyes are cold, moving down slowly to inspect Mitch from head to toe.

Mitch smiles nervously, looking towards his Chief of Security. But Sobero keeps staring straight ahead. "I appreciate that," Mitch says. "That's fantastic, thank you."

Hernández waves his hand as if to swat away Mitch's gratitude. Then he throws a different kind of look at Sobero — one that makes Mitch feel distinctly left out — then exits the room, appearing a moment later through the door visible through the one-way glass. The other man steps out.

Hernández takes a seat and he and Marta Ramos occupy the space in silence for several minutes. Marta, whom Mitch has never met in person, is chubby and mannish. Mitch thinks she looks tired, totally unthreatening.

"It is obvious that you are responsible for the abduction," Hernández says, finally. His voice is being pumped into the room where Mitch sits, but arrives thinner and distant, without the gravelly wheeze it carries in person. Mitch has the sudden realization that he isn't going to understand the proceedings. His comprehension of Spanish is decent, but not when native speakers are conversing quickly and, in this case, as if from the bottom of a well. "Shit," he says, and turns to Sobero, who sighs loudly, then translates. Mitch wishes he had decided better than to be here. He could be in Los Pampanos overseeing that forensic team in person.

Hernández raises the back of his hand towards himself like the truth of what he's just said is so self-evident it bores him. He examines invisible dirt under his close-cut fingernails. Marta tries not to be unnerved, putting aside thoughts of what this hand might have been responsible for during the war, what necks it wrung, and death orders it signed. It's only a show.

"You are famous."

Marta shakes her head.

"Yes. You are. People are sympathetic to you. You lived in what you call 'exile.' This makes you heroic."

Marta pictures the morning she landed in Toronto in 1987, when the threats had become intolerable. Trembling at Arrivals in her thin blouse, clutching a piece of paper where she'd scribbled the name of the contact person with Partners for Justice, Neela Hill. Marta was widowed, her children terrorized. Very heroic.

"I think that, for you, we don't need to waste time. We'll come right to the point. If you tell me where the foreigners are, you will be free to continue struggling for *justice*." Hernández obviously finds the word funny. "You will be immune to prosecution. Your brave little Committee for the Environment will be finished, naturally. But you will start again, I'm sure."

"I'm not saying anything until my lawyer arrives."

"She arrived several hours ago, *Señora* Ramos. We've decided she can wait a few more. I felt we should talk first."

The hair on the back of Marta's neck stands up: after everything, in El Salvador, this is the reality.

"*Señora* Ramos? Are you listening? We have direct evidence from the office you keep in Los Pampanos. Emails that show you planned the kidnapping."

Marta says nothing. She remembers her unfulfilled wish for an alarm system.

"Let me describe this in greater detail, and you correct me. You have no means to stop the mine's expansion at El Pico. According to your emails, you plotted with two members of your committee to hire these four kidnappers. You got one of them, Rita Santos, to offer the bus driver money. You knew he wouldn't ask questions. A sad story, the poverty of our country.

"Then these men, Cristóbal Santos Molina, Pepe Molina Domingo — cousins. One with military training. Quite advanced. But you know this! They took the hostages to a safe house. You have so many contacts in Morazán. And from there?" Hernández shrugs. "Maybe into the *mountains*." He emphasizes his last word as if it's the most important he's pronounced so far. "You've been communicating. We'll know soon how. We are searching your house. And you've published these letters in the newspapers, signed 'Enrique.' Your alter ego, maybe?" Here he smiles at Marta like a parent who's caught a child in a lie.

"Perhaps now you have found them other places to hide. You even convinced the daughter of one of the hostages to stay with you, this. . . ," he consults a piece of paper in front of him, "Aida Byrd. Good for the media."

Marta could laugh at the entire scenario he has described, except it sounds plausible, even to her.

Ten minutes later, the door opens and Hernández bursts back in. "What do you think, *Señor* Wall?"

"Great. Great." Mitch has been enjoying himself after all. Watching Marta shrink in her skin has been enormously satisfying. "You really grilled her. She's obviously guilty."

"You think so." Hernández sits down on the other side of Sobero so that Mitch has to lean forward and twist in his seat to see him well.

Sobero shakes his head and Hernández nods. It seems to be the equivalent of a verbal exchange.

"Am I missing something?" says Mitch, chuckling.

Hernández hits Sobero gently in the arm and Mitch's Chief of Security extracts a cigarette from his pack, handing it to him. Both men light up. "Everyone is very concerned about terrorism these days," says Hernández. "Washington? Oh, they are serious."

"As they should be," says Mitch. He doesn't see the connection.

"Absolutely. And Manuel, he does his best so that your mine will never be touched by these kinds of criminals."

"You think Marta Ramos is a terrorist?"

Sobero shoots Mitch a look that says he should listen before speaking. These men don't talk straight. Mitch values straight talkers.

"The Americans are not satisfied with their war in Iraq — our war. We are part of it, you know?"

Mitch is vaguely aware of this. He still doesn't see the relevance.

"But they are also concerned about terrorism right here, in our hemisphere. They've started a program. Of course, we support it. We support everything they do, and, in turn, they help us." Hernández gestures at the walls, thanking his American patrons for the surroundings. "It's a beneficial relationship. As we speak, they are flying small remote-controlled planes — drones. You've heard of these, at least?"

Mitch hasn't.

"Oh. Well. These go over our territory and all the way up to Mexico. Systematically. Imagine the resources!" Hernández sounds genuinely awed. "They say that *el famoso* Al-Qaeda might be smuggling operatives into the U.S. on the illegal migrant routes that start right here in El Salvador with the help of our very own gangs, who make such a healthy profit from that business. It is ironic, no? Our problems serving the subversives of another part of the world, and our soldiers in Iraq fighting the same subversives. It's globalization!" Hernández slaps his hands together to punctuate his observation.

Sobero nods.

Mitch shifts in his seat. "I still don't think I —"

"Today I called in a favour among the people who run this program. They owed me for some files I was able to provide them on one of our leading gang assassins who freelances in Los Angeles. A small thing, really. They shared with me the fact that they are currently analyzing some unusual photos their drones have taken of a small group of people travelling at night on an uncommon route — infrared, of course, only the best — through northern Morazán. What if I told you that the hostages will be among them? And that the Americans are prepared, as a favour to me, to resurvey this area, starting today, and to send us updated shots, at which point we will be in a position to act? We have excellent capacity." Hernández looks at Mitch eagerly, waiting for a reaction.

But Mitch is too freaked out to deliver the expected awe. Hernández, he's just realized, is a gearhead. Geology is full of guys like him. People who love their polymer-capped chipping chisels as much as the minerals in the rocks they're bashing with them. Hernández wants to use all the fancy equipment the Americans have bought for his unit. An image of Catharine Keil's face floats across Mitch's mind, the horror she displayed during their meeting at his suggestion that she let Hernández handle the kidnapping. Then Carlos's words from last night: ". . . Maybe there are problems. Casualties." Mitch's stomach turns. "And her?" he says, nodding towards the one-way mirror, behind which Marta is still sitting, her arms crossed now, staring down at the desk.

"What about her?"

"You'll keep questioning her, right?"

Sobero, who hasn't said a word since Mitch arrived, suddenly chimes in. "It's always useful to shake the confidence of individuals like *Señora* Ramos."

"But the documents." Mitch cannot — will not — believe that Carlos's sources lied, that Marta and her Committee are innocent. How could Carlos have been fooled?

Sobero and Hernández both smile. "Someone must have been bored," says Hernández, shrugging as he did earlier in the room with Marta.

Seeing Mitch's dejection, Sobero claps him on the shoulder, displaying a familiarity completely at odds with his usual manner. "You never know. If Antonio gets the coordinates and locates the delegation, they might still be convinced to use the name of Marta Ramos — whether they've heard it before or not."

"If they all make it out," says Hernández, pausing a moment before adding, "You'd be amazed what's possible once we have control of a situation, *Señor* Wall."

Mitch tries to write this off as joking exaggeration, looking between the two former military men for a humourous edge, but he doesn't find one.

TUESDAY
APRIL 12

11:20 AM. *27 KM south of the Salvadoran-Honduran border*

This last stretch before they're close enough to cross is rough going. Straight up to about 2,400 feet and through some of the only dense pine forest left in the country. These stands haven't been cut in nearly a generation. They were owned by the patriarch of one of El Salvador's richest families until he died in Miami, where he was living off the money he stole from the public coffers. His nine children have been fighting in court for the right to clear-cut the area ever since. Pepe has followed the case in the press, and he takes his time describing these ins and outs to Cristóbal in a clipped monotone as they set up camp together, digging a fire pit and latrine, then recovering the supplies — matches, bottles of water to fill the canteens, cigarettes, cans of food — that they buried here two months back. "These trees are thriving on lawsuits," Pepe says, in summary, and horks loudly.

Cristóbal shakes his head in an exaggerated manner and smiles at the inexplicable behaviour of rich people. He's happy to listen. They haven't spoken much since their disagreement about Rita except to confirm that they will continue to travel in this general area for the time being in a back-and-forth pattern, taking a slightly more northerly route every night. Suits him. Cristóbal loves the freshness of the air up here, the pine scent on the breeze, so different from the sweet, damp heat at the lower altitudes. Plus, when this is over, he and Rita can go north quickly. When Pepe finishes his story, Cristóbal tips his head towards Tina and the other hostages. He doesn't normally venture his opinions, but he wants to keep up the exchange with his cousin. "The antibiotics are working," he says.

"We should have started them sooner," Pepe barks back. "To-night, walk more slowly with her. Don't push. If she collapses, we'll have a bigger problem than going slow." He's lit a cigarette from one of the fresh packs, but now he throws it, barely smoked, onto the ground and heads in the other direction.

Cristóbal pulls the last cans from the plastic bag they were buried in, rolls the bag small and tucks it into his pack. He thinks Pepe overreacted during that last phone conversation. He should not have committed himself to taking the life of a hostage over some small problem of a time limit. They have plenty of supplies. They're prepared to keep up their evasive tactics. There's no real deadline on their end, no rush. But Pepe sent that message out to the press and now it's too late. If Tina can't walk, she'll be the one to go. It's a shame. She's very nice.

Cristóbal takes a few steps forward and grinds Pepe's butt out, then picks up the stub and puts it in his pocket. He goes about the rest of his daily duties then switches off with Rita and Delmi while the hostages finish their long morning sleep. When it comes time, he tells Pepe that he's free to go rest, but Pepe shakes his head and ignores him. Cristóbal tries to think of the right thing to say. He sees how Pepe is struggling with himself, which makes Cristóbal feel love for him and deep regret that the mine hasn't been more compliant. He's never been convinced that Pepe will find what he's looking for at El Pico, even if a team of people is allowed to dig for weeks. But he wants Pepe to succeed and hopes that if he does, his cousin will find inner peace.

The hostages pick up on the change in Pepe's mood as soon as they wake up — mostly because he's usually off sleeping by now. Cristóbal watches their eyes fill with questions. Curiosity keeps them quiet a long time. Eventually though, unable to stand it, they revert to their normal means of communication, using their hands and a sprinkling of quiet words in English, which Cristóbal half understands. But seeing them relax has the exact opposite effect on him. He and Rita and Delmi have been less than strict about the talking rule. Now that Pepe is agitated, the trigger won't be important. It could be something small. Cristóbal can only hope that if Pepe goes off, the impact of his rage will be minor and won't harm Rita.

It's odd. The kidnappers never give up sleep time. But even after Delmi and Rita get back from their daily food preparations and Cristóbal goes out for his afternoon sleep, Pepe sticks around. Everyone waits to see what he'll do, but for a long time he pays them no attention, stomping in and out of view. Then, abruptly, he sits, takes off a small, dirty looking pack Danielle hasn't seen before, then his rifle, and puts them on the ground. From the pack he tugs a heavy-looking pouch, which he lays open to reveal some containers, a cloth, a rod, a thick screwdriver and a brush. He disconnects the strap from his gun, removes the magazine and loudly pulls back a lever, making Antoine jump. A round falls into Pepe's palm. Everyone leans forward to see the ammunition. Pepe takes the rest of the weapon apart and lays its sinister black components on an enormous, oversized leaf. Danielle looks between this spectacle and the others, who are transfixed, Rita included, her gaze moving rapidly between the gun parts and Pepe's mask, maybe as concerned as everyone else that he's getting ready to put the weapon back together for a specific use.

The cleaning process is slower and more tedious than Danielle imagined, though Pepe tackles it with a manic verve that implies speed, every move an act of aggression. At some point people begin to relax their attention away from him and focus instead on their own tedium: Tina lethargically digging dirt from under her nails with a bit of wood; Pierre murdering ants. Martin, meanwhile, dares to pull Tina's chess set closer to his side. He requested it earlier from Delmi. Soon he emits a cheerful sound as he begins an early attack against Antoine. Pepe lays down the barrel he's been plunging with the long brush, gets up, kicks over the pieces of the game, grabs the board and throws it, leaving the young men dumbfounded. Danielle watches Delmi resist as long as she feels is necessary to guarantee her own safety before getting up and recovering all of the pieces.

Danielle can't decide if Pepe is just making a point, letting them know he's their only authority, or if there's more going on. She's slept better since speaking to the others. That was quite a moment, saying exactly what she felt, naming the problem and doing something about it. Feeling more confident than she has in days — maybe years — she channels her newfound energy into reading Pepe's signals as he pulls an oiled cloth along the outside of the barrel over and over. Did something go wrong? Does he know of a rescue operation? A refusal of some demand of his — whatever those are. Danielle realizes that she's already come to rely on Pepe to manage the situation for everyone. Right now, he looks unsteady, like he's coming undone with his weapon.

The pines swish endlessly above her. The area reminds Danielle of her ignominious departure for Honduras in 1980, but it actually looks and smells like Canada, evoking memories of pleasant weekend trips to Northern Ontario with her parents shortly after her father moved them back to Toronto to take the job at the university. Danielle lets the latter association soothe her. It seems, for a while, that the gun cleaning is just a routine thing, that the day will pass as usual.

Then Pepe forces the magazine loudly back into its chamber, reattaches his strap and rises with the gun in one hand. Danielle hopes he's leaving. She promises herself that if he does, she'll warn the others again, using this as an example of his capacity for violence. She's getting to like herself as a risk-taker.

"*Daniela*," Pepe says, not bothering to turn from where he stands with his back to her. "*Vente*"

Oh no. Danielle is genuinely afraid of going anywhere alone with him suddenly. Also, humiliated to be called like a dog. She looks around at the others. Their eyes are simultaneously pitying and bitter. Something in her resists.

Pepe turns to see what's taking her so long. In a swift motion he's at her side, lifting her with one strong hand in a grip that feels like it will crush her upper arm. Danielle doesn't know what's got into him, but she's relieved, at least, for the effect it has on the others. They gape, open mouthed. Danielle hopes it too will reinforce how useless it is to defy Pepe, how stupid to side with Rita.

Stepping past Tina, whose colour has returned somewhat today, Danielle distinctly hears her whisper to Martin, "He should leave her be," and sees Martin nod. Pierre, who's been sitting apart from everyone, apparently still preoccupied with whatever Rita told him, acts as if the scene has nothing to do with him whatsoever. He chews a blade of dry grass like beef jerky, the sore on his lip dried into a hard scab. As she is pulled out of view, Danielle glances towards Antoine, who seems to understand her meaning and tries, in turn, to make eye contact with his friend, though as far as Danielle can tell before Pepe draws her out of range, he fails.

Eventually Pepe pushes Danielle ahead of him and provides clipped instructions for where to walk. She rubs her arm where he's bruised it. The skin is already rashy from a prickly bush she brushed up against during the night, and now it throbs and itches simultaneously. She tries to ignore the discomfort, to put aside her worries over her physical health for once. They go further into an area where the huge, low-growing plants Pepe pulled his big leaf from grow at the feet of tall pines. Danielle's footsteps disappear beneath them and into a thickness of dry, skeletal leaves and fallen needles. Behind her, she hears Pepe breathing loudly. She turns to look and sees that she's got some distance on him. Pepe's tired. He's missed a good chunk of sleep and it shows.

Eventually, he yells at her to stop. Danielle doesn't see anything special about the spot except that it's far enough away that no one else can hear. Pepe sits and takes his phone from his belt, as he did before. Danielle sits too. She assumes they'll be using the phone again. But Pepe must just be trying to get comfortable in his underslept state because now he rests his immaculate weapon on his other side atop that same small pack he was wearing earlier, further unburdening himself. He reaches into his pants pocket and hands her two blank pieces of paper, then reclines somewhat into the pine needles. Even after all that, he still doesn't seem relaxed. The papers are much dirtier than the pieces Danielle's written on before. She wonders if Pepe took them from that house with the children. She visualizes those wide-eyed little ones deprived of even paper to draw on. She gives the sheets a shake, though they remain gritty, and accepts the ballpoint Pepe offers.

For a long time, Pepe just looks down at his gun. He seems to require a moment to go into his memories. Danielle is conscious of his energy shifting, becoming weightier. His eyes are empty, somewhere else altogether.

"As I said last time," he begins, finally, a little too loudly, as if lecturing to a crowd, for he still does not look at Danielle directly, "in the middle of the war — '85 — I got out of the military. My unit was on patrol in the south end of this province, at the edge of guerrilla territory. A dangerous place for us. It was early morning. I can still feel that air on my face. Very cool."

The air on his face? Pepe hasn't used such intimate description before. It's at odds with his gruff tone of voice, the way his sentences come in short bursts.

"We were on our way to a village that was only accessible on foot when one of our scouts picked up on something about a hundred feet off, up a hillside. He came and told our commander that he was sure it was subversives, sleeping.

"Something about it wasn't right. We'd been hearing that the guerrillas were changing tactics, moving in smaller units, using ruses. Why would they just be lying there, in a contested zone? But it was war, and you never knew what to believe. The commander got excited at the prospect of an easy kill, something to get him promoted. He ordered us to move forward in formation."

Pepe sits up. Danielle sees the butt of his handgun shift a little on the back of his belt.

"Maybe ten feet on, we set them off. Our feet activated the land mines. Arms and legs and blood went flying. Some of those things were hitting me. In the chest, in the thigh. I heard, like it was after, the sound of the explosives. My ears hurt and I was on the ground, dirt and leaves and wet substances all over me. I made out voices over the ringing in my ears. 'Cristo Santo!' someone yelled. There was laughter too. 'One's alive,' someone said. 'Shoot him!' said a different voice — a woman's. But the one who'd laughed refused. 'No, Compa. No. He must be a true survivor.' This man stayed with me. He walked beside me, and when I eventually got my head clear, I remember registering his face: the face of the man who'd saved my life. It was painted dark green, with twigs floating above his camouflage helmet, and just the whites of his eyes showing.

"Later, I was well enough to stand and march. They gave me the choice of going over to the Red Cross or joining *la guerrilla*. I knew if I went to the Red Cross, the military would find me and torture me. I wanted to die, but not like that. Anyway, I still thought these guerrillas would kill me. Or maybe I would kill them and get away. I took their offer.

"They named me *Milagro*, cleaned me up. The blast had torn my clothes off so they put me in a uniform that belonged to one of their own who'd been shot. A dead subversive's uniform. Even though my training had been to find this insulting, I didn't care. I'd been dead for so long, what difference did it make to me which side I was on? It was going to be more killing. More getting killed.

"Just a few hours later, reinforcements from my military base came in looking for my unit. Dropped down from helicopters. We all ran and I got separated from the guerrillas. It was me and the man who'd stopped the others from shooting me. We hid in a hole in the ground. Twenty-four hours or more like that, like worms. At first I didn't want to talk. He was going to try to get information out of me. Or murder me. But he kept going on about things I'd never heard of. He said there were lots of jobs inside the guerrilla that didn't involve killing. Lots of people were just growing food for the rest. Learning to read. I said I could read fine. Better than any brainwashed *campesino* with their priests telling them what to think. But then he had me talking. Once I started, I couldn't stop. There was no light in there, so it was like talking to myself. We didn't have any food except a bit of sugar in a bag and a canteen of water. We could hear gunshots everywhere. Finally, there was no sound. We got out and started walking.

"But they were still there, the government soldiers. We walked right into them. They were about to shoot — I know I would've. So I yelled out. "We're military! Hunters!" That's what we always called counterinsurgency specialists. And these guys, they hesitated. Just for a second. The man I was with was quick. He didn't miss the chance. He jumped in with a whole invented story, gave details. Said we were posing as guerrillas and infiltrating controlled territories. Said these soldiers better keep their mouths shut or they'd hear from the general. He used names we'd all heard. Important names. They bought it. They were like me — stupid and young.

"We marched with them back to the helicopters and they flew us to a garrison I'd never been to. There we were, this *subversivo* and me. The others were looking at us strangely. I knew we only had so much time. We went to the mess to eat. We stuffed ourselves and then, without saying a word, we walked out the door. Casually, like we were going for a stroll. We didn't stop walking until we'd reached the main road. We put our guns to the head of the first truck driver who pulled over for us and told him which way to go. That's how I joined the *guerrilla*.

"I had to retrain. The guerrillas had a different system. Didn't kill anyone unless there was a specific mission. Never non-combatants."

Danielle swallows a lump forming in her throat. This story just confirms how unlucky she was to see a breach of the guerrillas' rules by Adrian when he killed that boy.

"The man who'd saved me more or less adopted me," Pepe continues. "He taught me how to live invisibly, as a commando has to. I got good at their way of making war. I'd been trained to be vicious by the military, and the guerrillas channeled that. I ran my own four-man unit, doing long-term mission planning. We'd spend days lying on the ground, snakes crawling right over us — whatever.

Totally silent. Each in our position, watching a target — a dam or a bridge or a storage facility. We could get inside and make a mental map of any place without them ever knowing it. That's how we were. But their way was also more fair, more reasoned. I spent the rest of the war behaving like them, like a human being.

"At the end of 1988, we started hearing talk about a decisive battle — a general insurrection. The guerrilla leaders were going to provoke it with actions in each of the major cities. Surprise attacks. It was going to take a year to plan. I was still close to the man who saved me. Whenever we were both in the same place, we would talk, eat together. He was part of the top tier of guerrillas who were planning the actions for the capital city. By then, people were calling him *'Comandante'* — though he was never a real commander. But he was important and people loved him. Women loved him. He knew what to say. He was the kind of man who —"

Danielle is listening intently to this story, scribbling quickly to keep up with Pepe's telling, which has become more and more hurried, almost automatic, like he has rehearsed this version of the events of his life to himself many times before, and this is a preamble to the part where everything goes wrong. She waits for it.

But now, suddenly, a howl startles them.

They look towards the campsite. Danielle recognizes the voice as Pierre's. Her heart flip-flops. What has Rita done? She gets to her feet, pine needles falling from her pant legs.

Pepe picks up his rifle, stands too and grabs her arm again, seemingly all at once. This time, Danielle feels no pain. She's already being dragged towards the scream.

Another howl. "My head! My head!" screams Pierre.

Danielle hears herself say his name under her breath: "Pierre."

Pepe keeps pulling her forward and Danielle thinks she should speak up. "It's Rita," she mouths, in Spanish, but Pepe isn't listening. "It's Rita," she says again, much louder, and realizes, as they come into view of the others, that maybe Rita hasn't done anything to Pierre, that this could be the event she's been hoping against: Pierre doing something he planned with Rita. Danielle says to him, or to Pepe, "Don't do it!" but the words come out in English and are lost as Pepe lets go of her arm and pushes her aside. She stumbles and falls. Pepe stops in his tracks. Pierre is writhing on the ground with his hands on his head as Antoine tries to comfort him. Tina is lying on her side, her hair half out of its ponytail, her eyes wide with terror. Martin has his palms on the ground and is scooting backwards towards a nearby tree.

"*Qué tienes?*" yells Pepe, pointing his gun at Pierre.

Cristóbal comes jogging into the clearing with his gun in one hand. His hat is off and he's still tugging down his balaclava, the eyeholes not quite in place. He's obviously been asleep.

"Where is she?" says Pepe, turning towards his cousin, but Cristóbal just stands there. Delmi looks at the ground.

"My head, my head, my head," says Pierre.

But Pepe is suddenly ignoring him, his gun going down to his side. He seems to realize something. He tears out of the clearing back in the direction he and Danielle have just come from. Cristóbal hesitates a split second before running out after him.

The moment they're gone, Danielle watches as Pierre stops moving and takes his hands from his head. He sits up, alert and apparently not in pain. If she had a gun, Danielle would shoot him for his stupidity. "What are you doing?" she says, but he ignores her. He's breathing hard from his performance.

Delmi stands, her rifle up, her eyes darting about in confusion while they all listen as the men run further off, through the trees, branches snapping and the thumping of their steps growing fainter.

Cristóbal catches sight of Pepe in the place where he must have been with Danielle just now, judging from the papers strewn on the ground. Pepe is standing over Rita, yelling at her not to move. Rita is on her knees, holding Pepe's satellite phone.

Rita looks hopefully towards her husband, which makes Pepe turn too. Cristóbal catches his cousin's eye and something passes between them, but Cristóbal doesn't have time to understand what it is because in that flicker of hesitation, Rita drops the phone and runs from them both before either can stop her. Pepe follows, making a grunting sound, pushing branches out of the way, and Cristóbal chases just behind. "*No, Primo. No,*" he says.

———

Danielle hears the noises becoming louder again: they're coming back. Her heart beats in an unusual, unhealthy rhythm. The pine smell in the air is suddenly cloying, sickening. She sees Rita rush into the open space of the campsite and pivot on the heels of her boots as she pulls up her rifle. She's shooting back into the trees. Loud, fast, echoing shots that hurt Danielle's ears. Rita looks un-practiced, one hand unsteady around the muzzle. Everyone takes cover. Danielle is down low, her face against some pebbles, her legs stuck into some bushes.

More shots snap, this time coming from the trees. And then Rita's gun rattles, going off several times more in reply.

Cristóbal finally reappears. Everyone is on the ground except Rita, who is standing, shaking, holding her gun, the hair at the bottom of her mask sticking out, seemingly electrified, her eyes like saucers. But she isn't hurt. Danielle, still hugging the earth, is strangely, hugely relieved. She has time to wonder what the relief means about her feelings towards Pepe and Cristóbal, and even Rita — despite everything, she doesn't seem to want them dead — before Pepe breaks through into the clearing. Cristóbal has already gone to stand in front of his wife, looking her over as if searching for holes. He shakes his head slowly but determinedly at his cousin until, eventually, Pepe lets his weapon down.

Delmi takes this as her signal to get up from the dirt and begin to push the hostages with the tip of her gun, forcing them to return from wherever they've crawled or run to and get back onto their tarps. When she reaches Antoine, he won't move. "Get up," she says, adding one of her reflexive giggles. She pokes him again.

Danielle, on her scraped knees now, feels herself melting back towards the ground: there's blood.

"Get up!" Delmi says, more loudly, but Pepe walks over quickly and pushes her away. He puts his hand on Antoine's back. He's been shot there. There's a lot of blood.

Pierre panics. He gets up and starts to run. Cristóbal goes after him, grabbing him after just a few unrushed steps on his long legs and bringing him back. Cristóbal does not raise his gun. He doesn't need to. Pierre looks like he's had all of his bones removed. When Cristóbal lets him go, he falls to his knees and crawls towards his friend like an insect.

Pepe turns to Danielle and tells her to translate. "He's dead. It was an accident." His voice is even, despite his heavy breathing, despite the blood. His face is as closed as it was on that very first day, when he lined them up against the bus and let them believe he was about to shoot them all. "We will bury him and then we will move at sunset, like normal."

Danielle can't say this the first or second time she tries. "He's dead," she finally articulates. Two words like small fires igniting in her mouth. Martin promptly throws up. Tina tries unsuccessfully to hide under her own hair and shakes where she sits.

Pepe takes away Rita's gun and orders Cristóbal to tie her hands. The cousins, who, moments ago, were struggling for control, who might have killed one another over Rita, work in concert. Cristóbal seems to understand that his wife has betrayed him. He pulls her hands tightly behind her back. Rita is as silent as if Pepe has cut out her tongue. She and Danielle exchange a look. It's not regret, but it's not gloating either. Rita seems shocked to be alive. As soon as she's tied up, Pepe pushes her to the ground onto her stomach and orders Delmi to keep guard. Then he rushes back out through the trees.

Danielle wants to hope that Rita at least managed whatever she was trying to do — make a call out, likely, remembering Rita's words to Pierre that night: "*El teléfono. . . distráelo.*" Distract him. Danielle hopes Rita was prepared with the right phone number, a name, whatever will guarantee her precious transit across the border. If so, the shooting might not have been for nothing. They could all be freed. But Danielle is quite certain there wasn't enough time. And anyway, such an unlikely success won't change what has happened to Antoine. There's no going back.

Aida argues with the taxi driver, but he refuses to take her any closer. She wonders if she's using the right words. *"Me voy a la catedral,"* she repeats. I'm headed to the cathedral. The young man glances into his rearview from under a cap decorated with a stylized image of the blessed heart of Jesus wrapped in a thorny crown. He tells her firmly that he can't risk his car by getting any closer, that she'd be smart to let him take her someplace else and that otherwise she should pay up and get out. Aida counts the fare they agreed on, hands it over and slams the door. Four blocks to go. She assumes the aggressive look on her face — like an indifferent scowl — that she's learned deters harassment from men, and starts walking. Quite a lot of people seem to be moving in the same direction. Two come to a stop in front of her.

"Hey," says one of them, a girl about Aida's age, her hands stuck into the back pockets of low-slung jeans. "Sorry about your mother. We are really grateful for her writing."

Aida just looks at her. How dare this person lump Danielle in with the kidnappers' cause? "She didn't have a choice," Aida replies, altering her course to go past the girl and her friend.

But the young woman steps back into her path. "Salvadorans need to read what she's said about that man. Especially our parents. They don't get many chances to express their feelings about the war."

Aida sidesteps her yet again. "Half of it's probably not even true."

The girl looks like she'll laugh. She swings out one elbow to indicate the crowd. "True enough for all of these people."

Aida hurries on. How can anyone be so delusional? Probably that girl also buys Marta's logic that the violence of the abduction is comparable to the supposed violence NorthOre's mine is causing.

Which is insane. A gold mine is a business, not some random act of criminals. Aida continues to berate the girl inwardly until the cathedral comes into view. And then her breath goes out of her in amazement: there must be a thousand people crowding the plaza, maybe more. The girl's words echo back: *true enough for these people.* Aida wonders if that's how things are measured in El Salvador — in increments of truth. She can't remember ever being surrounded by so many bodies, except once, as a teenager, when her friends dragged her downtown for an appearance by the Spice Girls. Not exactly the same scene. Haven't they heard that the very committee that organized the rally is now implicated in the kidnapping? Aida can only conclude that people feel a personal connection with Marta Ramos, the woman who'll hug you like you're her best friend and fight for whatever cause you throw at her. A sentimental reaction to her arrest must be drawing them here. Aida has to compel herself to mix with them.

Suddenly, several people block her way. Reporters. She tries to avoid them, veering right, but they're like a swarm of mosquitoes. Their microphones prod her as they did at Neela's vigil in Toronto. Except Aida doesn't have Neela or André to shield her now, and she's cornered into doing several short interviews with Canadian and Salvadoran outlets before she can move away. "How do you feel about the kidnapper breaking his promise to release a hostage?" one asks. "What do you make of the arrest of Marta Ramos?" shouts another. "Which of the hostages do you think the kidnapper has chosen to die first?" Aida turns to glare at the reporter who's blurted out this question, a man not much older than she is. He wears an innocent expression of curiosity. Finally, she breaks free, but the question lingers.

She hasn't gone far when a police officer asks to see ID. Several curious people gather to stare as Aida produces her passport. The officer orders them all to back off and scrutinizes the picture, then pulls up his radio, presumably to check with someone more senior, let them know that one of the family members is on hand. Chances are such a person will order him to send her home, so Aida straightens her back and interrupts the call loudly, explaining that she's here to meet Carlos Reyes. He's already warned the police not to interfere with her movements, and she will be forced to report anyone who causes her to be late. Her bullying seems to work. The officer puts down his radio and gives her back her passport.

On two sides of the plaza fronting the cathedral, police cars are parked end to end, like opposing teams. Two officers stand in front of each car, legs slightly apart. Aida isn't particularly bothered by them. Actually, they reassure her. The crowd itself feels like the unruly element here. As she presses forward with difficulty, she sees yet more people pouring from two dilapidated school buses. The passengers wear cowboy hats and patterned dresses and carry cooking pots. Real *campesinos*, like the ones Aida has seen in pictures.

Far across the way, on the cathedral steps, Aida sees some people clustered together where she knows the microphone stand will eventually be placed. She strains to see if Marta has arrived yet — part of her hoping she has, as this will prove that Marta has been released from custody. But another part of her resists this scenario. Marta won't be fooled like that officer. If she has the slightest inkling that the demonstration might get out of hand, she'll make Aida leave. Which only makes Aida want to stay as long as possible. She's embracing spontaneity, breaking from the habits of acting, of feeling, that have locked her and Danielle into an impasse at home. She's staying, no matter what anyone says.

When the embassy called last evening with word that the kidnapper had faxed a map and instructions for how to locate the remains of "Enrique's" family on the grounds of *Mil Sueños,* Aida was ecstatic. She'd left Marta's by then. It was too lonely there after her phone call with Carlos. When Ralph rang to see how she was doing, she jumped at the chance to spend the evening with the other families. Staying with them felt natural.

They only had an hour to celebrate, however, before the embassy called back with bad news: the kidnappers were refusing to release anyone and were now imposing their own Thursday deadline to match NorthOre's. Benoît, who'd taken the call, picked up the phone to throw it across the room in frustration. Only by rushing over with her freckled arms up was Sylvie able to stop him. Aida slumped into a chair beside Ralph: no one was coming back. She got up a moment later and left the room, wandering through the common space of the guest house to a desk where there was another phone for visitors. She dialed Carlos. She needed to tell him, needed a better ending to their conversation than the one she'd had earlier. A woman answered his cell, sounding groggy.

"*Está Carlos?*"

The woman — his wife? girlfriend? — hesitated, but a moment later Carlos came on the line. "*Sí?*"

"*Carlos. Habla Aida.*"

"Aida. It's 1:00."

"It's just — the kidnappers. They're going to kill someone. Thursday. No matter what — unless the mine lets the exhumation go on indefinitely. It'll be Danielle. I know it. I don't know what to do. I wish I was home right now."

Aida heard Carlos walk somewhere with the phone, then a faint click as a door closed. "In Toronto," he said. "Maybe this is a good idea."

"What? No. I didn't really mean —" Aida felt idiotic. How had she ever imagined she could call a near stranger in the middle of the night for comfort?

"I'm only saying that if you decide to go home, you'll be safer. You'll have more support. Whatever you do, let me know. And tomorrow, please do not attend the Committee's demonstration. My police contacts tell me it could be dangerous. I would be very concerned."

Aida held the phone tightly. "I'm planning to be there," she said, which became true as she uttered the words. Carlos just wanted her gone, didn't want to have to listen to her read him old letters or babysit her anymore.

"No, Aida. Going will be a mistake."

She hung up on "mistake." She walked back to Sylvie and Benoît's room, where she found the others descending into their blackest mood yet.

Now, continuing to walk through the crowd, Aida tells herself she made the right decision. Benoît's anger and Sylvie's crying, Ralph's restrained disappointment, and Neela's endless phone calls would be too much to endure.

"*No a la mineria! No a la mineria!*" a group of students chants as she passes. Aida mouths the words, just to see how it feels. But a call of disapproval follows, emerging from a different group of people to Aida's right. "Booooh! Baaahh!" The students lose their rhythm and go silent a moment, then start back up with verve. "*NO A LA MINERIA!*" The second group chimes in again, and it's a mess of voices and calls.

"*Buenas tardes,*" says a man's voice over the crowd, interrupting them. Someone is testing the microphone on the cathedral steps. "Good afternoon," he says again, and the microphone squeaks. One of Marta's committee members. "We are very happy to see so many of you. Welcome! We have had word that there are some individuals in the crowd today who represent forces working against us, and against our committee."

Aida looks around. Only some of the people nearby are listening. The students are bunched together, rehearsing a new chant. Others are laughing, enjoying the get-together. Still others are readying banners and drums.

"Do not react if someone tries to provoke you. I want everyone to remain calm. We are going to keep our program short, and then we ask that you please disperse. Now, I want to introduce our only speaker today, whom we are very happy to have among us: Marta Ramos —" his voice is nearly drowned out by a loud cheer.

So she's out. Aida checks herself and finds that she is mostly relieved. She strains to catch a glimpse of her host.

"Thank you," Marta says, her voice a little shaky. "I want to acknowledge your presence and to tell you that I appreciate your support. My arrest yesterday morning was unwarranted. Another instance of the reverse justice that still predominates in this country, where the people who work for democracy are persecuted, and those who oppose it walk free." The crowd makes a variety of noises. "This is why tomorrow we will not be gathering here."

Aida is surprised. Many nearby are booing. Is Marta giving up?

"But wait! I said we will not gather *here,* where the police can harass us, and where people hired to do so can provoke us. We reject these tactics of NorthOre. We reject police brutality. But we will meet! At a different location. One with great symbolic value. The *Río Rico* has fed our land for a millennium. Currently, it is being poisoned by NorthOre and the *Mil Sueños* mine. This will be our gathering place. We do not exist only to shut down mines, as our critics will try to make people believe. We support clean water, clean air, healthy soil, healthy futures."

The crowd erupts in a roar of cheers. But there are nearly as many heckles, and Marta is forced to stop speaking for a long while. When the yeas and nays finally settle, she picks back up. "We've arranged for buses to leave from the *Estación del Oriente* tomorrow at 6:00 to take people to the mouth of the river, one hour north of here. Our committee members will contact the various organizations in the next few hours to determine how many will come. And now, all of you, do what is safe and go home. And Aida Byrd —"

Aida freezes.

"— please make your way to the east side of the cathedral, beside the steps, so we can take you back."

Aida is at once self-conscious and happy. She checks around her; no one recognizes her as the object of this address. They're too busy with one another. The mood is changing. A restlessness has gripped people. Aida looks for an easy path. Despite her tough self-talk, she suddenly wants to go exactly where Marta has suggested. She starts in a beeline east, but an older man puts out his arm to stop her. "*Señorita*. There's a fight that way. Don't go."

"But," Aida begins, trying to explain. Before she can, everyone around them seems to get the same message and they turn like a wave, forcing Aida to either squeeze through or be swept along with them. She decides to let herself go with the flow and double back at a distance. A few steps on she turns to see that a scuffle is indeed spreading to where she just was. Several men jostle one another and a tense line has formed between the students and hecklers. "A thousand nightmares for a thousand years," say the students, in a play on the *Mil Sueños* name. "*Viva El Salvador!*" say the others, less imaginatively.

Sticking close to the older man Aida makes a left towards the centre of the plaza's garden, but five paces along she narrowly avoids being punched by a man who's just taken a wide swing at another, who receives the hit directly on the left eye. His hat goes flying, and Aida marvels as someone else manages to catch it and quickly lower their arm, claiming it. She stands in shock watching the punched man fall to the ground in a heap before tearing herself away.

"Everyone, *por favor*," Marta is saying, but it's becoming more difficult to make out her words over the racket. Aida starts to hope Marta will use her name again. "Please leave in an orderly fashion. Please do not —"

And then Marta's voice is lost and the world slows considerably as Aida hears an entirely unfamiliar sound: a *phhooomff,* a whistle in the air, a sharp plonk, a rattle and a hiss. A puff of silver smoke appears, maybe forty feet away. Aida tries to retreat from it, but the smoke moves at tremendous speed and is quickly around and beyond her. She stops, her toes tightening in her sandals. An intense burning sensation comes over her, buckling her knees, and she's down, the bare skin of one of her kneecaps smacking hard earth below the grass. There's gas in her mouth and her ears, her eyes and her nose. She gropes at the damp blades, unable to breathe.

Suddenly, two people, women, pick her up by the arms so firmly Aida grimaces. They drag her along, she doesn't know which way. But she's willing. She's grateful. She'll go anywhere that the smoke isn't. Wherever they want to take her. Aida asks herself how a single scuffle turned into tear gas. It seems disproportionate.

Eventually, they get clear of the thickest smoke. Aida hacks and coughs, but is able to keep up, to inhale enough air. That's when she looks over and sees them: riot police, advancing, slapping their batons against their shields like in a movie. *Thud. Thud. Thud.* The two women just stare. *Vamos*," Aida says, and encourages them to retreat with her. They press past people in the direction Aida first came from after the taxi dropped her off and are nearly at the mouth of a side street when another set of sounds — *phhooomff, whistle, plonk, rattle, hiss* — sends a huge cloud of gas up into the air just behind them.

Aida is momentarily paralyzed. Her stomach folds over itself and she throws up, her eyes burning, her lungs feeling like they're being fried inside her chest. Only when she's finished heaving does she realize that the women have gone on running without her. She calls after them, stumbling around, eventually coming across several people sharing splashes of bottled water. Still bent over, Aida reaches out her hand and she groans with relief when she feels her palm fill with liquid. She brings the water to her eyes, catching a small amount in her mouth.

Many others stumble as she does, through clinging silver wafts of gas, hurriedly tying scarves or t-shirts around their noses as they scatter, each carving their own path, but everyone with the same goal: to leave behind the emptying canisters that Aida now understands are being lobbed from the tops of the buildings lining the central plaza. But what about the riot police? Why aren't they helping? How will she get home? Where is home? Marta's house? Her host's paranoia about the police returns to Aida now as a warning she has been too stupid to heed. And this, in turn, makes her doubts about Marta waver dramatically. Nothing seems as clear as it used to.

Aida has never been more aware of how unprepared she is to face real violence. She cries unabashedly for defying the others, for leaving that taxi, assuming things would remain in control, as they always have for her until this week, for wearing these clothes — an impractical skirt and flimsy sandals. The skirt is splattered with the blood of that man who was punched earlier; one of her shins is cut where she's fallen. Aida is filled with the sudden knowledge that if anyone really looks at her now, instead of just bumping into and streaming past her as they are, they'll see something truly pitiable: a fake, a war orphan.

"Marta! Marta!" Aida screams out Marta's name because she has no one else to scream for. But now her eyes widen at a new sound and her pupils burn for it. An echoey rat-tat. Gunfire. Aida hits the ground like everyone else around her. People scream. She can tell that the chaos is more intense closer to the cathedral, and she wonders how Marta got out — whether she got out. Aida is suddenly convinced that she will be shot. She clasps her hands over the crown of her head.

An arm grabs her shoulder. Aida lifts both hands and turns from the ground to protect herself, or to accept help if it's the same two women as before. But it's Carlos she sees. Carlos Reyes.

"*Vente!*" he says, and with the sound of bullets firing not far away they run towards one of the old yellow school buses Aida saw earlier. When they get to them, they round one, Carlos puts his arm over her and they press against the side of the vehicle. Ahead of them and behind, others also take shelter this way.

Carlos turns Aida's head left, then right to look her over. Behind him, people are running. He wipes her mouth with his hand and Aida realizes she must still have vomit there. Carlos pulls out a handkerchief and, using a small bottle of water, wets it and ties it around her face, covering her nose and mouth. "When I say so, we are going to get up and run to that street corner — over there."

Rat-tat. Aida jumps.

"They're not aiming this far from the cathedral," says Carlos. "They're mostly scattering them. Take a few more breaths," he says, and nods at her as if answering all the questions she might come up with.

Aida looks more closely at him. Carlos is dressed incongruously again, this time, in a collared shirt and thin sweater. He doesn't fit. Doesn't want to.

"*Vamos!*" he says, and takes her hand.

Aida goes with him, but there's a catch, something off about the way it feels to hold Carlos's hand — the one with the scar. The feeling is so strong she momentarily lets it go. "I have to get to Marta," she says, turning back to see what's happening at the cathedral, if Marta is still on the steps. But it's hopeless. There are too many layers of people and clouds of smoke.

Carlos finds her hand again and pulls. On they go, stopping and starting, out of the plaza and down the same set of streets Aida came in on, all of which are packed. They move around people, ducking flying objects (people are breaking glass, it seems) and hiding briefly in doorways. "*Vamos*, Aida. *Vamos*," Carlos says every so often, and Aida does her best not to lag.

And then they're at a locked door and Carlos is banging loudly, saying his name. They wait, listening as a helicopter makes a huge racket flying low along the next lane, moving towards the crowd. Carlos has just put down his fist and is turning to leave when the door opens a crack.

A moment later it's over. Aida is in the same café where she and Carlos had their first meeting. Rows of clean glasses behind the gleaming bar. Two clients crouching in one corner below window level, puffing nervously on their cigarettes. The thick door closes and the sounds beyond it, of the helicopter and approaching sirens and people yelling, are muffled. The person who's let them in, a big man, brings a large bucket of water and a rag, and Carlos starts washing Aida's face and her neck. But she pulls the rag from him and finishes the job herself. Then she drinks some water that the big man offers her before he goes to check on his customers. Tears pour involuntarily down Aida's cheeks.

"I have to leave," says Carlos. "I am very late. One of the family members, Sylvie, called the cell number I gave you all. I came to find you. But I can't stay. You'll be alright. Don Felipe will give you a phone. The others will be worried."

Aida shakes her head. Her vague distrust of Carlos has burrowed in somewhere very deep. Of course he's going. He will never give her his time. She no longer even wants it. She starts to cry in earnest, and Carlos looks away like he's seen something ugly.

"I should not have spoken to you the way I did before. I'm

going to do something important," he says, then pauses. "I have to repair things."

Leaning against the cool bar, Aida feels strong revulsion building inside. There is no repair for the damage Carlos has caused. She reaches into her skirt pocket and slides an envelope towards him across the polished wood. "Before you go," she says.

Carlos looks at the letter with genuine fear. He starts shaking his head. "Aida, no."

"Okay. Then I'll do it," she says, grabbing it back, pulling the sheets from the envelope so roughly both nearly tear. She scans the text for the final section of the letter she read to Carlos at the mall. She withheld it before, from him and from André, out of embarrassment and, she thinks now, because she didn't really want to understand Danielle's reasons for abandoning her. "Nine months before I was born," she says, then reads the passage aloud.

Back in camp, neither Isidrio nor I breathed a word about what happened in the village, but people knew I never made it to the literacy centre for my story. They must've. No one asked me anything.

Then last night I was alone in the spot I told you about before, reading with my flashlight, when I heard a noise. My heart almost stopped when I saw it was Adrian. I wanted to say the words: murderer, traitor.

He didn't ask if I was okay. Didn't talk about the incursion or that kid. He said we must always be willing to be truthful about our mistakes. I couldn't tell if he meant his "mistake" of having shot the boy, or my mistake for being there. Did he want me to admit I'd seen him?

I started shaking. He put his arm around me. I froze. Then, without another word, he started to feel me all over. He looked me right in the

*eye, but it was like he was staring at a blank wall. He took off my
clothes and had sex with me. The whole time I was like a statue.
And then he got up and left.*

*Now it's almost morning and I haven't slept at all, and I'm writing
this letter fast because my flashlight battery's dying. I think you will
never want to speak to me again after reading this, but I had to tell
someone. Don't be mad. Please. I thought I loved him.*

DB

Aida glares at Carlos. "You did this."

Carlos's handsome face comes apart and puts itself back together
more than once, the performer trying to overcome the guilty party.

The man from the café, Felipe, approaches, excusing himself,
saying he's checked and it looks safe for Carlos to leave from the
service door.

Pale now, sweating, Carlos nods, then leans towards Aida and
whispers, "I would like to know you, Aida." He stays close a moment, so close that he could touch her face or lay a palm on her
shoulder, maybe add something more, but probably knowing he
has no right to contact, to any claims to her affection. Then he
leans away, passes into a back room and is gone.

After a moment, Felipe asks if Aida would like to use the phone
to call home. How can he know she doesn't have one?

4:00 PM. Mil Sueños *mine*

Manuel Sobero normally dislikes this time of day. The guards' shift change, followed by routine paperwork, keep him from what he most enjoys: sitting in his office where he can plan in peace. But this evening is unique. He has an unexpectedly pleasant task to perform. "It's not possible for you to see *Señor* Wall," he says, stepping closer to the front window of the mine's reception area, his phone pressed to his ear. He can just glimpse the car Carlos Reyes has arrived in. It's parked at the main gate of the mine. "You'll speak to me."

"You made Mitch change the plan," says Carlos, on the other end of the line.

"In fact, I didn't. You did."

Sobero watches as the door to the car flies open. The two guards standing nearby hike up their rifles. "You forget yourself," says Sobero.

The car door stays open, but Carlos makes no move to get out. "Mitch has to override the Thursday deadline," he says. "He has to let the exhumation go on."

Sobero laughs out loud. Mitch's assistant appears where the reception room abuts the main hallway, but Sobero sends her back with a pointed finger, as he did a few minutes ago. He isn't finished.

"If this is about the documents implicating Marta Ramos," says Carlos, "my source says he can get more evidence that will prove definitely that she's involved."

Sobero clicks his tongue admiringly. "You would do this? For *Señor* Wall? How kind."

"Put Mitch on."

"Yes, such a friend you've been. Coming all this way! You must have rushed from the capital. One of my colleagues watched you leave your office and walk to the cathedral just a few hours ago. You have been so generous with your time, really since the day you met *Señor* Wall. You remember that day, don't you?"

Silence from Carlos's end.

"I'll remind you. You gave a speech to which, at the last minute, *Señor* Wall happened to receive an invitation. You used the example of this mine to illustrate your point. Very flattering. And yet, it's odd that this example came to you when you had a different one in the written version of the speech — an Australian water filtration company, I believe. Truly odd. Almost as if you changed the example on purpose to create a pretext for getting to know *Señor* Wall."

Carlos swears under his breath.

"I have to say I was surprised to learn how little some of the employees at your *Consejo Policial* are paid, *Señor* Reyes. I had no trouble finding one who was open to incentives. And your office has many interesting files. Hard copies of all your official speeches."

Sobero hears Carlos's engine start up. "Wait," he says. "Don't you want to know how *Señor* Wall reacted when I gave him the original version of the speech? The one that had nothing whatsoever to do with him?"

The door to the car slams closed and a moment later Sobero sees the vehicle backing away. The phone line remains open.

"We know where they are," says Sobero, nearly shouting now, tasting success. "And I am the only one who can do anything about it. The police, they are still sitting on their hands because of the Canadian Ambassador who, you'll agree, has been very troublesome to them."

Sobero pivots from the window to face Mitch Wall, who is sitting in the receptionist's chair, a fist to his lips. "Curious that your friendship with *Señor* Wall has coincided so closely with this crisis," Sobero says to Carlos. "Could it be that you knew someone was intending to ask for the mine to be closed? That you wanted to influence *Señor* Wall's decision in favour of meeting that demand?"

Carlos hangs up on him. Sobero holds out the phone to Mitch in a gesture of mock helplessness. "I guess now we will never know."

WEDNESDAY
APRIL 13

11:15 AM. *Main Road*, Mil Sueños *mine site*

Dear Mr. Wall,

We who have gathered peacefully outside your gates demand that you extend the deadline you have imposed on the exhumation at El Pico. We believe that if there are human remains on this land resulting from a crime committed during El Salvador's civil war, they must be brought up in the name of our country's collective memory.

We want to acknowledge your decision to impose a stop-work order this week, including an end to blasting, and we call your attention to the silence and peace this pause has brought throughout the municipality. We thank you and our children thank you for the respite. We hope we can now enter into more meaningful dialogue about the mine's responsibilities towards local people.

Sincerely,
Concerned Citizens of Los Pampanos

Marta holds the note out to the guard who is preventing her from stepping from the bus. "Give it to the boss." The guard looks at the note like it's made of uranium, but calls back to one of many others manning the roadblock. Each is dressed like him, with the stupid MaxSeguro logo of a breached lock stitched on the upper sleeves of their black shirts. One guard breaks from the line, trots up, retrieves the note, turns and runs past the barrier all the way down the road to the front gate of the *Mil Sueños* mine.

Ten minutes later, Marta is still perched on the bus's lowest step, still staring at the first guard's puffed chest, when something beeps on his lapel. He presses a button there, then puts a finger to his miniature earpiece. He nods and steps aside.

It takes Marta a moment to realize this means they can pass. *"Adelante!"* she says to the driver, and everyone on the bus cheers. Except the Canadians, Marta notices. Sitting at the back, they've been completely silent since the convoy was stopped.

Marta fibbed. It's an old trick — but a good one — to throw off police and hired agitators, at least for a while, by announcing a false gathering point for a rally. It works best if you can make sure the media find out otherwise, which of course she did. The *Río Rico* is nice, but *Mil Sueños* is the only place worthy of continuing the demonstrations.

Yes, she's afraid. Of more police, tear gas, rubber bullets, arrests. Two people ended up with gunshot wounds yesterday, scores more beaten, handfuls unlawfully detained. But every one of the people on these buses has chosen to come here of their own volition. They're used to risk. As for Marta, she doesn't believe in destiny, but if she did, she'd say she's going to outlive all the Hernándezes and MaxSeguros. In return, she just has to keep working, organizing. She'll do it for as long as she can find anyone willing to be organized. Today she has six buses' worth. So what if MaxSeguro has somehow gotten wind of her plan? The police will too, sooner or later.

Now, as they clear away the roadblock and the lead bus moves forward, approaching NorthOre's main gate, followed by the rest of the convoy, Marta waits for what Manuel Sobero has planned for them next. A line of guards is converging at a slow, military-style jog, taking up places along the road, to the east and west of the main entrance. Yet another set of guards has formed a pen around the journalists who, Marta sees, have already arrived. Two satellite trucks, camerapersons and their gear, photographers and individual reporters with notebooks and cell phones are clumped together, looking frustrated and hot.

The buses go right past them and park further east, on the south shoulder of the road. Marta takes her bullhorn and gets off, seeing the other senior committee members do the same at the doors of the other buses. She announces that everyone will have to work together to ensure an orderly demonstration. As people step out, she asks for volunteers to set up a makeshift cooking facility; of course, only women respond. As she speaks, the reporters come alive, hurrying to film or write notes about the protesters' movements. The guards keep pace with them but take pains not to interfere with all these cameras around. Manuel Sobero isn't that stupid.

Marta turns and sees that Aida Byrd is standing at the top of the bus steps, ahead of the other family members. Marta gestures for them to descend. She really didn't expect the families to come — Aida least of all. But last night, Ralph called to say that they'd taken a group vote and wanted to be here. Poor souls. They look like they fear an ambush. Marta leads them to a slightly shaded spot on the gravel shoulder, where they pass around drinking water. Paco stands nearby, as Marta has asked him to.

"*Hola*," she says, hugging each of the Canadians in turn, nodding at Aida to please translate. "A change from the plaza in San

Salvador, no? When the demonstration is over, Pedro will take you into Los Pampanos. There's a family in town that you will billet with."

Sylvie and Benoît hold hands and force smiles.

"You really going to camp out here?" Ralph asks.

"Of course. This is normal for us," says Marta in English, smiling, then switches back to her own language. "Aida, can I speak with you?" She steers the girl away as the others watch. "I was so worried yesterday." It's true. Marta was frantic until Neela called with the news that Aida had returned by taxi from the demonstration to the guest house, unharmed.

Aida keeps her eyes averted.

"Those documents they have about me. They're not real."

"I know."

Marta sighs, surprised. Aida has been suspicious of her from day one, but Marta has tried not to interfere with whatever process she has needed to make up her own mind. "You weren't hurt?" she asks, checking Aida over. She looks fine, as put together as always, her light hair tucked neatly behind her ears. Maybe more fidgety than usual — biting a fingernail. She seems to be on the verge of unburdening herself, trying to decide whether to speak her mind. "You were really in the thick of it."

"Some people helped me," says Aida.

Marta smiles. Aida is giving her a half-truth of some kind, but she won't probe. She feels great sympathy towards Aida Byrd. She has been foolish, but daring too, in her own way. An essential combination in a young woman. There's still the self-confidence bordering on arrogance that Marta noted from the start, but it seems to have been productively troubled. "Some people helped me too," Marta says, smiling. "Our members have a lot of experience with these kinds of situations."

Aida manages her own weak smile. "I'm sure they do."

"So you'll stay with me again? When we go back to San Salvador?" Marta asks, but doesn't have time to wait for the answer, because now several reporters approach, and the Committee needs every bit of this coverage.

Aida nearly says "Yes." Or more: "I'm sorry about your husband," or "I heard you call my name." But none of it feels necessary. There'll be time later. Instead, Aida tries to sort through her feelings about being here. Sensorial bombardment. That's what it's been so far. The surprise meeting place for this demonstration. The two-hour ride from San Salvador on that dirty bus. The ugliness of the mine, which, really, Aida can only glimpse behind the massive fence that extends as far as she can see, but that seems like a wasteland of broken earth. Nothing in Aida's experience can help her here. She can grasp the business side of running the mine, but she has no context to understand what's going on right now behind NorthOre's gates. She doesn't know about digging up bones. Until now, she has genuinely preferred to let the past be.

Meanwhile, moments from the demonstration keep returning to her like clips from a film. People scurrying. The sound of guns. The look on Carlos's face when she slid the envelope down the bar. Riding back to the rooming house in the taxi, her ears buzzing. Waiting, weakened, for Neela's call, for her to say whether Marta had made it out of there alive.

Today, her host has swept her up again, this time depositing her on a distant planet, the Salvadoran countryside. Aida's brief glimpse of the famed town of Los Pampanos didn't make much of an impression. It was bleak. Low, cement-brick buildings jumbled together on either side of an insignificant stretch of highway. But what made it strange for Aida was her certainty that the town is part of her now. All of El Salvador is. She was made here, by two parents. Danielle tried to reduce that number to zero from the start, substituting in her own parents, and later claiming to Aida that the man who fathered her had been nobody, that he'd died. Aida gets Danielle's choices more than before. Danielle had her reasons for wanting to remove herself; she'd been an idealist and was played for a fool. She took Adrian out of the equation because he's the one who played her. Still, she lied. And still, Aida has managed to have two parents. She wonders how she'll react when — if — she sees her mother again, whether she can forgive Danielle for her selfishness. At the same time, she understands in a new light her own reasons for being here. She needed to apologize too. For trying to hurt her mother back all these years, for making it her business to keep Danielle at arm's length and ignoring the toll it's taken on them both. She has failed just as badly as her mother at rigging the numbers and making the past nil.

An old woman approaches and hands Aida a faded scarf, indicating that she should cover her head from the sun. Aida accepts it, pulling it tightly over her head, then returns to rubbing the cut on her shin and thinking about the new dynamics introduced into her life by having a living father. A bad man. A good man. Adrian. Carlos. Gone now to repair the unrepairable. How?

"You think we're nuts to be here?" says Ralph, who's come to sit beside Aida on the gravel. The way he says it is funny and Aida can't help but laugh a little. She's assumed they've been in some kind of fight since she suggested that Marta's arrest might have been justified. She nods her assent, widening her eyes for effect.

"Me too." Ralph takes a swig from a dusty water bottle. He has on his signature dark shades and a red kerchief tied over his substantial hair. "But where else we gonna be?"

Aida still says nothing. She doesn't know where. Part of her wants to blurt out what she knows about Carlos, which she hasn't told anyone yet — not even André. But it feels too strange to say aloud. Too soap opera. Her own certainty about him arose so quietly she didn't even notice it reach the surface until she held his hand as they ran from the cathedral.

"I'm not really impressed with the embassy," Ralph goes on. "They said, 'Stay in the city. Don't go to this, don't do that.' Forget it. This makes more sense."

"Not to me," says Aida, looking back at the guards along the fence. Beyond them, in the distance, are scrubby hills, and behind those, actual mountains. Then she catches herself. "But yeah, I'd rather be here than sitting alone in San Salvador."

Ralph clears his throat. "If it's true there's bodies in there, they should get them out. We've had that situation at home."

Aida assumes he's referring to the kind of conflict between golf courses and traditional grave sites that occasionally pops up on the news. Until now, Aida has tended to dismiss these sorts of claims. Now, Ralph's words provoke a strange feeling of regret, for stories she hasn't read carefully enough, at the knowledge that much has been lost while she's been busy looking away.

"Anyways," Ralph says, pushing his sunglasses up his nose, "Benoît brought some sandwiches from the hostel. You want one?"

Though the white-bread sandwich looks decidedly unappetizing, Aida takes half. She wants Ralph to stay with her and to keep talking.

"Excuse me."

Alejandro Reverte looks up. He's been so immersed in his work he hasn't noticed anyone approaching. A big man stands at the site perimeter, accompanied by an armed guard. The man has his hands shoved into the pockets of pressed pants and wears a white hardhat with a green NorthOre logo stenciled on the front.

Reverte stands and starts moving towards him, but his assistant walks up with the latest status sheets. Reverte stops to quickly review and sign them.

"Excuse me," the man repeats, more impatiently, and Reverte, who is accustomed to people breathing down his neck, understands that whoever this is won't go away. He winds along one of the paths they've cleared for movement in and out of the dig site.

"Mitch Wall, CEO," the man says, extending a chunky, freckled hand. "You're on my property."

Señor CEO looks uncomfortable under his helmet, his grinning face blotchy and red. It's as hot as it's been every day so far. Reverte's used to it. This guy isn't. Reverte takes the moist palm and smiles coolly. Ownership does not impress him. Neither do mines. It's not the big holes in the ground he's interested in, but the small, careful ones. But due to his life of conducting digs under all kinds of circumstances — with guns pointed at him, politicians defaming him, local press insinuating that his work is bogus — he's learned that of everyone he makes nervous and angry, landowners have a special place because they are also, in their hearts, embarrassed, and their bluster, which covers this fact from themselves, is comical. This keeps him smiling as he gives the CEO's hand a hard shake. "Alejandro Reverte," he says.

Wall looks a little disconcerted by the enthusiasm. "I wanted to introduce myself and see what kind of progress you're making.

We're going to need you off the expansion site relatively soon," he says. He could be speaking to his own child.

"Yes, the deadline. That gives us today, all night — we have flood lights — and tomorrow still."

"Yes, but. . . I wanted to —"

"We are just beginning," says Reverte, interrupting. "Normally, we have several days, even weeks, just to choose an ideal site. Normally, families of the deceased are permitted to watch and to help us. Your security people have refused to let anyone through. We can only go so fast. We cannot afford interruptions."

"How do they know where to look?" says Wall, changing the subject. He looks peeved to have been reduced to an interruption, but also curious, Reverte can see, as he watches a team of local men turning up small shovelfuls of the reddish, dry earth under the tent they've erected over the upper quadrant of the dig site.

Reverte follows Mitch's eyes over to his labourers. "*Despacio!*" he calls, seeing the speed at which they're removing the soil and gesturing to them to please be as gentle as possible, even with the deadline pressure. The men immediately slow their hands. Reverte knows more than one of them probably had family members disappear during this country's war. Which is why the skill level of local hires is never important. They nearly always want things done just so.

"We have that map they sent," says Reverte, addressing *Señor* CEO again. "But usually, as I say, we have more to go on. Our last project — in Iraq — we had exact coordinates. Those were recent burials, mind you. Very systematic." He pauses, returning to a set of memories he knows the CEO will want to know nothing about.

"Can I see it — the map?"

Reverte scrutinizes him. There is very little to lose in satisfying the curiosity of local authorities, and much to gain, Reverte knows. They tend to be as awed as everyone by his work. He calls his assistant back over and has her hand Mitch the single piece of paper sealed into a see-through plastic cover.

"We think that stone over there is this one on the map," Reverte explains, pointing at a rough shape on the homemade diagram. "We measure along a straight line up the slope to where that southernmost peg is." Reverte watches as the CEO tries to make sense of the poorly rendered map that was faxed anonymously to the Canadian embassy Monday night. An arrow points right and upwards from the stone, the words *"aprox. 50 pies"* written along its trajectory. Where the arrow ends, there's another drawing, a crude tree, with the words *"arból de fuego"* written below it. Near that tree is an X, marking the spot where the team should dig. "Unfortunately, there are no instructions about how high he means for us to go uphill from the stone, just the distance," says Reverte. He runs his finger across the brief typed instructions on the bottom half of the page, reading them aloud for Wall — who knows if *Señor* CEO reads Spanish? " 'The grave will be a 15-min walk straight uphill from the site of what was once Ixtán, on the western side of El Pico.' "

Reverte shakes his head. "Of course, we might have guessed wrong. The stone we found could have been moved here recently when your company built this road extension. The tree the map refers to was probably cut down for firewood years ago. Luckily, one of our workers from Los Pampanos, Lionel, at least remembers where Ixtán was. There isn't anything left of it — as you know. One of our senior team members was kind enough to walk the fifteen minutes, up and down, four times, from where Lionel pointed us, to estimate an approximate location. You see why our work takes time."

"Well," says Mitch. He now looks positively faint with the heat. "I guess I came up here to say that likely this is all a figment of a deranged man's imagination. No one has any business taking any of it seriously."

Reverte stares at him hard. He doesn't mind a challenge. His never-ending dig in Guatemala — that's a challenge. Negligible supplies. Very little money. No help, except from unskilled family members, who've at times been too afraid of retribution to identify gravesites where they absolutely know relatives are buried. And constant bureaucratic and police interference. But there, he's had the necessary time. This assignment is far less reasonable. Three days is laughable. And they've been treated like prisoners from the minute their van pulled up to the *Mil Sueños* gate. Especially by the mine's head of security, a rat-like little creature who took time out of his busy schedule to threaten Reverte directly. "I have friends in the Guatemalan military who would enjoy paying greater attention to you when you return — if I call," he said through his rodent teeth. Of course, he is only the heavy. The final word rests with *Señor* CEO.

"I always take my work seriously, as I'm sure you do," says Reverte, shaking away a mounting rage. In reality, snooping capitalists and insecure men with guns only make him more eager to find whatever he can in the earth and place it on public display. For Reverte, exhumations are the true language of justice, wordless but undeniable. Cruelties do not decompose. They can be hidden, lied about, covered by the earth's incessant sedimentation, by laziness, by denial and fear. But they're there, underneath. And Reverte knows how to speak to them, how to coax them out so that they have to say what they really are, what they've really done. He is exhilarated at the thought of helping something emerge from NorthOre's property, which he knows *Señor* CEO is busy tearing apart for totally different reasons, to unearth wealth, to try to erase the land's memory, cut its tongue.

Wall looks ready to leave, but now he snaps back around. "It's senseless!" he yells. "If you knew the kinds of lies that have been involved in this case. I am not the bad guy, believe me. I am responsible for letting you be here at all." He points a finger in the general direction of the dig. Both the team members and the local hires have stopped working and are staring at his raised voice.

Reverte puts out his bottom lip and nods in acknowledgement of this generosity, then picks up his trowel and returns down the marked path to within the dig's parameter, putting the small blade in the dirt to cast a little of it in Mitch's direction.

After Reverte's assistant politely reclaims the map from him, Wall stands there a minute longer, unsatisfied until, finally, he signals for his guard to follow and goes back down the road towards wherever it is a man like him prefers to spend his time.

Danielle is back in Toronto. Aida and Antoine are set to marry, but her invitation names only a date and time, not the place of the ceremony, so she's on the subway, guessing which stop is hers, frustrated by endless delays, wearing an uncomfortable and un-flattering outfit of her daughter's choosing. She's retying the strap on one of her too-tight high heels when blood begins to pool at her feet. It fills the subway car, rising to her armpits. She tries to scream, but no sound comes out. The blood is pushing past her lips when the car begins to shake. Someone has her by the shoulder.

Danielle blinks. Pepe's palm is over her mouth. He signals for her to get up. She rises, trying to shake off a feeling of horror as she steps over the rest of her group, all asleep, then past Rita, who is sitting, wide awake but refusing eye contact. The reality that Antoine is dead and buried somewhere behind them, that they've left him there and walked away, returns to Danielle like the taste of blood.

After the shooting, Pepe ordered everyone moved out of sight of Antoine's body. The hostages protested, crying and refusing to get up. Cristóbal took Pierre by the arms and lifted him forcibly. After that, the others followed. They carried their backpacks and tarps like sacks of stones and went into the trees in the same direction from which the bullet that killed their friend had come. All of them were sweaty and shaky. Rita was especially dirty, her balaclava torn on one side, revealing a pale bit of forehead. Her hands tied behind her, she kept her eyes on the ground. Delmi and Cristóbal held a steady watch over everyone, Cristóbal's mask taking on a grim flatness as he stared at his wife in plain disappointment.

Early in the afternoon Pierre became hysterical. Half lying on the ground, he started grabbing at the earth and weeds, pulling up random handfuls and mumbling in French about Antoine. He was only calmed by a lot of effort from Tina, who gently persuaded him to sit back down, putting her head on his shoulder and an arm around his waist and rocking him. After a time, she reached her free hand out and clasped Martin's wrist. Martin let her hold him that way as he prayed aloud. In turn, he reached over and put his free hand on Danielle's back.

Danielle had become so unaccustomed to being offered physical support that she jumped, but then relaxed some. They all cried together, knowing Pepe had moved them so that he could bury Antoine. He'd refused any help, which Danielle offered on the group's behalf. And so they had to wait, watching the sun drift across the sky and fall, eventually growing less visible to one another in the darkness.

When Pepe finally returned it was so dark only his bulky outline was visible. A stubby Grim Reaper. *"Cinco minutos,"* he said to Cristóbal, who went about getting everyone into line.

Danielle could see that for Pierre, leaving was worse than knowing that his closest friend was dead. It was punishment. She watched as he called upon all his strength just to get up. She and the others helped, easing on his pack and sticking close until he found his feet.

They hiked all night, as usual, but more slowly than before. Each focused on the physical labour of their nighttime, fugitive life. They were allowed a longer rest in the middle, but it felt superfluous. There would be no whispering now and no escape plans to excite or worry anyone.

Just as Danielle started to notice gritty light opening across her field of vision, the predawn set to turn blue, they reached the new campsite — an abandoned shack with crumbling earthen brick walls and no roof. Cristóbal had everyone wait outside, shivering and fatigued, as he quickly fashioned several beams from tree branches, spacing them evenly across the top of the structure, then covering them with bows, as they'd seen him do before, ensuring no one would notice them from above. Finally, the hostages were ordered inside, where each fell into their fitful sleep.

"We'll be over there," Pepe says to Cristóbal. He pushes Danielle behind the shoulder to hurry her out the doorway and about fifteen feet away, but still within sight. No more leaving Cristóbal and Delmi alone with Rita.

To her surprise, Pepe pulls out the papers Danielle assumed had been lost before the shooting, the ones she'd been writing on, and thrusts them at her along with a pen. When he speaks, his voice is as dull as the first grey light of day. "Write what I say."

Danielle physically aches with resentment. "We all need to bathe," she says.

"There is inadequate water here for that. I want you to write."

"We need time to mourn our friend." What's the worst he'll do to her for talking now? Hit her? Truss her up like Rita? These feel diminished as punishments. Danielle realizes for the first time how much Pepe needs her. For her language and her writing skills — maybe more. As a sounding board. It makes her brave. "There should be a ceremony. It's only right."

Behind his mask, Pepe's eyes roll in a strange pattern, as if he can't take in the visual of an open-air funeral for someone he's so recently killed. A beautiful young man. An innocent. "I can consider this later," he all but grunts. "Now, write."

Danielle wants to scream. How can he still care about ancient history? How could he leave Antoine back there? She's replayed the shooting over and over. She wants to pity Pepe the way she did before, but she can't feel anything about what he's done except confusion. Why? Why has he really taken them hostage? Maybe, she thinks, feeling ill at the prospect, it's as simple as the fact that

Pepe was trained to distill everything into violence. He never had the chance to exploit a different range of reactions. What else could you expect from a wild animal? Then again, maybe Pepe is just evil.

She looks for a place to sit. There is none. So she drops onto her haunches with her back against the nearest tree. Despite her dwindling forces, Danielle's legs have become much stronger since this started, and she feels a shameful glimmer of pride at the thought of how she can now do things she hasn't been able to do since her thirties, at how she might look to others at home if they could see her so transformed.

Pepe sits directly on the ground with his knees ahead of him, his black army boots scuffed and worn-looking, his mask stiff with dried sweat. "This will be the last report. To let people know why we are here."

So. He's going to own up. Finally. Danielle is all ears.

"I described my transition to *la guerrilla*. I believed in what I was doing. The man who saved me, my friend, was admired. But he was like some of the other highly placed combatants. He'd spent a lot of time with *internacionalistas,* had gone on training and fundraising missions to Europe and Africa. He was from a different class. He didn't like to talk to some people. Probably he started to hate the poorest among us. I don't know. I know I saw him one time and he was talking about how this great offensive was going to work, how we would knock out the government and the military, and I had my first moment of distrust.

"I'd been hearing rumours that the very top commanders only wanted to use the offensive as a bargaining chip. They wanted to do just enough damage to shock the military and the elites. Just enough to make them negotiate an end to the war. They were sick of fighting. We all were. But some of them were tired of living like peasants, too. My friend was. He came from a rich family. That never leaves you. Like being poor.

"I had a foreign acquaintance of my own. An Italian photojournalist. Someone respected by the faction. I ran into him when I was travelling near the Guazapa volcano. This was after my mentor had started to take clandestine trips to the capital to prepare for the offensive. The Italian had pictures. He didn't know what to do with them. He was a supporter of our cause and didn't want to publish anything that would hurt us internationally. I looked at these pictures. In them, the man who'd saved my life was in San Salvador. Dressed in civilian clothes, but it was him. He was meeting with an American. CIA, probably.

"I thought no, it's a mistake. I told the Italian that this man was a friend, someone I could talk to. The journalist and I, we had a history. He trusted me. He gave me the photos and his negatives. It didn't matter. I never saw him again. He was killed a few months later.

"I travelled here, to this province, near Los Pampanos, and eventually my mentor came back too. By then I was suspicious. I said to him, 'What you're doing is wrong. You're selling secrets.' He said I was crazy, that I should get my head checked. I said I had proof. He told me it was all part of the plan by Command. But I knew by his eyes that he was lying.

"A week later, some guerrillas came and said I was to come with them. They wouldn't explain why. They took me to the place where the faction handled internal conflicts. Finally I was told I was being charged with treason. They had a witness willing to say I'd been in contact with my old military commanders on the government side, that I'd been working as a double agent. They confiscated all my belongings, including the photos.

"It was him, of course. My old friend. He wanted me gone. By this time, he'd gone underground for good in San Salvador and there was no possibility of contacting him. The punishment for what I'd done was death. They were going to keep me under guard until they made their final decision. I thought I was a goner. I didn't mind so much. But I was sorry that he'd done away with me like that, like I hadn't been worth anything to him.

"Security in those camps was not ideal. It was late in the war. People got lazy in the controlled zones. The good guerrillas were either on the fronts or dead. I was experienced. I got out of the place they were keeping me by overpowering two guards. Just country kids. I retrieved the negatives of those photos, which I had hidden, just in case. But what was I going to do with them? Who would believe me? I'd left both sides of the war. And both sides were everywhere.

"I must be fated to spend time in holes," he says, and Danielle looks up to see if this is meant as a joke. It isn't. Pepe's mouth has a slackness about it that repels humour. "I lived in one again, a large cave. Several weeks underground. I wasn't alone. There were other *campesinos*. They always shared the bits of food they had. You probably met some like this," he says, throwing Danielle a harsh look to make her return to her notes instead of ogling.

"I took what they offered, went to San Miguel and blended in, tried to look like I'd been there for the whole war just praying not to be killed. I had no ID. If they asked me for any, I was a dead man. So I moved and moved again. Survived for two years that way, until I nearly starved.

"The general insurrection was a failure for those of us who'd wanted victory, but it was exactly what my mentor had hoped for: it let both sides sit down and sign off on Peace. They did the deal in Mexico City and the big boys in the *guerrilla* came out of the mountains and formed a political party. It was over. For them. But for many of us it was like an amputation. People who'd been in the mountains since they were seven, who'd been carrying a gun all their lives.

"I was one of those who couldn't claim any benefits in the

government programs. I was nobody. I was not human. I drank so that I would die, but my body wouldn't let me go. . . . Then I met up with Cristóbal — you'll change the name in your story. Call him David. They were handing out meal tickets to dig holes and fill them in again. UN money. The drinking didn't stop, but with him, I could continue.

"I liked the news. I read all about the Truth Commission. The political parties. All about the things they were doing 'for the people.' I saw that a lot of the commanders I'd worked under on the military side, some of the cruelest, were doing very well, starting businesses, private security mostly. On the other side, some of the guerrilla commanders were doing okay, too. The man who'd been my friend was placed in charge of all kinds of things. Cooperative farms. Micro-credit schemes. Then he took his big job overseeing police conduct. Because people trusted the *Comandante*.

"I watched all of it and did nothing. Too drunk. I'd always intended to go to the place where I'd last seen my parents. But I'd been too ashamed. Just when I finally decided I would do it, the mine came. They cleared Ixtán — wiped it out, bought the land the *guerrilla* had won for the people. They installed guards and their big electric fence. You know the rest."

A strange sensation makes Danielle shiver: this really is about the mine. The same gold mine Partners for Justice sent the delegation to observe. Pepe's asking something from the mine; he wants his family acknowledged somehow, or he wants the right to — to what? Visit their grave? But he doesn't even know for certain that they died there. Whatever it is, the mine hasn't conceded to it. Or she'd be home by now. And Antoine would be alive. She suddenly burns with a brand new hatred for a company whose name she can barely remember. North — something. "All of us came here to support the people who want to shut that mine down," she says, gulping air, feeling like she'll hyperventilate. "Why would you choose *us?*"

Pepe's eyes narrow. "What do you think the Committee for the Environment has gained, so far, from people like you? They get visitors all the time. The *jefe* there, at *Mil Sueños,* has never agreed to meet with anyone face to face. Not once. El Pico will be gone in weeks — days. Dynamited. My way was the only way."

Danielle's mind continues to race. "And this man, your friend, who tried to get rid of you, is he still alive? Is our being here connected to him?"

Pepe stands, adjusts his pants.

Danielle senses she's touched on something, though, in reality, the possibility that Pepe might be looking for revenge interests her less than what it means that her capture is directly related to that Canadian-owned mine. She can't wait to tell the others. It might help, might make them feel that there's some meaning in their abduction, in what happened to Antoine.

"You'll write it now. The phone will ring later and I need this done."

"What if these stories don't change anything? What if your demands aren't met?"

Pepe shakes his head. "Write," he mumbles and settles in to watch her do her work, his mask an expanse of gloom.

Danielle tries to hurry through the report, but she keeps getting stuck on Pepe's story and has to start over. The betrayal he's described is so much like her own. Memories return to her from the day in November, 1980, when she handed all her features — a year's worth of writing, her future as a journalist — to her senior contact in the guerrilla faction. He'd been assigned to vet them before she brought them back to Canada for publication, a deal she'd struck at the outset. He took the stories, sealed into a plastic bag, and Danielle never saw them again. He needed time to read them over and recommended that Danielle visit the guerrilla's literacy centre to alleviate her boredom while she waited. He thought he was doing her a favour. But it was on that walk that she saw Adrian murder the boy. Adrian must have made something up afterwards. That she'd gone to that village expressly to undermine the faction. That she was untrustworthy. Danielle's contact wasn't a man who would've been easily fooled. But Adrian had clout. He was convincing. Then, not long after she'd returned to camp, after Adrian had come for her that last time, on a day when a group of *campesinos* was going to be led over the mountain pass to the refugee camps in Honduras, Danielle was informed that she would have to go too. No explanation. Nothing to negotiate. A low-ranking guerrilla simply advised her that her term with the faction was up.

Danielle tries again to leave her own past aside and get through Pepe's, but it ends up taking all afternoon. Pepe pops up every now and then to prod her, swearing and pacing around. The feeling that he has no intention of letting them have a ceremony for Antoine becomes more concrete with the passing hours, which also slows Danielle's hand.

When the phone finally buzzes on Pepe's belt, he answers and hands the phone over. Danielle delivers her text, ad-libbing the end. Then Pepe takes his phone back like it's a part of him, hooking it onto his belt. He lets her return to sit with the others.

Danielle is starving, has missed two meals. She doesn't really care. She's bursting to tell the others about the mine: the company could still concede to whatever Pepe's demands are; they could still be freed. But Cristóbal orders her and Tina to follow Delmi. Everyone freezes with the same question: follow where? They've never been asked to go out alone, just the women, except to bathe, and Pepe said that can't happen here. What else is there to do, alone, out of view? Still ashen with grief, Pierre and Martin stare nervously as Danielle gets back up, then Tina, to trail Delmi out the door of the shack. They walk several minutes in a different direction than Danielle has just been with Pepe. "*Allá*," says Delmi pointing to a tree. Tina looks at Danielle with intense negative anticipation as they step towards it. They both flinch as Delmi tosses something at their feet. "Open those," she says. The women look down. It's a can opener. A stupid can opener. Danielle looks around. There are several cans to one side, really dirty, like they've been dug out of the ground. Tina sees them too, relief smoothing her face. Delmi throws something else: a tied plastic bag. Danielle unknots it. It's filled with rubbery tortillas. Finally, Delmi passes them a stack of plastic plates. All in all, the makings of a very unappetizing meal. But they're only being asked to help assemble it now that Rita is incapacitated. A deep tremor of satisfaction runs through Danielle at this manifestation of Rita's demotion.

Tina works scrupulously to achieve fair distribution of the food, sometimes brushing up against Danielle as she works. Danielle enjoys their physical closeness, the fact that whatever barriers previously existed between them have dropped away. Her mind turns to Aida, to how little real physical contact they've had.

Arriving back at her parents' house after a lengthy transit through Honduras in 1980, Danielle didn't know how to go on. She didn't have the guts to tell them what had happened or to end her pregnancy. After Aida was born her parents were so willing to help that it was easier and easier to let them bring the child her happiness. Danielle occasionally felt a deeper attachment to that small person. It was like sensing something alluring in the distance that she couldn't, or wouldn't grab hold of. The thought of doing so was exhausting. No one blamed her. People saw Danielle and Aida together and figured everything was fine. But they couldn't see the missed connection, that Danielle wasn't making the effort.

They went on for so long that way that the gap between them came to seem natural. Danielle travelled. Worked. Had affairs. Took her time. Then her dad died of a heart attack, less than a year after her mother's last cancer. Danielle rushed to Aida's school to find her in the principal's office sitting beside a terse school counsellor. Aida was barely twelve that year, and Danielle wanted to embrace her, to say and to do the right thing. But Aida's face, still a child's face, forbade it. The counsellor put Danielle through the wringer, tossing judgmental looks her way, calling Social Services and administering all kinds of useless paperwork before letting Aida leave with her. That one moment seemed to establish a no-pass zone between mother and daughter, one that Danielle accepted. The loss of her parents had fixed a border in place. She would have to stay on her side until Aida told her otherwise.

But now, as Tina plops the last portion of beans onto the last plate and hands it to her amiably, Danielle questions her easy assumptions. It wasn't only Aida who was angry that day. Danielle resented her too, for forcing an end to what she had always defined as freedom. To be alone. Come and go. Figure things out slowly, in order, and without too much painful looking back. The shock of knowing they would be together full-time, from there on in, made Danielle claustrophobic. It's not that she didn't love Aida. They didn't even fight much in the first years after that. Instead, silence floated like a laden raincloud through the house Danielle had inherited from her parents — never quite bursting. Aida was practically never around anyway, always in her room, studying, or out adding some achievement or other to her résumé. Things got ugly when she moved out just four years later with her first serious boyfriend. That event marked the beginning of their more vocal period of mutual attack.

But to Danielle it was also a huge relief. She didn't admit it. Not in her failed attempt at therapy with Aida. Not even to Neela. In

a way, taking herself out of the country after leaving those letters on the dining room table was another act of evasion. She's
given Aida access to a partial truth. Danielle did plan to explain,
when she got back, why she lied about Adrian being dead, how it
would've been cruel to tell a child that she had a liar and a killer
for a father when he was still out there, unabashedly alive. But
picturing Aida reading through the letters, perhaps even pitying
her, makes Danielle feel wretched and regretful.

Tina must sense it. She puts her hand on Danielle's back. Delmi
frowns at her under her mask, but Tina leaves the hand there
defiantly.

"I think I've really been a shit to my daughter."

Tina nods. "How old is she?"

"Your age." Danielle catches herself. "Wait. How old are you?"

"Twenty-eight."

"Oh. She's younger then. How old's your brother?"

Tina gives her a strange look. "Twenty-four," she says, warily,
as if she thinks Danielle might have another motive, but also
obviously happy to speak of her sibling.

"Aida turns twenty-four in August. She'll be in Paris by then."

Delmi doesn't intercede in this exchange. Her sister's failure
seems to have subdued her. It's like she doesn't know where her
safety is anymore now that Rita isn't controlling her and Pepe has
no time for her.

"Tina," Danielle says, as Delmi prods them back to a standing
position with their arms full of plates, then marches them towards the campsite. "I think I know why we're here." Danielle is
relieved to say it, her eagerness to share the news returning. "It's
about that gold mine."

Tina starts to ask what Danielle's talking about, but Delmi
hushes them: Pepe is visible through the trees. Danielle and Tina
hurry forward to place the food in front of everyone. Then they

sit, Danielle across from Pierre, on the packed earthen floor of the abandoned shed. She eats quickly, waiting for a moment when Pepe will be out of earshot.

Ten minutes later, he finally steps out with Cristóbal. "Pierre," says Danielle.

Pierre turns lethargically towards her. His hair clings to his sweaty, pale face. His slender nose seems tragic now.

"I think this has all happened because he's against the mine — the one we were going to see. In Los Pampanos. He wants to find out what happened to his family. They were killed in the war."

Pierre takes the information in without reaction, like Danielle's words have seeped through his skin rather than being captured by his ears.

"But PJA's against the mine too," says Martin, overhearing. "We're on the same side?"

"Sort of. He knows. But this still gives us something — we could convince him. Slowly. Or the mine meets his demands."

Pierre finally enters the exchange with two half-nods. The first signs of life. Then, in the lowest voice, like a faint whistle, he says, "It's good that it's not for money."

Tina and Martin both nod back. It's a strangely beautiful moment, like a fragment of a eulogy. Everyone seems to analyze the nugget of information Danielle has passed on, along with Pierre's comment on it, and to extract from these the same faint hope.

An hour later, they leave and begin walking into the descending night. The moon is now nearly full, strong enough that the kidnappers haven't bothered with the LEDs. Danielle follows Martin. She can see him clearly enough, the way his arms swing heavily, the outline of his hair.

They seem to be on an actual trail, and for a time Danielle doesn't have to concentrate as much as usual on her aching feet.

Her mind wanders again to thoughts of Aida. Danielle tries to conceive of a plan, a concrete set of steps that will bring them closer. She is considering the words she should start with — something straightforward, "I missed you" or "I'm sorry" — when she hears a voice up ahead, somewhere off to the side.

"Stop where you are," yells a man, in Spanish.

Martin's swinging arms go rigid. Danielle looks into the dark black where the sound is coming from. Nothing. The moonlight can't reach far enough into the trees. Maybe she's fallen asleep standing up. But when she turns, there are Cristóbal and Tina, behind her, Cristóbal's gun glinting, real as anything. He has his hand on Tina's back, pushing her protectively towards the ground.

Danielle turns towards Martin and chokes out the words "Get down!"

"*Pepe*," says the voice, urgent now. "I'm above you. In range. Put up the rifle. Your pistol too. Throw them in front of you. Same for the others."

Pepe. If this is the police, how do they know his name? She used "Enrique" in all her reports. And if they know his identity, why aren't there more sounds? Helicopters? Troops moving through the trees? A torturous silence follows, each moment vibrating with unnerving, unanswerable questions like these, from hostages and kidnappers alike. Then the man's voice comes again, eerie as it snaps the intensity like cutters through a wire. "Don't move."

Danielle has visions of another member of her group being shot, of someone else not getting up the way Antoine did not. She fears it could be her. She hears herself promise to embrace Aida if she makes it out alive. Truly embrace her. She wishes she were young again, that it was 1980 and that she could start over. She would still come to this country. But she would do things differently. She would accept people as they are.

"The photos will go out. I won't stop them." It's Pepe, screaming back.

The only photos Danielle can think of are those Pepe spoke of in his last report, the photos of his mentor selling secrets. But why mention these to the police?

"They don't matter to me anymore," the man yells back.

And then, after yet another strained silence, Pepe, who is ahead, as always, maybe twenty feet from Danielle, amazingly, raises both his weapons in the air and throws them to the ground. They barely clatter.

He's giving in. Danielle can't quite believe it.

"*Primo, Delmi,*" says Pepe.

A noise makes Danielle turn. Tina is pressing herself into the base of a pine tree as Cristóbal, his ever-present hat on a slight tilt, starts walking forward. A metallic clunk as his gun comes into contact with Pepe's.

Delmi does the same, then goes to stand beside her brother-in-law, unarmed.

Danielle hears a loud crash and snap as someone hurries towards them through the trees. And then he's standing ahead of her, still in shadow, between the guns and the kidnappers. He has a rifle pointed at them. "Someone come here and pick these up."

At first Danielle can't imagine doing it. She isn't going to touch Pepe's guns. But no one else moves. They haven't understood the Spanish — or don't want to. Danielle pushes herself up, pine needles stuck to her palms. Slowly, shakily, she walks past Martin, then Pierre, and finally Rita, who is standing stock still with her wrists tied. Danielle gets so close she can see the familiar guns clearly and Pepe's eyes staring back at her. Delmi whimpers.

"Hand them out," the man says, this time in good English. And Danielle looks more carefully at who's talking, who has come here to rescue them. He wears fatigues and a cap over his thick hair.

She recognizes something. The stance, or the shape of him. She picks up a gun, which is much heavier than she expected, then moves backwards, still facing the man, until she's reached Pierre. He grabs it from her with eager hands and she returns to the pile. She does the same twice more, giving Tina one and Martin two, keeping only Pepe's handgun for herself. All the while Danielle has the sensation of floating above the scene, like it isn't for real. Soon, she will be riding the subway to Aida and Antoine's imaginary wedding.

When the group is armed and Pepe and his crew stand defenseless, the man steps up, the moonlight illuminating his features.

"*Hola, Daniela.*"

"Adrian."

"Carlos," he corrects her, warily. "We must walk."

THURSDAY
APRIL 14

12:30 AM. *7 KM northeast of the hamlet of Zarcero, Morazán*

They head downhill, gravity finally on their side, kidnappers in the lead, followed by Pierre and Martin, who hold their guns the way the man named Carlos has showed them, except badly. Pierre's face is set in hatred, his gun up high as if he will shoot at the slightest provocation. Martin follows, hauling his two weapons more tentatively. Then comes Tina, who lets her rifle hang loosely on its strap across her back. She doesn't look like someone who's been so ill. She has untied her long hair and it swings in thick sections. If they're confused about how Danielle knows Carlos, how Carlos knows Pepe, none of them asks. They're afraid of upsetting the balance of things. Danielle, a few steps behind Tina, knows the questions will come later. Right now, Carlos is at her side, walking in step.

"I don't understand," she finally gets the courage to say.

"He blackmailed me. But it's not important. We need to walk to —"

"Why?"

"I hurt him." Carlos is older, of course. But still handsome. And the same. Truly the same. Danielle feels a sexual energy begin to take hold, despite herself. She tries to focus on what Carlos is saying. And then, what must have been floating in her mind as a possibility for some time clarifies: Carlos was Pepe's mentor, the one who sentenced him to his life after the war. All of which happened long after Danielle was sent home, but nonetheless involves her, involves everyone here. The sexual energy seeps away and Danielle is left with a hollow feeling and the knowledge that she will never be able to make this man understand what he did to her, to Pepe, or to Antoine.

Nor can she bring herself to admit to Adrian — Carlos — that he was the real object of her return to El Salvador, that she'd long fantasized about a cathartic encounter in which she would tell him exactly how he'd ruined her. She cannot find her voice to say that he fathered her child. The imaginary version of these revelations, of the confrontation she'd pictured, dies so suddenly she has to struggle to find any words at all. "Why did you do this? Intervene this way?"

"I had to."

Danielle considers his meaning. "You're the one who took my reports. On the phone. You're the contact. Did you know where we were? How did you know?"

"I had a signal, yes." Carlos is walking briskly, slightly ahead of her now, as if trying to get away.

A signal, Danielle sees the blood pooling around Antoine's body. It was preventable. She remembers the top popping abruptly off Pepe's satellite phone. Was there a bug in there after all?

"From the video camera," Carlos adds, answering her silent question. He holds up a device Danielle doesn't recognize, but which she presumes is the gadget that reads the bug's position. "He needed good gear. I had access to police equipment. The bug was insurance for me. I had not planned to use it."

"You were going to let us die," she says, putting it together.

"Even after you knew I was one of the hostages. My name — it was out there, in the newspapers. The video — you saw me."

Carlos just keeps walking.

What changed? Danielle thinks she knows: the phone calls. Pepe's stories got to Carlos. He felt guilty. "You were the only person Pepe ever trusted. You tried to get him killed, in the war, to save your own skin."

Carlos stops and turns. His eyes are stern. "Our war was unwinnable. The Americans were going to fund the military indefinitely. It would've been easier for us to trap people in endless warfare."

In another situation, with distance, Danielle would laugh heartily at this level of self-justification. Here, close up, with her former lover, it stuns her into silence.

"The war was a world unto itself," Carlos goes on, as if she didn't hear the first time. "There were many intrigues. Many. Some ended badly for us. I can't hold even a portion of them in my conscious mind." He puts up two fingers and pinches them together, as if measuring what little he can hold. "I did what I did because our country was being transformed, and we were the ones transforming it."

Danielle accepts that beyond coming here Carlos will never own up to his betrayals. She wonders if he even remembers that boy, the one he killed, whose death changed the course of her life. Even if he does, Carlos has probably filed it away with the other "intrigues." If she had the misfortune to witness that one, if Carlos had to make sure she didn't write about it, he was probably left long before now with just the general impression that he did it for the greater good, for the struggle.

Carlos looks at her impatiently. "We have to hurry," he says, taking Danielle by the arm and pulling her forward.

She violently shakes herself free.

"The nearest hamlet is more than an hour away," he pleads.

"Who is the weakest among you?"

Danielle looks over at her fellow hostage. Tina is walking forward in big confident strides. "Her. But I think she'll make it."

"I'll take her backpack." And then Carlos looks at Danielle once more. He dares to reach out and touch her arm again.

She doesn't know what to expect. A denial? An apology? She isn't convinced that she prefers to be under the power of this manipulator and murderer than under Pepe's.

"*Daniela,* you should know that Aida is in the country. She's with Marta Ramos. She's fine. Now, really," he says, tightening his hold of her arm and pulling her back to walking speed, leading the way, as he always did. This time, Danielle is too dumbfounded to resist. Her elbow feels like jelly.

"Where is the other one?" Carlos asks. "The other hostage?"

"Antoine," Danielle mumbles, trying to understand: Aida has come to El Salvador. For her. And Carlos knows. Does he know? That she's his? She tries to picture Carlos and Aida together, but the idea is too far-fetched for an image to form. "Antoine's dead," she says flatly, feeling faint.

Carlos stops.

So, Pepe has not informed his untrustworthy accomplice of Antoine's death.

"His parents are also in San Salvador," Carlos says. And then he gently lets go of Danielle and hurries ahead to relieve Tina of her backpack.

Danielle steadies herself, controlling her shock, her breathing. She watches as Tina refuses at first, thinking Carlos is asking her to give over her weapon, putting a hand protectively to the strap on her shoulder. Danielle has the exact opposite instinct. She walks up to them and hands Carlos Pepe's handgun without a word, not wanting anything more to do with firearms, and then drops back again to walk alone and think her way through this strange night.

By sunrise, the members of the group are beyond exhausted, but exhilarated too, while Pepe, up front, walks as if being pulled along by an invisible thread he can't resist but does not acknowledge, followed by Cristóbal and Rita. At some point Cristóbal asks Carlos if Rita's hands can be untied, to which he agrees, and so she and Cristóbal walk side by side, occasionally touching hands, Delmi not far behind them.

As far as Danielle knows, there hasn't been any direct contact between Pepe and Carlos, even during bathroom break, when Pepe avoided everyone. She nearly decided to approach him then. She wanted to acknowledge something, if only the truth of his stories. She doesn't feel the same compulsion towards Carlos. He has his reasons for coming, and even whatever Pepe has blackmailed him with — likely those CIA photos from the war — hasn't stopped him. He's risked his reputation to be here, and she knows that's significant for a man like him. He has physically travelled all this way, even bringing news of Aida. Danielle is grateful for all of it. But she feels nothing more. Maybe Aida had something to do with him coming. Danielle won't ask. She'll find out from her daughter, as soon as she gets out of here.

Danielle plods on. How did Aida pay for her trip? Certainly not with her savings for Paris! But the means, as amazing as they are, pale beside the question of Aida's motive. Was it pity after all — over her letters? Danielle refuses to believe it. She lets herself incline instead towards something purer. She visualizes Aida with an eraser working the border between them to nothing.

They take a second, longer rest. Using a map that he's brought, Carlos explains in English what he's planning. "We will walk to this hamlet here, where I know some people, and I will call in help."

Danielle is only slightly disheartened to see proof that they are so near an actual human community and to the road Carlos has used to get here. Pepe has simply steered them away from it all like blinded pack horses. But the young members of the group don't register this. They listen eagerly, their weapons laid across their laps. They could be inexperienced guerrillas, Danielle thinks, getting to know life in the mountains, learning from the master.

"Once you are all safely out, I will stay behind, with them." Carlos motions towards Pepe and his crew. "Then, I will call the police. Drink your water and let's go."

—

Cristóbal is sitting beside his cousin when Carlos approaches. The hostages are talking excitedly to one another nearby. Cristóbal can see how happy they are to speak so openly, like they're trying out new voices, little birds sing-songing.

Carlos addresses Pepe. "I am not going to call the police. I'll make up a story that you escaped."

Cristóbal has known of Pepe's loss of trust during the war. But he never asked about the person who was responsible for it. Now he is looking at that man, face to face, someone he has detested out of loyalty for a long time. Yet Carlos says he'll let them go. Cristóbal can't make sense of the concession. Nor can he figure out why Carlos has not forced them to remove their masks in front of the group, which also seems confusingly decent.

"But only if you have the photos destroyed and give me the negatives," Carlos adds. His eyes never leave Pepe.

Pepe makes no move to indicate one way or the other that he has even heard this request, let alone what he'll do about it. Cristóbal stares at the ground, just as his cousin does, but he hopes Pepe will agree to whatever condition is being discussed, because he has already decided to forgive Rita, and he knows their only chance is to leave across the border together. Today.

"You can think about it," Carlos says, and the familiarity in the way he says this, like Pepe is close, practically family, takes Cristóbal aback. "By the time we get to Zarcero, though, I need to know."

Cristóbal sees his cousin watch as Carlos turns from them and walks off, the satellite phone bulging from the pocket of his pants. The little birds take his place, approaching with wobbly guns up.

The man with the beard and his fellow tracker, whose arms droop heavily from the rack of his shoulders, were happy enough to receive the GPS coordinates from their boss, despite the abuse Sobero heaped upon them over the phone for not finding the group on their own and therefore requiring him to do all the work he's been paying them to do.

The man with the beard knew better than to say aloud what he knew: that the Americans' drone coordinates, already more than twenty-four hours old, were practically useless. After the call, he plotted them on his maps amid all the other locations where they'd found evidence of the fugitives. The pattern he saw emerge was not reassuring. He and his colleague both understood that there was nothing more to go on except instinct.

Not long after the call from Reverte, they'd come across a nearly overgrown trail running north and south, likely unused since the war. They'd decided it was unrealistic that the kidnappers would follow any known trail system.

This morning, the man with the beard rechecked that logic. Probably by now the fugitives are tired. One has diarrhea. They will be more eager than before to reach the Honduran border. They won't be so quick to bypass a shortcut. The trackers both agreed to double back and follow that trail.

They move silently and steadily uphill, keeping their thoughts to themselves about the consequences of returning to Sobero empty-handed. The man with the big shoulders clasps his hands and makes a foothold, heaving his bearded companion up a particularly steep section of trail, where they stop for several minutes to drink water. They have just picked up the pace again and are rounding a corner when they stumble into a man of medium but bulky build, wearing a facemask, at the head of a long line of people going downhill.

Everyone is running. The strangers' guns fire. Their shots receive replies from terrified, inexperienced hands alongside more experienced ones. It's difficult to determine whose shots are connecting with those who are hit. Danielle definitely sees Carlos running towards Pepe and passing him the handgun he received from her earlier. She sees Pepe fall to the ground to begin shooting. Sworn enemies, yet they're working together against whomever has found them. She cannot understand this and doesn't try.

At some point, one of the strangers — they don't look at all like police, but then who? — collapses within sight of her and is bleeding from the head.

Danielle watches Rita go down too, though it's unclear whether she has been hit by a bullet or has merely tripped. Probably the latter, because Rita gets up again and runs screaming, very much alive, a section of her forehead still exposed, moving uphill and past a rocky outcrop until she's clear out of sight.

Martin takes a bullet in his thigh, which leaves him bloodied and screaming for help and for his lord Jesus Christ in a high-pitched voice about thirty feet from where the second stranger is still firing. But Cristóbal crawls over and drags the young man over a sheltered dip in the land, ensuring that all of Martin's limbs are hidden. Then Cristóbal takes a gun from him and rushes back out, still shooting.

Tina sees Cristóbal get shot in the stomach. After the first of the intruders took a bullet in the head, she rose from where she had dropped to the ground when they first appeared and ran as fast as she could away from everyone, her gun bouncing painfully against her back. She ended up slightly uphill, which is where she is when Cristóbal goes down. Tina has to swallow a cry of concern, an uncomfortably strong feeling that adds to the overall confusion of the situation. Not long later, Delmi passes very nearby, moving with a swiftness and silence that Tina could not have foreseen into the tall trees.

———

Danielle sees Carlos on the ground, firing his own weapon. He seems confident to her, young in his movements, the way he was when she knew him. Invincible. But not so heroic now. More like resolved. She's aware of a feeling of pride on Aida's behalf. And then something makes Carlos jerk twice. He slumps over himself awkwardly, landing on his stomach, and Danielle knows he's gone without even having to go over and check, which she can't do anyway because she's hiding, her lips coming into contact with the dirt, her palms burning from having skidded over pebbles. There, she cries silently for her daughter as she waits for whatever will happen next.

Nothing does. What Danielle has hoped for since that long-ago first morning is suddenly real: their capture is over. The thrashing and screaming and shooting have abated, and the sounds of the day fill the void. Insects. The breeze steadily brushing over pine branches. A distant, indifferent airliner arcing far overhead. Danielle rises slowly and goes over to the body of the man she knew as Adrian. She looks at him in the face, closes his eyes. He's done something good after all, hasn't he? She pulls the satellite phone gently from his pocket. Then she removes her own backpack and withdraws a piece of paper where she knows she wrote down a phone number before leaving San Salvador. With trembling fingers, she dials.

12:30 PM. Mil Sueños *mine*

"You're not going to believe this," says Neela.

Marta puts a finger to her ear to hear better. One of the foreign reporters standing beside her is speaking loudly and self-importantly in English into his own phone. "Is it over?" she hears him ask, as if he too is speaking to Neela. Then the reporter drops the following line in Marta's general direction, nonchalantly, as if it were equal — no less valuable but no more — to all news updates he's ever passed along: "Three dead. Lots injured. Being flown in to the hospital in Gotera now." He turns to his photographer. "Let's go!" They rush down the road towards their vehicle.

The scope of what Marta can think shrinks momentarily to those two English words: "three dead."

"Marta? Are you there?" Neela sounds frantic.

"*Sí*," says Marta, but she can't focus on her friend's voice. At the mine's main gate, everyone halfway important among MaxSeguro's army of guards is speaking on their phones too. The police, who did eventually join them before yesterday's demonstration, are also abuzz. Something is happening.

A lens is shoved up close to Marta' face. She pushes it back. "*Un momento*," she says to the reporter and to Neela too, because beyond the cameraperson she has caught sight of a familiar car on the main road. Pedro. "Intercept them!" Marta calls out to anyone who might help. "Tell them to go back!" But before those within earshot can figure out what she means, Pedro drives straight up and all the reporters who've begun approaching Marta turn to swarm the car.

"What's going on?" says Neela. "Talk to me."

In the car, Pedro seems to realize what's happening. He brakes and puts the vehicle into reverse. The reporters surround him anyway, their cameras making contact with the windows, stopping his progress.

"The families are here," Marta says to Neela. "I'll call you back." She feels horrible cutting Neela off, but Marta has to get to the Canadians before the reporters bombard them with the news. Three dead. And there's the demonstrators to think about. MaxSeguro and the police now have no reason to hold back. Marta quickly charges people with the task of disbanding the protesters. Everyone is to calmly gather up their things and be ready to board the buses. She has just started towards Pedro when someone calls her attention to the mine's gate. Marta turns. The unbroken line of security personnel has shifted. Guards are moving to one side. The human barrier breaks open completely as the gate is withdrawn and two minivans, flanked by more security personnel, are slowly escorted out.

It's too soon. Too fast. "*No!*" Marta yells. But there's absolutely nothing she can do to stop their expulsion.

———

A bewildering mass of reporters scream over one another as Pedro honks and Sylvie, in the back middle seat, screams. Ralph, on the right, is giving an overeager camera the finger. Benoît, in the front seat, reaches back to take his wife's hand and shush her comfortingly. Pedro's phone rings and he answers, all the while reversing, inch by inch, in a wide half-circle.

Aida trusts him to take them to safety. They'll be fine. No tear gas here. But suddenly, every camera, every palm that's been banging on their windows, turns away and the area around the car clears. The reporters are all running towards two vehicles — vans. Now that she can see again, Aida scans the area where they held the protest yesterday. Her eyes find Marta Ramos. Short, badly dressed Marta, who nonetheless looks like a general. She's pointing at the vans, advising someone beside her, talking on the phone, visibly upset — all at once.

"It's the exhumation team, isn't it?" Aida says.

"*Quoi? Non!*" says Sylvie, straining past her with her perfumed head to get a better look at the vans, which are disappearing beneath three layers: first guards, then police, and now the reporters. Sylvie makes a horrible animal noise. Aida wants to get away from her panic, but she feels it too. She realizes that the exhumation has started to matter to her, and as more than just a way to get her mother home. She's wanted them to find something — anything. Now the process has been cut off. She puts her index finger to her teeth and peels away a sliver of nail.

"Maybe they found what they looked for," says Benoît.

"If they did, the mine probably took it," says Ralph, and Benoît turns to challenge the remark before registering that it's likely true and letting himself turn back towards the front, his shoulders folding in.

A moment later, the van is gone. The front door to the car clicks open and Marta gets into the front seat. Benoît shoves over and Marta closes the door, which Pedro immediately locks. His hand on the horn, Pedro finishes his delicate reversing, moves into forward gear and ploughs ahead. Some reporters who have already come back from the vans reluctantly move to spare their own feet.

Then the car is driving down the access road to the place where it intersects with the main highway. Pedro signals and they turn south, headed right back to where they just came from.

"What's going on?" Benoît says, finally, as they join southbound traffic. Aida watches the back of Marta's head. She seems to be choosing her words.

"The abduction has ended. We'll go to San Francisco Gotera. That's where they're bringing everyone." Marta gives Pedro the subtlest nod, acknowledging their destination.

Aida translates what Marta has just said as exactly and

economically as she can. She holds Sylvie's hand, and Sylvie reaches out and takes Ralph's. Marta uses her phone to make a series of calls in a low voice, all of them to do with reaching Alejandro Reverte, the head of the exhumation team. But she does not pass on any more details to the families about the hostages and none of them asks. They spend the long, haunting hour on their way south to the provincial capital suspended in a silence each is afraid to breach.

Sobero returns to Mitch's office. He has just overseen the withdrawal of the final bus of demonstrators. His guards used the utmost restraint, he says. No reason to add to the tension now. He sounds invigorated, upbeat.

Mitch nods, stares out his window. On his cluttered desk is the white hardhat he wore to meet Reverte yesterday. "They slept out there. On the road," he says. "Last night."

"A handful. They were probably paid agitators working for the Committee. Or given free food. It's unimportant now."

Mitch meets this comment with a long silence. His fingers tighten on the window's edge. Free food in exchange for an entire night on a road, under guard. He flashes back to the dig site and the story of that worker walking four times up and down El Pico, up and down, looking for a grave. Mitch hates the feeling that has been dogging him since Sobero showed him how he was duped by Carlos Reyes. A pang that won't let go. Not sadness or hurt pride — though it's got those things in it, sure. It's just that he believed in that future, the one Carlos always seemed to be gesturing towards. One that blended economic and political prosperity. One where Mitch would never meet anyone as morbid as Alejandro Reverte, or cold like Antonio Hernández. That future will never be. Mitch has met them. And they've seen him, too, in ways that, when he thinks about those parts of himself, deepen the pang into a sinking throb.

"We should discuss security for the coming weeks as the expansion begins, *Jefe,*" says Sobero.

Mitch isn't in the mood for one of Sobero's chipper planning sessions. "Yes. But not today."

The intercom buzzes.

Mitch eases himself down into his leather chair, resigned to a call from the media. But his assistant surprises him: it's Mitch's wife, calling from Vancouver. Can he talk? Mitch hasn't expected her to know yet. The world of his family and the West Coast — his garage, their yoga studio, his view of the Burrard Inlet, the twins — opens suddenly before him, overwhelmingly appealing, palpable. There, he is a successful man. A father. Real things. Light years from the house of cards he was building with Carlos. "Put her through," he says. ". . . Honey!. . . Yes, I know. We just heard. . . Of course, we're thrilled." And Mitch, letting himself feel this thrill over the end of the threat to his mine because his wife feels it for him, sees another future open up in a way that did not seem possible just moments ago. His legacy at Pico. He raises his head and shifts it ever so slightly, indicating that Sobero, who is still waiting, should vacate the room during this personal call, which his Chief of Security does after only a slight hesitation. Sobero probably wants to say more, to receive some tribute. Probably he thinks this is all his doing. But Mitch is aware that he and Sobero are not actually in this together. Sobero has his business to run, which he mostly does just fine, and Mitch has his.

"How are the girls?" Mitch asks. He picks up a piece of paper his assistant deposited on his desk earlier and glances at it. Another letter from the Committee for the Environment — this one thanking him for the shutdown. Like he closed his mine for them. Mitch shuts the letter into his bottom drawer without a second look.

2008

JUNE 14

Northern Mexico City

Danielle and Pedro follow the man named Jorge. Without him, it's not worth bothering. At least, that's how Marta put it when she handed Danielle the note.

They're on a dead-end street abutted by a three-sided shack piled with old ovens, dirty microwaves, leaning blenders and toasters. A heavily muscled man stands outside the shack with a shotgun. He stares indifferently at Danielle, who clutches the note and keeps close to Pedro, who's negotiating a small patch of grass that some hopeful soul has planted beside the road and surrounded with barbed wire.

Jorge approaches the armed man. "We're looking for Lane 14, lower end — blue rooming house."

"Evangelicals?"

"*Barrios Seguros.*"

Danielle knows this is the name of Jorge's organization, which works with gang youth in this part of Mexico City.

"*Por allá,*" says the man, indicating with a turn of his thick neck that they should go left.

Jorge, who is exceedingly calm, leads Danielle and Pedro down the uneven road. Pedro, meanwhile, is the picture of alertness. He reminds Danielle of the best guerrillas she knew so many years before. Just like Aida said he would.

"People want to believe he didn't die," Marta said when she first produced the note for Danielle. They were sitting together on Danielle's couch, Neela facing them in an armchair. Neela had arranged for Marta to give a talk in Toronto.

The note had appeared in Marta's hand in April during a rally in Los Pampanos to mark the third anniversary of the temporary shutdown at *Mil Sueños*. Someone shoved it at her and left. No signature.

Danielle took the piece of paper and read through its directions. On the one hand, she was relieved. When the police had failed to turn up any sign of Pepe after their release, she'd decided he had been shot by those strangers and gone off to die somewhere. The note meant that maybe her kidnapper had met a less cruel end. On the other hand, the directions felt like they could lead her backwards. Life has gone on. Over the past three years, it has become easier and easier for Danielle to accept that everyone involved in the kidnapping is either dead or has moved on too. She has crossed a threshold. On the surface, things look the same. She's still editing, hanging out with Neela. But she's sold the house. She's back in therapy, reads the news.

"I want to go," Aida said that day, grabbing the note from Danielle's hand and moving towards the windows that look out from Danielle's condo building onto a green space. "We have to know."

Marta shook her head. "You? No, no, no."

"Send Pedro with me," Aida said. She smiled knowingly at Marta, a woman Danielle had met many years ago through Neela when Marta lived for a time in Toronto. Danielle feels she owes a huge debt to her for having hosted Aida during the abduction.

Marta and Aida have since remained close, talking on the phone occasionally. Aida even stayed with her again when she decided to meet with Carlos's other adult children. Danielle doesn't quite understand why Marta and Aida get along. Aida is basically the same conservative businesswoman-in-training that she ever was, married now, though thankfully not to the man she was with when she met Marta. But somehow the two women click.

That afternoon, Marta was feeling protective. "It's too dangerous," she said, like the subject was closed.

"What can happen?" Aida insisted. She slapped Danielle's arm lightly. "You think he'll kidnap me this time?"

Now shanties close in around her as Danielle makes her way forward, dogs and small children staring nervously. They are crouched in doorways or leaning against the wooden walls of their homes, tin roofs above, hand-strung power lines dipping low enough nearly for the tallest among the children to touch. One woman operating a tiny *pulpería* and framed in her windowless window between silver bags of corn and yucca chips shakes her head disapprovingly as Jorge walks past.

"Many here have been converted by American *Evangélicos*," he explains to Danielle, shrugging off this rude behaviour. "They know we're a secular organization."

Danielle can see that though the slum is very poor, it's not the poorest. It has the density, but its low, overlapping structures make a strange kind of sense. Jorge told her earlier that lots of money passes through this place because there are so many illegals in transit here, running drugs, doing sex work, or acting as enforcers until they pay off their "debts" to the gangs who got them this far north. A volatile hub even the police are afraid to enter.

Danielle reminds herself that the risk to her own safety here is small. Marta has checked everything out. And there's the group to think about.

Tina said it was the last, crucial step to healing. She's back at her yoga practice and into what she calls "completion." Martin, in Vancouver, started out cool to the idea. "If that's your path," he said, noncommittally. But by the time they'd talked it out, he admitted, "Yeah, I'd like to know. I would." He's given up his short-lived career as a smoker and become something of a fitness buff. He's recently quit his job, too — though not his church. Danielle even sent Pierre an email, letting him know. After their individual interviews with the police and Foreign Affairs, he stopped talking to the rest of them. Danielle knows he's doing a Ph.D. at Laval, but nothing more. He never replied. Still, she infers from his silence that he isn't opposed to the idea, and probably that means he's curious too.

In those first days after the abduction ended, the four of them were able to agree on a few crucial points. When they were grilled over and over about the sequence of events, none wavered on the fact that the shooting began only after they ran into the two strangers, not when Carlos Reyes had intervened. Pierre and Tina admitted to firing the weapons they'd been handed, in self-defense, but said they didn't know if they'd managed to hit anyone. Martin explained that Cristóbal is the one who protected him after he was shot. They all said they believed that it was Cristóbal, or Pepe, or Carlos, and maybe even Delmi (who was caught the next day when she was spotted, badly scratched up and sunburned, trying to steal eggs from a chicken coop several hours' walk away) who likely struck and killed the two men. No one knew who'd shot Carlos. Everyone put the blame on the strangers. They insisted it wasn't Pepe — even Pierre did. In short, the ex-hostages formed a kind of bond over the way they kept to their version of things. It's a bond Danielle still feels. But in the end, that wasn't what convinced her to do something about Marta's note.

A week of picking up and putting down the phone passed before she finally called Sylvie Duchamp and her husband, Benoît

Thériault. She knew Benoît had been living with their adult daughter for nearly a year, and Danielle reached him first. "It is a hole I cannot fill," he said, a bit cryptically, when she explained about the note and her idea to see where the directions would lead. Then, after a minute, he added, "It's a sinkhole. For me, there is no way out." His voice had the same thin, scratchy quality that Danielle remembered from the funeral in Montreal. Sylvie was more together. "Anything to bring justice," she said. Danielle made clear that she was not planning to contact the police. Sylvie paused. "Police? I don't mean them. I mean, just knowing this note is a lie and he's really dead."

Sylvie never forgave the police or Foreign Affairs for the way she and Benoît were treated after the abduction. How they weren't permitted to recover Antoine's body for several days while the other hostages and the captured kidnappers — Delmi and Cristóbal — were questioned. The police didn't believe the story that was emerging, one in which a future politician had inexplicably gone to end the abduction but had passed a weapon to one of the kidnappers when two strangers appeared out of nowhere. They insisted it was illogical for Carlos, a man who had just disarmed the kidnappers, to have re-armed Pepe, the leader of that group. Besides, the police maintained that the two strangers, both dead, had been found unarmed.

Marta Ramos, who didn't leave the families' side for days on end, had prepared them for resistance from the authorities. The strangers had probably been working for MaxSeguro, she said. Marta didn't know how they'd managed to find the kidnappers, but said it was entirely possible the security firm had collaborated with the police, especially Antonio de la Riva Hernández, who she knew had been friendly with Manuel Sobero for many years. She pointed out that following Danielle's call to the embassy, she and the others had been whisked away within minutes after the police arrived. Who knew what Hernández had ordered done at the crime scene, whether he'd disposed of the trackers' guns and anything else linking them to NorthOre, and therefore to Hernández himself?

When Sylvie and Benoît pleaded with their embassy to follow up on these allegations, they were told to be patient. Their son's body had been located and would be exhumed shortly. Embassy staff claimed they had no jurisdiction to act, that the Salvadoran police were not requesting any further help in the investigation.

The couple eventually took their son home. After that, the Canadian embassy quietly let the whole matter go. They'd lost one hostage, yes, but it had been an unavoidable consequence of the actions of the kidnapper named Rita, who had mutinied and caused the leader, Pepe Molina Domingo, to fire. A single bullet had passed beside Antoine's lower spine and pierced his bowel. Nothing could have prevented it, from the point of view of the embassy. It didn't help that the then-Ambassador, Catharine Keil, left her post not long afterwards to take over the Canadian embassy in Costa Rica. Her replacement was not keen to reopen the file. Hernández, meanwhile, refused to speak to anyone about the abduction, and no one will ever know exactly what arrangement he made with Sobero, if any, because he had a massive stroke in 2007 that left him in a twenty-four-hour care facility. After that, Sylvie and Benoît stopped caring what any official had to tell them, and even about each other's words of comfort.

Jorge has to ask directions twice more, once from a group of teenage boys sitting on stools outside a one-room house playing a video game on a console hooked up to a small television, the power cord running through a window and inside. They're taciturn, absorbed in their game, dressed in jeans and armless undershirts. But one, whose back is to Danielle and whose handgun is clearly visible, tucked in above his back pocket, gets up and offers to show the way.

"*Gracias,*" says Jorge, but the boy ignores him. He leads them through several more left and right turns to a particularly long, low building with several doors opening out of it. It's painted blue, as the note said it would be.

"*Quién busca?*" the boy asks, lifting his arm to indicate that Jorge should choose a door.

Jorge turns to Danielle.

She doesn't want to use the name on her tongue. It feels magical, like it could unleash danger. After a long pause, during which the boy starts to look agitated, she takes a stab: "*El boracho,*" she says. The drunk.

The boy half-smiles and points to the leftmost door. Jorge thanks him, passes him a decent quantity of pesos, and, circumventing a pile of still-smoldering burnt garbage where a chicken pecks, they reach it. Danielle turns, she and Pedro nod at one another, and he and Jorge withdraw. Danielle stands at the door alone, feeling extremely nervous. She knocks.

No answer.

She knocks again.

After a moment, someone speaks from inside. "*Sí,*" says a sleepy, muffled voice. Danielle pushes the knobless door, finding it unlocked, and enters into a pitch black, windowless room with a linoleum floor. Its warped edges ripple under her sneakers. The space is so dark she's afraid to take another step. A strong smell envelops her, prominently of tobacco, but also of burned corn and rum.

"Close the door," says the voice from the far right corner. Before she shuts out all the light, Danielle distinguishes a figure on a mattress. It's oppressively hot. She waits for her eyes to adjust before announcing herself. "*Soy yo, Daniela.*"

The man, who must not have been curious enough to wonder whom he'd permitted to enter, gives a start. "No," he says.

"Yes. It's me. If I could sit down..." she says, feeling weak. Danielle watches as the vague outline of the man shifts, sitting up and reaching. A click, and a television, the volume turned down low, comes on. Its flashing, bluish light fills the room, imprinting itself on and dimly illuminating the face Danielle has hoped she would find here and also has long hoped never to see again. It doesn't look like the newspaper photos. It's older, thicker. The hair is too long at the sides and matted, drooping clownishly. Pepe Molina Domingo has survived, again. *Milagro.* Danielle feels a physical sadness at this theme of his life. She realizes that she has never met him, not properly, with his face exposed, which is strange, because she feels she knows him so well.

"You think they'll let you take me out of here," says Pepe, swinging his feet to the floor. This starts out as a question, but ends like a dare. He lights a cigarette.

Danielle thinks of the man they saw on the way in, of his muscles and his shotgun. "Someone in Los Pampanos gave Marta Ramos a note."

"Marta," he mumbles, like he's running through memories. "Marta Ramos Ramos."

"Yes. She's still working against the mine. They dropped the charges against her. . . . Anyway, the note said we might find you here." Danielle fingers the worn piece of paper, now damp in her palm. She looks deeper into the room. There's very little to it. On her left is a plain wood table. Making no sudden moves, she steps over and leans against it. "You're alright here?" she asks.

"I work nights. They come and get me. It's temporary." There's real sorrow in the way Pepe admits to whatever he's admitting to. Violence on behalf of the gangs, probably. The price he pays for hiding out in this place. Or maybe just fear that he's wrong, that this situation is permanent.

"Will it cost you? Talking to me?" Danielle asks, but she receives no answer. The light from the television flickers more quickly over Pepe's round face. "I brought you something," she says, and reaches into her shoulder bag. "The *Liberador.* A whole issue from spring of

2006 devoted to. . ." Danielle can't make the word "kidnapping" come out. ". . . to what happened." She holds up the weekly. Its articles each place the abduction in a different context: NorthOre's destruction of the land in Los Pampanos, post-civil war economics, mass migration of Salvadorans to the U.S. Marta thought Pepe would be interested. Danielle agreed, but now she doesn't feel like she should cross the small space that separates her from him to present it. She indicates that she's leaving it on the table. "And two more things. One is a letter. From Antoine's family."

At this, Pepe's face clearly shows fear. Danielle feels the same. That letter has been like a radioactive rock beckoning from her desk ever since she received it about a week after speaking to Sylvie Duchamp. It was accompanied by a short note for her, signed by both of Antoine's parents, saying they felt strongly that if Pepe is alive, he has to know what their son's death has meant.

Danielle's hand shakes as she places it on top of the *Liberador*. She planned to say something more about Antoine, but it's like the room is erasing all her careful speeches. "I knew Carlos," she blurts out instead.

Across the room, Pepe puts his hands to his face.

"I knew him in 1980. That's why he came." She doesn't mention the hurt Adrian caused her, the child they had together. Aida's name doesn't belong here.

Even using Carlos's name aloud is jarring. Danielle decided the moment he was shot never to say a bad word about him again in public. Her last report about Pepe's life, the one she'd scribbled down and read to Carlos over the phone (a call, she later realized, that he must have taken from very nearby), disappeared with Pepe, and Danielle said nothing to the police about what she knew of the connection between the two men. Only Aida heard everything, and she was awed enough by the profound contradictions in her late father to feel protective of the information.

A subsequent police search of Carlos's home and office computers turned up nothing. Not a surprise, Danielle thought, considering Carlos's expertise in covering his tracks. Those who'd seen Carlos in public with Mitch Wall in the preceding months assumed Carlos had simply called upon his guerrilla background to end the abduction in order to help Wall out of a bad situation and save some lives while he was at it. If the photos had appeared — those with which Pepe had blackmailed Carlos into collaborating — maybe Danielle would have corrected this version of events and exposed Carlos as an operator who'd used NorthOre's CEO to ensure Pepe's demands were met and, therefore, hold on to his future. But nothing ever came of them. "You destroyed them, didn't you?" she hears herself ask now. "Those pictures."

Pepe seems preoccupied. Maybe busy reviewing the events that put an end to his plans. It dawns on Danielle that maybe all this time he has believed that Carlos went into the mountains because he really did regret betraying their friendship. "I'm sorry," she says. She feels compelled to provide some shred of good news. "Marta has seen Cristóbal. He's fine."

In fact, Cristóbal has become a kind of pet cause of Marta's. She visits him often, has a lawyer filing every paper towards his early release. He claims to be out of touch with his wife Rita since the abduction. When Marta once presented him with a newspaper clipping about returned migrants, from four months after it ended, with the headline: "Migrant Claims Kidnapper Among Those Who Crossed Border," in which a young woman said she had met Rita while a group of illegal migrants was waiting to cross into Texas from Mexico, Cristóbal remained stone-faced. The woman in the newspaper had reported that Rita told her she was headed to Miami to live with her cousin and planned to send for her husband and children later. It took four more visits before Cristóbal would even use Rita's name again.

Danielle doesn't know what to believe. She can only hope that Rita will forget about him, but she doubts it. "He's never said anything to the police about you. Nothing."

Pepe still doesn't respond.

Danielle is suddenly aware of the time. She knows Pedro is waiting. He might be getting nervous.

"The last thing is this," she says, and, overcoming the inertia that seems endemic to the room, she walks over to Pepe with the gift in her hand. It's a soiled, torn piece of thick cloth, maybe ten centimetres square, its colours set in a check pattern, terribly faded.

Pepe snatches the cloth from her hand and glowers at it.

Up close, Danielle gets a better look at his face. He's younger-looking than she thought earlier, with a wide nose. "This is all that wasn't confiscated. The head of the exhumation team gave it to one of his local workers, who kept it. Then the man gave it to Marta Ramos."

Pepe looks at the cloth again, this time with different eyes. He turns it over in his hands, which Danielle, looking down, can see are dirty on the backs. Familiar hands. And then Pepe puts his face into the cloth and breathes. Danielle knows she should back away, let him have his privacy, but she doesn't. She wants something too. Something of Carlos's to give to Aida so she can hold it to herself. As it is, her daughter has to make do with an idea of him that's only half good.

Danielle wants to believe what she's seeing. But she has a doubt. No one really knows if this cloth is what Pepe thinks it is. Reverte can't say for sure. There wasn't enough time. And nothing more came out of the ground to prove anything. The rest has been blown apart in a million ways with El Pico, now that NorthOre's expansion is complete.

A sharp knock at the door. Pepe instantly lifts his mattress and places the cloth under it, gets up and stands protectively in front of Danielle. "*Sí!*" he yells with a voice that sets off a chain of memories for Danielle. It's his voice of detachment, the one he used throughout the abduction.

The door opens and the man with the shotgun stands in the brilliant sunlight like a large cardboard cutout of a cowboy. Behind him, Danielle can see Pedro tensed, ready for anything.

"You must be someone quite special to receive such an honoured guest," says the guard. "All the way from Canada. Maybe you would like to tell us what makes you so special."

"She's a friend of my family in Toronto. She brought me a letter from a relative. Here," Pepe says, retrieving the letter from Sylvie and Benoît from the table. "You want to read it?" he says. "I dare you to understand a word. It's in English." He flaps the letter aggressively in front of the man Danielle realizes is both jail guard and protector, here to ensure that a valuable illegal, an asset to the gang, is not getting any ideas about leaving. Not yet.

"You've already caused a lot of gossip," the armed man says, beaten, letting the issue of the letter go. "We don't need a past here."

Pepe holds his letter carefully at his side. "She's leaving. She won't be back."

"No," says the gunman, stepping aside to indicate that Danielle should exit immediately. "I say she won't."

As they both approach the door, Danielle sees Pepe and he sees her in broad daylight for the first time. His breath smells of alcohol. For a moment, Danielle wonders, in her faded vanity, how she must look, how it makes Pepe feel that his former hostage is thriving. She wants to ask how he plans to get out of here, how he bears it. She wants to know if his motives were ever pure, or if it was always as much about hurting Carlos Reyes as recovering something of his lost family.

"Tell my sister not to write again," says Pepe. Then he turns and closes the door.

ACKNOWLEDGEMENTS

Many people gave their time to help me understand gold mining, Central American politics and culture, kidnappings, stock market investment, helicopters, guns and more. I thank them all, particularly:

In Canada: Grahame Russell and Rights Action, Mining Watch Canada, Sandra Cuffe, Chantal Venturi, Don Venturi, Robert Sparks, Bert Struik, Gina Wang, Gordon Smith, Bill Morgan, Sara Koopman, Ken Leigh, Mary Morgan, Jeff Hodgson and Marc-André Pigeon.

In Honduras: Carlos Amador and the members of the Comité Regional Ambiental del Valle Siria; in La Esperanza, Berta Caceres and the members of COPINH.

In El Salvador: Jaime Martínez, Jesus Morales, Damian Alegria, Katherine Miller, Juan Carlos Hernández, Remberto Nolasco, Helda Consuelo Molina, Wilma Angelica Santo, José Santo Márquez, Sister Noemi of the Bajo Lempa, and, especially, Padre Rogelio Ponseele in Perquín, the esteemed Mirna Perla, and generous hosts José Martir Pineda Nolasco and family.

Thank you to the Fundación Valparaíso, where I revised an early draft, and to Cindy Patton, my generous employer during much of the writing process.

The editors and readers at NeWest reviewed my manuscript with careful attention. I thank them, especially Douglas Barbour. My own readers were Adam Frank, Jeff Hodgson, Marc-André Pigeon, Jean-Claude Pigeon, Anar Ali, and (twice, and with heart) Nick Kazamia. Sanchita Balanchandran checked a portion of the book.

Lynn Coady, Madeleine Thien, Greg Hollingshead, Andreas Schroeder, Ann Shin, Nick Kazamia and Anar Ali all guided me through the labyrinthine publication process, for which I am grateful.

My friends deserve a medal for years of encouragement, especially Nick Kazamia and Anar Ali, whose phone lines must be burned clear through. Thank you to my family for believing in me, starting with my mother, Dolly Pigeon, and my siblings, Marc-Andre Pigeon, Jeanne-Claire Sloan and Jean-Claude Pigeon, soul sister Colette Gignac, brother-in-law extraordinaire Kevin Sloan, compatriot Chris Guppy, and all of my cherished Pigeon, Shea, Venturi, Goth, Mirka, Grenier and Abolins aunts, uncles and cousins.

Thank you to Merle Frank for coming along, and, most of all, to my closest reader, interlocutor and companion, Adam Frank, who gave me space, time and so much more — even the book's title. Without these Franks, forget it.

MARGUERITE PIGEON is a former journalist and traveller turned writer of fiction and poetry. In 2001 she lived for several months near the Honduran-Salvadoran border working with a local indigenous organization, an experience that became the inspiration for *Open Pit*. She later attended UBC's Creative Writing MFA program. Since graduating, her short stories and poems have appeared in journals throughout Canada and internationally, and her first book of poetry, *Inventory* (Anvil 2009), was nominated for the Gerald Lampert Award. Originally from Blind River, Ontario, she currently lives in Vancouver. *Open Pit* is her first novel.